THE LOVE STORY

C. KENNY

For my Elena.

CHAPTER ONE

J ohn Buckston never thought he would do this. Taking a deep breath, he stepped forwards and entered the unknown.

"Welcome to Winter Wonderland! Here's a list of all the great activities you can do, have a good time!"

John smiled as he accepted the leaflet. "Thanks!" He stuffed the paper into the pocket of his coat and observed his surroundings. Hundreds of people were milling about as the light snowfall of the evening dusted their winter clothing. Even John who rarely felt the cold, was wrapped up warm tonight. Quite what had possessed him to go to this Christmas fun fair all alone was beyond him, he had always imagined he would come here with a girlfriend, or at the very least a group of friends. Yet here he was, alone and reminded of that fact every few seconds when either a happy couple would walk past, or a loud group would bellow laughter into the night sky.

"Remember why you're here," John said aloud, sighing as he trudged along. It wasn't that he was jealous of couples, quite the opposite actually, he liked seeing people in love. It was just that he really wished he had *someone*.

There was an intoxicating buzz in the air which meant that John couldn't help but get caught up in it all. He loved Christmas and he was really here for his mum; she loved decorating their tree with gaudy tinsel and tonnes of trinkets that often made her friends cringe, but John loved that about her; she didn't care. She had the tree her way, with it looking like it had all the decorations shot at it from a cannon. John decided he wanted to give her something for the tree this year and Winter Wonderland offered plenty of custom designs for him to choose from. As John was scanning the various kiosks, one in particular caught his eye, but it wasn't the items on offer that drew him in. It was the girl working there. Her dark hair hung beautifully around her face, framing her tanned skin. He noticed her brown eyes first, shining impossibly in the night, flickers of nearby fires illuminating them magically. He saw her delicately hand a carrier bag to a paying customer (another couple as it turned out) and her smile seemed to brighten the darkness. His feet began to carry him over to her and immediately his heart started to thump faster, his mouth suddenly became a lot drier and before he knew it, he was standing right where the couple had been.

"Hello. See anything you like?" the girl asked innocently. Her eyes glinted with a spectacular quality that seemed super-natural to John. What was it? Mischief? Happiness?

He suddenly realised that he hadn't responded.

She stood patiently, her eyes widening a little and her eyebrows raising as John's silence continued.

"Oh God, yeah, erm. Not sure. Maybe?" he finally blurted out.

"No problem. Take a look around and let me know if there's anything you fancy!"

John paused for a moment before answering. *You!* he wanted to say.

"I don't know what I'm looking for to be honest," John said, settling into himself a bit, yet still transfixed by her beauty.

"Well, I assume something *Christmassy?*" she inquired.

"Yeah. For my mum really, a bauble for the tree or something?" John responded.

"Aw how sweet, what sort of things does she like?"

"Anything that stands out and looks a bit quirky."

"Ooh, sounds like me!" the girl answered, smiling widely. "Hang on let me check this box." She disappeared off to the side and John exhaled deeply, steadying the nerves that were building up.

She's absolutely stunning, John thought, watching her rummage through a stockpile of various objects.

"What about these?" she asked, surfacing with a pair of intricately designed ice skates that dangled from a thin golden hoop.

"Wow that's...that's perfect! My mum used to ice skate. This is incredible! How did you know?!"

"I dunno. Just...it's the prettiest decoration we have. It's my favourite," she answered, burying her face a little more into her pink scarf as the wind blew stronger. John cleared his throat, caught up in her beauty, and felt a warm fuzzy feeling inside despite the rapidly plummeting temperature.

He began to laugh.

"What? Is it something I said?" said the girl.

"You look like a giant marshmallow! A pretty one, of course," he said before he could stop himself, and the pair locked eyes.

"I didn't know such things existed."

"Well, with that fluffy hat and humongous scarf, and your face, I can categorically say that yes, pretty marshmallows exist."

Time seemed to stand still for a moment as they smiled at

each other, the girl blushing and almost matching the colour of her attire.

"Can I get you anything else?" she asked, the question lingering in the air a moment, John wavering between answering with his head or his heart.

"That's it I think," John answered flatly, feeling immediately that this wasn't the right thing to say.

"Okay, twelve pounds fifty please," she said, turning away from John to wrap the decoration as he handed her a twenty-pound note. The girl reached into her pocket to give him his change.

"Don't worry about it, it's definitely worth this and more!"

"Oh, thank you, that's so kind. I'll tell my sister, she made this!"

"Wow. She's seriously talented. Send her my thanks as well, this will make my mum so happy." John shifted his weight and looked down at his trainers, now completely covered in snow. "Are you here every night then?" John probed, feeling the window of opportunity closing with every passing second.

"No, this is our last night here. We fly back to Seville tomorrow for Christmas."

"Seville? Is that where you're from?" John asked.

"Yes, well, us marshmallows need a warmer climate," she said with a smile.

John laughed at this. They stood in silence for a brief moment, John wanting with all his might to ask her for her name, phone number, anything. But he was too awkward. "Thanks so much, have a safe flight and a good Christmas," he said, disgusted at his lack of confidence.

"Thank you. You as well," she answered, waving and smiling, a hint of disappointment in her eye as she watched John turn and walk away.

∽

John arrived home late, and crept inside quietly, placing his keys gently on the sideboard so as to not wake his parents. He reached into his coat pocket and took out the gift he had bought for his mum from Winter Wonderland. Just to make sure it was still in one piece, John decided to carefully unwrap the present. To his surprise, a folded piece of paper dropped out. His heart leapt with anticipation and he hurriedly unfurled the note, eyes rapidly scanning the neat handwriting on the page.

I hope you and your family have a lovely Christmas. Elena x

John held the note in his hands, reading the words over and over. Cursing, he folded it up with care, sliding it into his pocket before re-wrapping his mother's gift. He once again regretted not saying anything to her. Finishing the task and heading into his room, he placed the handwritten note on his desk, willing Elena's phone number to magically appear on the piece of paper.

CHAPTER TWO

E lena Viegas walked towards *Brecchio's,* a cosy Italian diner that she often visited when in London, usually with her friends for a lunchtime gossip. Today however, after a particularly long day at work, she didn't feel like cooking so decided to head to the restaurant alone. Elena had been single for almost two years now. It had been by choice originally; she enjoyed her own company and wasn't afraid of doing things by herself. Yet as she approached the glass doors, her heart sighed as she surveyed the usual crowd of couples who filled the restaurant.

"Ah, Ms Viegas, a warm welcome to you. Table for two or..?"

"Just one tonight Marco, I couldn't drag anyone along last minute to accompany me!"

"Of course, no problem," he said. "This way please." He guided Elena to a table set for two at the back of the restaurant and swiftly began clearing away the extra place setting. Elena took her seat and smiled at Marco, illuminated by the spotlights above her.

Her table had a direct view of the front door, however she

was hidden from sight by foliage which adorned the tables, so when she saw him he didn't see her, or her mouth agape in shock.

John parked his black BMW, ascended the grimy staircase of the underground car park and emerged into the open air of the town centre. Staring down at his trainers, John continued around the bend to the restaurant where he would be meeting Kate Bradstock for their evening dinner. *Could it be called a date?* Truthfully, John had said as much to his mates, but deep down, he knew they were just friends (it was their seventh "date" and there had been not a single act of affection between them, except for a hug of greeting and goodbye). Usually, John felt nervous whenever he went on dates. He wasn't experienced with women and was never the one out of the group of his friends to pick up girls on a night out. Though he was an attractive, charismatic and charming man, John's confidence in himself simply wasn't there, meaning that he was unlucky in love. As he approached the restaurant, he saw Kate crossing the road and heading towards him. He waved and she returned the gesture with a smile. They drew closer and John examined her properly; her long brown hair hung limply over a denim jacket that was paired with black jeans and flat shoes.

"You look nice," John said as they embraced.

"Thanks, so do you, I like the shirt, Buck!" she replied.

"Well, I do try," he said. "Shall we?" he continued, opening the door for her.

"Welcome to *Brecchio's!*" announced the doorman. "Table for two?" His eyes directing the question to John, who felt like replying with "yeah, no shit", but instead politely nodded with "yes please."

Led to a booth in the corner of the dimly lit restaurant, the waiter guided them to their table and presented menus that were covered in dark leather.

John was oblivious to the fact that the girl from Winter Wonderland was sitting just a few feet to his left, on the opposite side of the restaurant, all alone.

~

"No way!" Elena whispered to herself, ducking down behind her own menu upon seeing a new couple enter the restaurant. *I can't believe it's him!* She kept her head buried, studying the choices under the "Appetisers" section as her waiter returned to her table.

"Are you ready to order?" he asked, far too loudly for Elena's liking, though she suspected it was her paranoia amplifying his voice.

"In a moment, I think. Can I have a bottle of still water though please?"

The waiter nodded and left.

He probably won't even recognise you, she thought, daring to lower her tightly held menu. She saw the man from Winter Wonderland engaged in conversation with whom she presumed was his girlfriend. *They look happy,* Elena thought. Suddenly, John glanced over and Elena frantically ducked below her table, fumbling with her shoes and trying desperately to stop her face from glowing red.

~

"How was your weekend Bucky?" Kate began.

"Yeah, it was decent, thanks," replied John, his mouth already dry.

"It was Freddie's birthday on Saturday," he added, now swivelling in his chair in an attempt to catch the waiter's eye.

"Ah yes, I remember you told me last week, how was it, any gossip?"

Any gossip? What am I, page twenty of the local newspaper? John thought as he returned his body fully to the table, his quest to gain attention from the staff having failed.

"Well, not really," he began, without truly digesting the question asked. He looked around the restaurant, trying to find someone to take their order.

"Usual antics with Carter which meant that Freddie got disgracefully drunk," John answered.

She laughed honestly at this.

"And Henry ended up taking us to a club near Victoria to finish the night off," John ended.

"Sounds fun. Did you get your dancing shoes out?"

"Well you know me, can't contain my moves."

"Oh yeah, I can totally picture you getting your groove on," she finished, just as the waiter arrived to take their order of drinks.

John stared at her for a second, *did she actually picture me like that?* Maybe he should invite her out clubbing one night, it might get things onto the next stage, he pondered.

"Fancy sharing a starter?" he offered.

"Yeah okay, how about a salad?" Kate replied.

John couldn't think of anything worse. "Yeah, sure."

An awkward silence hung in the air as they continued to stare at their menus.

Elena was desperate to finish her meal as quickly as possible and exit without being seen. She had so far managed to go unnoticed by the man who came to her stall, but that could only last so long. With her plate cleared, she resolved to get her mind equally as empty. *Why am I so hung up on him? He's just some guy who bought a bauble from me.* But she knew the spark between them had been real. *Was he with this girl at the time? Did he feel anything, or had it all been one-sided?* Elena heaved a great sigh and slumping down in her chair, she resigned herself to the fact that whoever this man was, no matter how much they got on, he wasn't available. However, running into him like this was making her question whether she should say something. She bit her lip, again studying him, watching him cut his meat up into neat chunks. There was something so *manly* about his actions, she thought.

"Thank you madam," the waiter said, appearing out of nowhere and snapping Elena out of her trance.

"Oh gosh, sorry, I was miles away!" she said with a small laugh, producing her credit card for payment. While he fumbled with the card machine, Elena looked over his shoulder and again took in the man from the stall, her internal conflict tearing her apart. *Should I stay here or go and say something?* The card machine beeped noisily to break her focus, so she hurriedly punched in her pin and reached into her purse to leave a tip for the service.

"Thank you, have a lovely evening!"

"Thanks, you too!" With a swift turn, he left, and Elena was alone. She knew she had a decision to make. Her heart started pounding in her chest, her body lifted from her seat and she began to walk towards the man from the stall.

"What you thinking Kate?" John asked, moreso to break yet another increasingly awkward silence.

"I think I fancy the chicken, veg and potatoes."

"There's a shock," he replied, with a wry smile. Kate usually chose chicken whenever they went out for a meal on a date (*was it a date?*).

"Oi, it's what I like," she responded, pretending to be offended but returning the smile.

"Well, it's going to be steak and chips for me then," John announced, closing the menu with a satisfying thud.

"Proper carnivore aren't you, Buck?" teased Kate.

"Growing lad aren't I?" John replied, making a point to try and draw attention to his biceps, which went completely unnoticed.

John was starting to think this might be the last time he asked Kate out on a date, it clearly wasn't going anywhere. All of a sudden, she reached out a hand and lightly held his, laughing as she was about to tell a hilarious story.

"Oh my god, I didn't tell you about this guy at work! It was so funny!"

John immediately lost interest but feigned a laugh and encouraged Kate to continue with her tale.

"He was trying to ask my friend Cassie out, which I thought was bad anyway. I mean he's hot, but not a lot going up there you know?" she pointed to her head.

He's hot? John heard, feeling more uncomfortable at being in this situation with Kate, the sinking feeling that he was being relegated to "The Friend Zone" more and more apparent.

"He tried to be sweet, he left a note at her desk, but he spelt her fucking name wrong! He put *Casey*!" she finished, laughing at this mistake and John, feeling obliged, joined in.

"Oh, I wish you would have been there Buck," Kate said, again clasping his hand.

John was once more conflicted. *Does she actually wish I had been there? Why is she touching me so much tonight?* Before he could process these questions, their dinner arrived, and John was grateful for the distraction as he began cutting his steak.

Elena took a step closer, then another. He still hadn't noticed her. Then she stopped, making direct eye contact with his girlfriend. Almost in response, the girlfriend became affectionate towards the man, holding his hand, marking her territory. Elena's heart was racing and her hands were clammy; she wanted to say something, *anything* to him, but she stopped herself upon seeing this display of tenderness between the two of them. As if to break the spell, the man knocked his knife onto the floor and quickly leant down to pick it up, returning it to the table so the other guests in the restaurant wouldn't notice that the noise had come from his direction. His girlfriend laughed and shook her head, clearly something she'd seen him do before. *Probably at home when they have dinner,* Elena thought. With that, Elena Viegas turned sharply and marched out of the restaurant, not daring to look behind her. She finally exhaled and let the cool night air whip around her face. "No more of this, I'm finding my man. Just like that lucky girl in there," Elena said aloud into the darkness.

John was watching Kate finish her food when he accidentally elbowed his cutlery and it went sailing over the side of the table, clattering loudly onto the floor. "Fuck me!" he muttered under his breath, which made Kate laugh. He quickly picked it up and placed it noisily into his empty plate, drawing yet more laughter from Kate. As he looked at her, John saw a woman leaving the restaurant over her shoulder. He couldn't help but get the feeling that it was somebody he knew, somebody important. The mystery girl's hair swayed as she walked, in such a way that John was mesmerised. Suddenly Kate was invisible and John was yearning to go and talk to this girl.

Where do I know her from? John puzzled as he racked his brain. He watched her exit and mentally returned to the present, seeing Kate Bradstock in front of him. For a moment, he thought he had seen the girl from Winter Wonderland.

Stop being ridiculous John, she lives in Spain, he thought to himself. *Focus on the here and now. Don't regret not doing something again, ask Kate out.*

"Do you want to come to my birthday night out? I know it's a bit early to ask, but it would be great to have you there," John blurted, before he could stop himself.

"Oh, an official invite? Sure, I'd love to!" Kate responded.

John smiled, for a moment still seeing the girl from the stall. Reality swam back into view and John immediately felt deflated, something was crying out to him that he should leave right then, get out of the restaurant and just go outside.

"Everything okay, Buck?" Kate asked him.

John shook off this feeling, instead allowing himself to feel pleased that Kate had agreed to come to his birthday.

"Couldn't be better," John answered, taking a sip of his drink. He could still feel an inexplicable pull from somewhere, telling him to leave. John stayed in his seat and would miss his opportunity.

CHAPTER THREE

ONE MONTH LATER

"How has this happened?" Dom said with despair, scratching his light stubble.

"Beats me," Henry said, taking a deep swig of his drink before putting it down on the wooden table the four men were seated at.

"Oh, get over it," Freddie said, his large pale arm knocking John's chest. "Can you believe these two?"

"Well they do have a point," John responded, lifting his own vodka and coke and taking a sip before continuing. "I mean did you honestly think Alex would get a girlfriend before us?"

Freddie laughed as did Henry, whilst Dom and John looked at each other.

"What's so funny about that?" Dom asked the giggling pair.

"You two strike out more often than I have hot dinners," Henry responded.

"Ah come on, we're unlucky in love!" John said.

"Yeah you are!" Freddie concurred.

"Well let's be honest, Alex isn't exactly who you'd think

would be able to get a girl, let alone an absolute rocket like this," Dom reasoned.

"What, you seen her then?" John asked.

"Yeah, she popped down the shop the other week when you weren't working."

"Typical. Ah well, soon they'll be here. What was her name again?"

"Helen weren't it?" Henry offered.

"Yeah, that sounds right," Freddie again confirmed.

"Well, I need to take a leak boys, do excuse me," John said.

John walked with determination. He really needed to use the toilet. Easing through the dense crowd, John climbed the staircase, avoiding wobbling drunk men and women as he did and entered the men's room. He walked to the sinks first to do a quick spot check of how he looked in the mirror. A receding hairline (styled with wax that did just enough to hide this fault) met his gaze. John was quite self-conscious of his hair, but so far, he was managing to get away with it. He adjusted his shirt, noticing how his hours at the gym had started to pay off. Stroking his shortly trimmed beard, John was satisfied that his appearance was good enough, maybe even so good he might meet someone tonight. He had always hoped to bump into a beautiful stranger on nights out like these, but that hardly ever happened. Suddenly, John reminisced about that night before Christmas, almost two years ago. The girl at the stall who had so completely mesmerised John, so much so that he hadn't even introduced himself, let alone asked for her number. Sighing and resigned to regret, John put that thought out of his head. He'd surely never see her again anyway, so what use was it holding on to such a distant dream?

John left the bathroom and began walking back to his

friends. He noticed that Alex and his girlfriend had now joined the group at the table. Turned away from John, he could see a girl in a white dress, long dark hair flowing down her back. At that moment in time he couldn't place it, but she felt familiar to him. Her tanned skin was flawless against her outfit, which only served to accentuate her glowing presence. He was close enough to see that she looked attractive, but still too far to make out the details of her face. It occurred to John that he had been standing perfectly still as he watched them and luckily nobody had noticed.

Composing himself and summoning as much faux confidence as he could, John approached the pair, ignoring his friends and instead focussing on making an incredible first impression. He realised as he was walking that this was a ridiculous intention; *why would a great first impression matter? She isn't here as a single woman to be charmed, she's here as Alex's girlfriend.*

As he drew closer and she adjusted her hair, John could smell her perfume; roses with a hint of orange. *Where had he smelled it before?* When he saw her face clearly for the first time, John felt a sudden spike of adrenaline. He stopped dead in his tracks; this was the same girl that had stolen his heart at Winter Wonderland. With a sinking feeling he realised that she was here, not for him, but for Alex. *With* Alex.

"Shit," he said aloud without realising.

"Oh, nice to meet you too!" said Elena, gradually looking up and meeting his eyes. "Oh! It's you!" she gasped with a wide smile.

"Er, sorry, do you know Buck?" Alex said to Elena, looking a little panicked.

"Yes, well, no, not really. He bought something from my sister's stall at Winter Wonderland ages ago. What is it, like, almost two years ago or something?" she asked, knowing precisely how long ago it had been, but not wanting to sound keen.

"Yeah, about that I reckon. Well it's nice to see you again!" said John, hugging her awkwardly.

"Yes, um sorry, I never caught your name?"

"It's John. Well, Buck, Bucky, John Buckston, whatever, call me Superman if you like!" The words spilled from his mouth making him sound like a nervous schoolboy.

"So many names! I'm Elena."

"Yes, I remember, from your note! I still have it!"

"No you don't! Why would you keep a note from a marshmallow?" she laughed, trying to still the fire growing inside her at the thought that he had kept a note from their first meeting.

"Ha, yeh, sorry I called you that. I dunno what came over me."

"Sorry, I'm so lost here. What are you two on about?" Alex questioned, looking more and more uneasy as the conversation between his friend and girlfriend continued in front of his eyes.

"Oh nothing, just something silly!"

John was completely disarmed, so he tried to make a joke to get himself back on track.

"So, all this time I thought you were a figment of Alex's imagination," he said, grinning. "I'm glad to have been proven wrong finally."

Elena smiled and looked John in the eyes, "I'm sure I can prove you wrong at most things, Buck".

Smiling himself now, he retorted, "Who you calling Buck? You just got here!"

With a broader grin she replied, "I think I can call you what I like, I've known you for years now!"

Laughing back and in the full flow of conversation, John

asked, "You didn't even introduce yourself, what was your name again? Who are you?!"

Smiling that intoxicating smile once again, she laughed and looked down, feeling herself blush.

The moment shared between them seemed to linger in the air for a magical, stretched period of time, yet it was also over far too soon. Elena was quickly ambushed by the rest of the boisterous group, Freddie unsurprisingly leading the charge both literally and figuratively as he grabbed Elena in a tight bear hug.

"Oh wow thanks so much!" she grimaced, with playful distaste on her face.

"Nah you love it!" Freddie beamed back, drawing further laughs from the group.

"So how did a dickhead like you end up with her?" Dom asked Alex.

Yeah, how in the hell did this happen? John wondered to himself.

"Well it's all thanks to me being great at pouring a drink," Alex said, somewhat boastfully.

"No, that's not it at all!" Elena said loudly before continuing in a softer tone, "I was having a meal by myself in what turned out to be Alex's pub."

"Parents' pub," Dom corrected, winking at John.

"Yes, alright Mr Detail!" Alex said with a smile.

"Anyway!" Elena said, interrupting the boys playfully. "He comes over and says do you mind if I ask you something?" she paused, allowing the anticipation to build. "So, I'm thinking, oh God, is it something I've done...what is it...and he says, how come you're eating alone?"

"Ah the old charmer," Henry said, interrupting, nudging Alex who grinned bashfully.

"So I tell him, it's because of my crippling loneliness and

the fact that I have nobody to be with," Elena continued. "Then he says, can I sit down with you? So I said, yes of course, and here we are!" Elena finished her story and Henry and Freddie congratulated Alex on his out of character confident approach.

"Right place at the right time I guess," Alex said, a hint of arrogance underlying the surface charm.

John didn't appreciate that and realised with horror just why. *He was jealous of Alex Wickerman.* He caught himself and was stunned with how he was feeling. He looked at Elena, then at Alex. It didn't make sense. They were polar opposites in almost every way, surely the others could see it. He'd find out later from Dom what he felt, his best friend was always honest. For now, John tried to stop his stomach from turning, the realisation that the girl from the Winter Wonderland stall was here with his friend was gut-wrenching. Yet, he had to be the better man and not let it consume him, for it so easily might.

"So you're coming to my birthday?" John blurted out, the question directed at Elena.

"Well, if you're inviting me then yes, I suppose I might," she flashed a smile at John that completely disarmed him and he was lost for words.

I can't believe it's him. Elena was still holding her smile for John, the boy who she hadn't been able to get out of her head for months.

"Want a drink, babe?" Alex asked her. She looked up at him, his narrow face smiling down at her. She returned the grin, yet it wasn't with the same warmth she reserved for John.

"Yes please, thank you Alex." He was good for her, she surmised. He had been there when she was in need of companionship; he was steady and honest. She turned her attention back to John, who was now laughing with the boys about something and she felt a wave of sadness wash over her as she realised that his girlfriend would likely be at his birthday party as well.

"Well, thanks for coming out tonight," Alex said as the group made their final preparations for departure, loitering by the underground station.

"Yeah was great to see you and meet the Mrs," Henry concluded.

"I had such a fun night," Elena said. "Bye everyone!" She made a move to hug each one of them in turn, Freddie holding on too long for comical effect, and then she was face to face with John.

"Nice to see you...again!" she said with a stifled laugh, her nerves surfacing.

"And you, glad I got to see you again," John said, forcing a smile, inside feeling his heart sinking. They pulled apart, Elena now returning to Alex.

"It was so lovely to meet you all," Elena said, waving from the top of the grey staircase.

John, who was closest to the couple, spoke just to Elena, "get home safe okay?"

"You too," she replied, taken aback by the intimacy in the tone of his voice. As she linked hands with her boyfriend and walked away, she turned and waved, reserving one last look for John.

"Come on Buck, train's here!" Henry proclaimed.

Looking at the girl of his dreams disappearing with every step, John boarded the train and just like that, was whisked away from her.

As they travelled home, Elena couldn't stop thinking about John. She sat next to Alex in silence, but her mind was racing and having thousands of conversations with itself all at once.

What had happened tonight? She felt like she'd been through a tornado of emotions, the events of the evening all replaying in her mind in a distorted highlight reel. *Is it fate? What are the odds that I have now seen him twice since Winter Wonderland? London is a huge place, could it mean something? He's so...*

"So, what did you think of them?" The question from Alex rudely cut through her thoughts like a knife.

"Oh, erm, yeah, amazing, I had so much fun!" she managed to force out of her mouth, her mind still very much elsewhere.

"Any surprises or comments?" Alex probed.

Yes, she wanted to say. *Yes, John was everything you described and more. He's so charismatic, good looking* (did she mean that? She decided she did) *and funny.*

"No, I mean Dom and Buck were really funny, so was Freddie too actually. But they're all very nice," she finished, her true thoughts hidden from her boyfriend and even herself.

John exited the station alone and trudged home in a trance-like state. Replaying the evening's events and attempting to process the coincidence of what had happened, he realised that he had never met a girl like Elena before. He was pleased for yet envious of Alex, and more importantly, wanted to see her again. He had wanted to join her on the train to her home, where he should have been many months ago if he had just had the guts to ask her out when he had first met her. He continued his solitary walk home, not even thinking about his birthday in a few weeks' time and forgetting that he had even invited Kate. In fact, he hadn't even thought about her at all, he was consumed with images and thoughts of Elena, the girl from the stall. His friend's girlfriend.

CHAPTER FOUR

E lena stirred from her slumber the next day around 8am. She was awake before Alex, as usual, and went about her morning rituals uninterrupted. Her road was tranquil, the occupants in the townhouses of her street in Notting Hill all peacefully asleep. Opening her downstairs windows to allow the warm air to fill her home, Elena prepared her coffee, along with Alex's tea. Her thoughts were just about to drift to last night when his voice suddenly pierced the silence, "Morning, darling."

"Oh, good morning sweetie, I thought you were asleep still?"

"I was, but here I am now, bright and breezy."

He was anything but, in all honesty. His blonde hair was matted to his forehead and his eyes were a bit bloodshot.

"Want to get breakfast? I feel like I didn't see much of you last night."

"Well, I was with my friends and I haven't seen them in a while," came Alex's response.

"Oh, I didn't mean that, just that I missed you my love," Elena said, circling her arms around his waist as she spoke.

"Oh, that's nice. Yes, I missed you too, of course," said Alex, his tone softer and his arms mirroring hers, easily enclosing her petite waist.

"Right, let's get ready and go!" Elena said, breaking the connection and making her way upstairs.

"Come on Alex, let's go before it gets busy!" she cried, grabbing her car keys.

Alex was still adjusting the spikes on his freshly waxed hair. "Alright, alright!" he said, lazily descending the staircase. He never rushed anything, which was a quality Elena both loved and hated. Frustrating at times where prompt action was needed, yet a significantly calming personality trait in times of stress. Though in truth, their relationship hadn't seen anything of the latter yet, so she was basing her thoughts on assumptions.

Setting the alarm and closing the front door behind her, Elena unlocked her car, relishing the new car smell as she slid daintily into the driver's seat.

"I really fancy a nice big breakfast today," Alex mused as he clambered into the passenger seat. Alex couldn't drive and had no desire to learn. He relied on receiving lifts from friends on most social occasions and used the bus to get to work.

"Hmm, I'm not sure, I think maybe just a croissant for me," Elena responded, eyes darting left and right as she checked the road both ways before pulling out of her allocated parking space.

"Oh okay, I'll let you choose the place then," Alex proffered, head down and eyes scrolling through various news bulletins on his phone.

"How about *Lolita's?*" Elena asked, somewhat pointlessly, as that would invariably be where they went anyway.

"Yeah if you like," Alex responded, without looking up from his phone.

"Great," Elena said, without much emotion, concentrating on the road.

The ten-minute journey concluded and the small parade of shops and restaurants was still relatively quiet, the odd person dotted around here and there.

"Right, let's go and pay for parking and get a table, it looks fairly empty," Elena announced.

"Yeah okay," Alex replied.

This wasn't what Elena wanted to hear, she had hoped he would take the initiative and either pay for parking or secure the table. Elena was very organised and fast-paced, especially for tasks such as this that required no thought process. However, she pushed these thoughts aside, linking arms with her man as they steadily walked to the nearest pay station, which was at the opposite end of the pavement to *Lolita's*. The short distance was covered in less than a minute, no words were exchanged, both of them content to let the silence sit easily between them. It wasn't an awkward or uncomfortable one, just that of familiarity, that you would have with a brother or close friend. Making their way back to where they'd been, they were greeted at the door by a middle-aged woman of Spanish descent.

"Welcome, come in, come in," she greeted, ushering the pair inside the cosy, family-owned restaurant. "Please, sit, sit," she insisted, pulling out a lightly coloured wooden chair, which matched that of the other fourteen tables neatly arranged in rows.

Elena graciously folded her patterned skirt beneath her as she sat, looking across at her boyfriend. He met her gaze and smiled with an open mouth, revealing a small but noticeable chip on one of his two front teeth, the result of a drunken stumble a few years ago.

A brief moment of quiet hung between the pair after they

had ordered, before Elena asked, "any news from your friends?"

"Erm, let me check, hang on." At this, Alex pulled his mobile phone from his dark blue jeans and checked the group chat that all of the friends shared.

"Ha, Freddie is hanging badly. Good." He didn't notice the look of disapproval from Elena at these words, as he continued to monitor the messages. "Nothing from Henry or Dom yet. Elena was leaning forward with expectation (though she didn't realise this), waiting for him to say one name in particular.

"Oh, John's gone to football this morning," Alex casually said, continuing his scroll. At this, Elena was suddenly not interested in hearing the rest of the news, though Alex, his head in the familiar downward position, studying his phone, continued on. *So, he plays football*, Elena mused. *Sporty guy, funny, good looking.* She caught herself at the last thought and suddenly coughed unexpectedly.

"You okay?" Alex asked.

"Yes, yes fine," Elena responded, somewhat flustered. Just in time, the waitress arrived with the drinks. Elena began drinking her hot chocolate a little too quickly and bowed her head over the mug to avoid Alex's gaze.

Regaining her composure, Elena set her drink aside and asked, "Has anyone uploaded any photos from last night?"

"Not sure, I'll look now," he said, scrolling through Facebook.

"Here we go," he said, finding the new album that had been created. Elena became suddenly anxious, even desperate. Alex silently scrolled through the pictures, laughing at some, neutral expressions for most.

"Well?" Elena impatiently asked (he was taking a while).

"Don't worry, no bad ones of you! Here," he offered the phone with a smile.

She realised that she didn't care about the pictures of her. She only cared about one thing. Swiping through the photos, she stopped on one particular image. There he was. Standing there, a perfect photogenic smile emblazoned on his chiselled face. She couldn't stop staring at his pink polo shirt which was filled out to perfection, and she studied every inch of his muscular frame.

"He's something else, isn't he?" Alex asked, leaning over the table to look at the picture himself.

"W-what?" Elena replied, startled and caught off-guard.

"Freddie. Look at the state of him." He gestured to the image, his finger landing to the right of John and on the drunken mess of Freddie.

"Yeah, I couldn't quite believe what I was looking at!" Elena recovered, thoughts of John smuggled away to the far recesses of her mind.

"I could tell!" Alex responded, returning back to his seat with his phone.

She hadn't even realised that Freddie was in the photo.

CHAPTER FIVE

"How do I look?" Elena asked, twirling as she did. "You look nice," came Alex's reply. "Nice" wasn't what Elena wanted, but it was the default response whenever she asked. "Are you ready?" he asked, adjusting the collar on his grey shirt.

"Almost, darling," she replied, taking one last look in her mirror as she made a slight, nervous adjustment to her hair. There was a heightened air of anticipation around her, a greater level of desire to look good and be noticed.

"Ready!" she proclaimed, beaming at Alex as she walked down the stairs. She stopped in front of her full-length mirror in the hallway and took a final glance, satisfied that the strappy top and white skinny jeans complimented her figure. These deliberate choices were the result of many failed outfit options, but she was confident that she looked good, no, *great*, for the evening ahead. Lifting her coat off the rack, she was ready to leave.

John pulled up to Fairway Street and turned the engine off, the rumble of his BMW abruptly ceasing. "I hope Mrs. B has got a nice big meal for us mate, what a day that was," chimed Dom from the passenger seat.

"Me and all mate, double busy today weren't it?" John agreed, unfastening his seatbelt and exiting the car, locking it as he and Dom shut their respective doors in time, as though they were part of a synchronised swimming team.

"After you, my good man," Dom declared, an exaggerated elegance to his voice.

"Why thank you kindly, good Sir," John replied, matching Dom's tone. John swung the small black gate open, which creaked in welcome as he walked the short path to his white front door. The terraced house was one of the nicer ones in the road, thanks largely to his Dad, who was a painter and decorator.

"Shoes off at the door boys," came John's mum, Tina's commanding voice from somewhere deeper in the house. Tina was a robust woman who ran a tight ship in the Buckston household. "And get those overalls straight in the wash, you too Dom," she continued with the loud instruction.

"Yes ma'am," Dom replied, saluting the air as he did.

"Aye aye," came Bob's voice from the top of the staircase.

"Alright, Dad, how was your day?" asked John, who had just finished removing his work overalls and boots.

"Not bad mate, not bad. Me and your Uncle are working on this gaff over in Chelmsford, fucking massive, should see the garage!" he made a large "O" with his mouth and tilted his head back as he thumped down the stairs, a towel still drying his bald head; dark shorts and a white vest his attire for the evening.

"'Allo Dom, how are ya son?" he said, clapping Dom on his shoulder as he did, finally at the foot of the staircase.

"Yeah good thanks mate," came Dom's reply, a broad smile accompanying it.

"Good, good. Here, you best have a quick wash, dinner will be up soon," finished Bob, walking past the boys and into the lounge. Both Dom and John stood half a foot taller than Bob, yet both respected him tremendously. He was well loved by his family, friends and of course his wife, Tina, who was shouting something else from the kitchen which nobody could quite hear.

"Yeah he's got a point Dom, get yourself washed and ready and we'll get a move on," John said in agreement, now wearing a simple blue t-shirt that was under his overalls and the bottom half of his work attire.

Elena and Alex walked side by side in a lazy stroll. They headed out a little earlier than required, so that they could enjoy a meal before the evening's celebrations. As they continued on, Elena recalled how she had felt when John had asked her to come to his birthday a few weeks ago. The initial delight at the prospect of seeing him again was merged with the unwelcome realisation that his girlfriend would be there as well. Elena decided that she needed to get confirmation of whether that girl in the restaurant was John's girlfriend or not. It started with her creating a Facebook account, which she had held off on for years due to an incredibly jealous and controlling ex-boyfriend. Coupled with her new and very public job, Elena thought the risk of privacy invasion was too great to compromise. Now, however, there was a reason to have it. Smiling as she continued to reminisce, Elena was reminded of the sudden panic and excitement that fizzed up in her stomach when that all-important notification she was waiting for hit her phone:

John Buckston would like to add you as a friend.

She had hurriedly accepted and within a minute, found herself added to a virtual group which was titled, "Buck's Big Birthday Bash". Elena then noticed the list of attendees. The familiar faces from their last outing were there, but there was also a stranger. A girl. Kate Bradstock. Elena had spent the next thirty minutes scrutinising her profile and spotted the evidence she was hunting; she and John had been out before and had pictures together, as well as exchanges on her page which looked very friendly. Delving deeper into Kate's photo albums, Elena saw that she was indeed the girl she had seen John with at the restaurant. Curiously, neither of them had their status as *"In a relationship"*.

"Everything okay?" Alex asked, noticing that Elena had gone quiet.

"What? Oh, yes, of course, sorry. Just thinking." Elena's memory of finding Kate Bradstock on John's Facebook page made her shudder.

"About what?" he probed.

"Just work stuff," she lied. Alex didn't bother to interrogate further, which Elena was very grateful for. However, breaking the silence, she changed the topic by asking, "Are you excited for tonight?"

"Yeah, be good to see everyone again, been a few weeks now."

"Good, it's nice for you to see your friends," remarked Elena genuinely.

"What about you?" Alex continued.

"Oh, very much so, been so long since I was out clubbing!" she excitedly responded, looking up at him with bright eyes shining with anticipation.

"Yeah, me too, let's hope we actually get in this time and Bucky hasn't used some dodgy website to get us entry."

"No, I think Buck's the type to get things sorted. I mean, he seems quite capable, you know?" she blushed suddenly at this, which again went unnoticed.

"Yeah, should be fine," Alex finished, in a non-committal way, making his way into the bustling French restaurant.

~

"Pass us the sprouts, son," came Bob's request at the head of the table. John duly obliged, handing his father the dish containing the vegetables.

"Ta," he replied, dishing himself a generous portion, adding to the enormous mound of food already on his plate.

"How is it?" Tina asked, matter-of-factly, but with an underlying tone that sought approval.

"Yeah, lovely."

"Amazing."

"Beautiful," came the garbled responses of the three men at the table, mouths presently crammed with food.

"Good," Tina commented, allowing herself a glance at the spread before her. A perfectly roasted chicken took centre stage, with roast potatoes in a dish on one side and an array of vegetables filling another bowl. Taking up the rest of the space were the aforementioned sprouts, a boat of gravy and a plate of roasted gammon (Dom's favourite).

"Cheers to tonight then boys," Bob initiated the occasion by raising his Budweiser, clanging it against the twin bottles of Peroni held by John and Dom, with Tina's glass of water meeting the trio with a gentle clink. They all proceeded to take a drink and Bob continued, "She gonna be there tonight then?"

"Well I would have thought so," John replied out of the side of his mouth, smuggling a potato on the other side.

"Good, maybe you can convince her to be your bird," he continued, half-joking, half seriously.

"You what?" John remarked, taken aback and somewhat flustered.

"Well, you've been seeing her for a while now, surely it's about time?" Bob answered.

He was talking about Kate. Of course he was. For a second, John thought he meant somebody else. His heart rate slowed and he steadied himself, buying time by inserting some more chicken in his mouth. Finally, John said, "Yeah, well we'll see how it goes. We're taking it slowly I guess," he finished, satisfied with his answer.

"You go any slower and you'll be going backwards mate," Dom chimed up, which drew raucous laughter from Bob and even a laugh from John, despite being the target of the joke.

"Yeah, yeah, alright," he grinned, nudging his best friend.

"Oi, no fighting at my table!" Tina commanded, brushing her blonde hair out of her eyes as she did so, letting it sit neatly on her shoulders.

"Yes mum, sorry mum," John respectfully answered, with a sly smile.

"Good boy," she replied, in a mocking tone, which drew more laughter from the table.

"Right, best get ready, ain't we," John announced, giving Dom a nod of direction.

"Yeah, 'spose we had," came the reply. "Lovely dinner as always Mrs.B, can I help clear up?"

"Oh that's alright Dom, Bob's gonna help, aren't you Bob?"

"Do I have a choice?" John's dad answered, still working his way through the various layers of food.

"Course you don't, besides, we can't let you get bored now, can we?" she joked, drawing additional laughs.

"Right, thanks mum. Dom, take the upstairs shower, I'll go down here. Evan's on his way in about half an hour, so don't take too long with your hair for once," John instructed as he left the table, taking his and Dom's plates.

"You only say that because yours will be on its bike soon, just look at your old man!" he joked, whilst making a dash for the door.

"Cheeky bastard," Bob said, shaking his head and smiling.

"Yeah, yeah laugh it up. See you back down here in a bit," John said, a raised middle finger accompanying the words.

The Glass Jar loomed into view as the private taxi that ferried John, Dom and Evan from Dagenham reached its destination. The fee was paid and the three men spilled out into the bustling street.

"Right boys, here we go, let's have a blinding night!" John exclaimed, sandwiched between Dom and Evan. They produced their driver's licences to verify their ages and entered the funky bar. A blast of contemporary music hit them like a wave as the doors were held open by the bouncers. An array of multi-coloured lights streaked across the moderately sized room, briefly illuminating the occupants within, revealing how near capacity the venue was.

"Good thing we booked," John opined, nods of agreement from his companions solidifying his conclusion.

"Have a seat John, I'll get the first drinks in," Evan offered.

"Ah cheers mate. Yeah, best see if some muppets are in our booth as it goes," John replied, hoping that his statement would prove to be inaccurate. He weaved in and out of dancing young adults, catching the eye of one or two and exchanging a smile with some ladies in passing. It was a good confidence booster this early into the night, which he would need. She would be here soon and he was getting more anxious.

"Ah, there we go," John said, pointing at the booth with his name on it.

"Wicked, I'll just nip to the loo mate, be two ticks," Dom announced.

John didn't mind being left alone. He approached the booth and sat in the middle, able to analyse the scene before him.

A packed dance floor was a few meters directly in front of the booth and to the right, an even busier bar that stretched the entire length of the room. He spotted the unmistakable figure of Evan there, who at that moment turned around and caught John's eye. They exchanged signs of greeting, Evan tapping his watch followed by an exasperated look to the heavens, which made John laugh. He moved his gaze to the entrance, of which he had a clear enough view, once the general throng of people had subsided enough as they moved back and forth to either dance or get more drinks.

John felt his heart thump in his chest; he was looking to make a big impression on her tonight. He'd had a fresh haircut and beard trim the day before, cleaning up his skin-fade and shaping his facial hair precisely in a smooth style. His polo-shirt was brand new and fit perfectly, complimenting his muscular physique, which was the goal. To finish the look, John had purchased some maroon chinos, paired with dark shoes. It was comfortably the most effort John had ever put into an outfit or night out and he pondered if *she* was the reason why.

"Is he still mucking about at the bar?" Dom said, interrupting John's thoughts.

Scanning the room to confirm Evan's progress, John replied, "Yeah, although he's just being served now."

"Might as well stay there, look who's just turned up," Dom replied, pointing to the door.

John's heart skipped a beat in anticipation and was quickly returned to normal as he saw Freddie, Henry and Leo arrive together, accompanied by their girlfriends.

"Oi oi!" John shouted, standing up in the booth and waving to the cohort who all looked in his direction, beaming smiles at him and returning the gesture.

"Night's about to begin fella, happy birthday!" Dom smiled and clapped John's shoulder.

~

Elena was shown inside whilst Alex had his ID checked. Her heart was beating faster now and she was more nervous than she showed.

"Is anyone else here?" she inquired.

"Yeah, think...oh, yeah there's Leo and Freddie at the bar," Alex replied, smiling and waving in their direction.

"Great, good," Elena replied, gripping her clutch bag tighter without realising.

"Come on, let's go and get some drinks," Alex led, not extending his hand out for Elena to hold, but instead desperate to get to his friends and presumably, start drinking.

Elena scanned the room and through the crowd, spotted John at a table, laughing heartily as he shared a joke with others who Elena couldn't quite make out due to the sheer amount of people in view. She turned back to the direction of the bar on her left and locked eyes with Leo, hugging him in greeting.

"Shall we go and sit down?" she asked, tugging Alex's shirt as she spoke loudly into his ear over the deep bass of the music.

"Nah, we'll just get our drinks and then go, won't be two seconds." he replied, turning his attention back to the bar and his friends, just as Leo moved out to head to the bathroom.

"*Scusa*," he said, his native Italian coming through, smiling at Elena as he passed her.

She decided to reach for her phone and check for any messages. She didn't notice that mere inches behind her, Kate had arrived and was heading straight for John and the table.

～

John took a sip of his iced strawberry daiquiri, shuddered a little from the sharp taste and set it back on the table. He looked up and saw Kate approaching, which was verified by an elbow into his ribs from Henry.

"Eyes up fella, you're on."

Oh fuck, John thought. He didn't have any sort of "game plan" for what to do in order to win her over and it occurred to him in that moment that he didn't really care. Yet he was nervous all the same, a by-product of being low on confidence. "Kate!" he exclaimed, banging his knee on the table as he rose sharply out of his seat. Pain seared through him, but he ignored it, shuffling past Dom in order to go and greet her.

"Hi!" she replied with a wave, and the two shared their typical, sibling-like hug. "Do you want a drink?" John asked, an air of haste to his voice.

"Yeah, sure, shall we?" she offered her arm to be taken, which John did, much to his own surprise.

"Well that's a good start," Dom commented.

"Yeah, still plenty of time for it to go south, though," replied Henry with a laugh.

"Stranger things have happened, boys," Evan offered.

"Yeah, apparently so, if *he* can get laid," Henry said, pointing a finger at Leo, who feigned insult.

"I'll have you know, the girls are lining up to be with me," he defended.

"Probably because they think you'll make a blinding pizza!" Henry responded, to hearty laughter from the group.

～

John and Kate joined the queue relatively close to the reserved table. As they turned their backs to the dancefloor and studied the drinks menu, Elena, Alex and Freddie walked past them, joining the rest of the group.

"Easy boys!" Freddie proclaimed to the mixture of men and women, proudly holding two beers aloft in each hand as he did, some spilling carelessly onto his shirt.

"Sit down you mess," Dom playfully said, embracing Freddie as he tumbled into his seat, more beer being spilled.

"Hi everyone!" Elena announced, waving as she did. A quick scan revealed that John wasn't there, much to her disappointment. A chorus of greeting met her back and she shuffled into the booth alongside her partner, as conversation droned on in the background. *Why wasn't he here? Probably in the toilet*, she thought.

"You're looking good tonight," said Dom, a little smile and a look of desire flashing in his eyes.

"Oh, thanks," she replied, caught a little off guard. "Do you like the glitter?" she asked, regaining her composure.

"Very sparkly," Dom affirmed, taking another sip of his beverage. It was then that John and Kate made their way back to the group, their arrival announced by Dom, "Here he is!" he said, beaming.

Elena turned around and her heart sank. Walking towards her was indeed John, but his gaze was fixed upon the girl he was walking with, both of whom were laughing at a shared joke. She had clearly put very little effort or thought into her outfit, Elena surmised, quickly looking her up and down, eyes stopping at her faded jeans and scuffed trainers. *He could do so much better than her*, Elena suddenly thought with a jolt, and then they were upon the table.

∼

John introduced Kate to the group, many of whom she had met before. He was then taken aback by what he saw sitting at the edge of the booth. *She was here at last.* Perched like a delicate flower, Elena sat and was staring right at him, her eyes swimming with emotion. *What was it? Excitement? Joy? Yet there's something else there,* he couldn't put his finger on it. Was she not pleased to see him? He decided to find out.

"Hey!" he greeted, hoping she would stand up so he could get a full look at her.

"Hi Buck, happy birthday!" she exclaimed, standing up and hugging him. John had been longing to embrace her again, and he could smell her sweet scent. Her arms wrapped around his back for the briefest of moments and ignited a spark of desire within him, that was hastily put out.

"Oh, sorry, I've gone and got glitter all over you!" she teased, looking down at his body, with a mischievous glint in her eye.

"Haha, so you have!" John cried out, lightly pretending to dust the remnants off. Their eyes lingered on each other briefly and John felt a presence at his left shoulder, which made him jump back a little.

"Hi!" Kate announced, leaning in to embrace Elena. "You must be Alex's girlfriend!" she continued.

"Hi, yes, I'm Elena, and you are?" she questioned, knowing exactly who she was. John definitely detected something in her tone.

"I'm Kate," she answered, apparently not sensing the same disdain John had. "I love your top!" she continued.

"Oh, thank you," Elena replied. "Do you want to sit down?"

she asked, moving up at the same time.

"Great, thanks!" Kate said, taking her seat.

"Let's get to know each other a bit, we're very outnumbered here!" Elena said, looking around at the male dominated group.

John watched all this unfold and with a last look at the girls, he turned his attention to the quartet of Dom, Freddie, Henry and Evan and joined their conversation.

CHAPTER SIX

"Why is this taking so long?" Henry moaned, hands firmly in the pockets of his dark jeans.

"I assume because it's busy, unless that fact escapes you," Dom replied, a few rows behind Henry in the huddle of people eagerly waiting to enter *Club Destiny*, which, despite the name, was actually an enjoyable venue that they had frequented on numerous occasions. John had learned from years gone by and numerous failed nights that finished in terrible clubs that it was best to hold celebrations in familiar territory. *The Glass Jar* had provided the ideal setting to act as the first meeting point, allowing people to unwind into the night and more importantly for John, give him time to cement his plan of action. He had intended to make this the time where he would ramp up his efforts to break free of the shackles of the friend-zone he found himself in with Kate. Yet he realised that his focus was not entirely on the task at hand. Instead, he cast a glance over his shoulder past Kate and saw the dark hair of Elena blowing gently in the evening wind. She was with Alex, but her conversation included Leo and Freddie. Something made her laugh, which caused John to smile.

"Come on," Dom said, giving John a slight nudge, which shook him from this momentary daydream. The queue had moved forward a few paces and they were next in line to enter.

"What's the plan then, big man?" Dom inquired, which caused a fleeting moment of panic before John realised he was asking about Kate.

"Well, erm. I guess, just get her alone, dance a bit, see what happens?" John answered, his mind still not really committed to the task and instead resisting every urge to once again look back and steal a glance at Elena.

"That could work," Dom started, "But it's pretty vague, mate. You need to think of *how* you're going to do it, what you're going to say. Those sort of things. No pressure," he finished, flashing a grin.

"IDs" the bouncer asked, looking completely bored. The boys dutifully obeyed, displaying their driver's licenses for the second time that night. Satisfied that they were indeed their age, the dark red rope was lifted and Dom and John proceeded down the wide staircase to the payment booth. Paying the familiar price of £10, they were given a stamp on the hand, enabling them to enter. Just then, the twin doors burst forth, revealing a deranged looking man with most of his shirt hanging open, firmly escorted by two large bald bouncers.

"That'll be Freddie in about half an hour," Dom joked, causing the pair to burst out laughing.

"Suppose we should wait here then so you can pounce on your victim," Dom continued, still laughing.

"You make it sound like I'm some sort of predator," John replied, taking no offence, but acting as if he had.

"Well, if the shoe fits mate," Dom answered, causing them to embrace in a grapple that turned into a genuine hug.

"Look mate, whatever happens, just enjoy your evening. It

doesn't matter if she says yes or no, you'll always have me and the other lads," Dom reassured, a firm hand on John's shoulder and a warm smile on his face.

"Ah mate, thank you," John said, pulling Dom in for another hug.

"Oi oi, didn't realise you two were together!" Henry brazenly proclaimed, bounding towards them, leading the remainder of the group who had now all been granted entry.

John smiled and then his heart skipped a beat as he saw her coming towards him. He noticed that she wasn't holding Alex's hand and in all honesty, they didn't look like a couple. Kate then swam into his view blocking out Elena, and he was again focussed. "Come on, let's grab a drink," he said to Kate, taking her by the hand as he did so.

Elena saw John grab Kate's hand and despite herself, she felt disappointed. In the brief time they had spent together at the previous bar, she had learned everything that she needed to know about Kate. Chiefly, Kate wasn't all that interested in John, as he didn't crop up in conversation once and she was more concerned with talking about herself, something about her twin sisters and her job as a secretary. Elena was somewhat relieved at this revelation, but simultaneously flustered at Kate apparently leading John along. Kate had eagerly accepted his hand, giggling away as they melded into the throng of the crowd. Elena couldn't hide her look of disgust which was noticed by Alex.

"Everything okay?" he asked.

"Yeah, fine. Just hate this song," she answered, still glaring into the space where John and Kate had been. "Do we have anywhere to sit?" Elena asked.

"No, there's no booths here, just two floors with bars and a huge dance floor on each," Alex explained.

"I see," Elena muttered, somewhat disappointed in the fact that it would be difficult to get to know the group better. She had only ever been to a club once before and didn't really drink much, so she normally preferred a bar setting where she could talk to her friends.

∼

"What do you fancy, then?" Kate asked John, which made him jump as he initially misheard the "what" for "who".

"Oh, erm. Vodka and coke, please," he responded, with a little less composure than he would have liked, his voice cracking.

"Great, me too," she replied and turned back towards the bar, making her order. John looked around, seeing some of his friends littered along the bar as well, placing their own requests. Leo caught his eye and gave him a thumbs up.

Does everyone know my ambitions for the night? John thought, smiling back at Leo and mimicking the gesture, just as Kate served up his drinks.

"Cheers!" she announced, lightly tapping her cup against his. They both drank, John a little more than she did, and a moment of silence settled noticeably between them.

"You having a good time?" he finally spluttered out, not really that interested in the answer, but wanting the conversation to resume.

"Yeah! Thanks a lot for inviting me," she replied, taking another sip through her straw.

"Of course," John answered. "Shall we?" He motioned towards the dancefloor, which was full of people, some dancing, some locked in passionate kisses and some just staring at the ceiling, shuffling their feet occasionally as their wide eyes scanned objects above that only they could see.

"Yeah, let's do it," she replied and extended her hand for John to take. He gladly accepted, noting that this was the most physical contact that he and Kate had engaged in outside of their friendly hugs. He led her onto the dancefloor and they moved their bodies in time with the music. His hands dared to grab her waist and she smiled, making no resistance to the forward movement. Her arms dangled around his neck and they locked eyes. John's heart started to thump, he was suddenly in a place where he had wanted to be, yet now that the moment was upon him, he was holding back. The music was pounding in his ears, the multi-coloured lights were dancing over his vision and in that moment, he had to act. He pulled her towards his body and leant in, kissing her cheek. He spoke into her ear saying, "Thanks for being here."

"I'm happy to be," she answered, speaking loudly into his ear. John had realised his opportunity had been and gone and continued to dance, his eyes now searching the crowd for someone else.

~

Elena danced, absently letting her gaze wander. She had given up looking for John in the crowd. One of the strobe lights flashed green and the whirling mechanism spun its beam of light perfectly into Elena's right eye. She squinted, looking accusingly in the direction from where it had originated and spotted John, his arms holding Kate's waist. A flicker of jealousy flared up inside her and she grabbed Alex's arm.

"Look, there's John," she announced, waving as she did, hoping he would see her. He didn't. Annoyed, she pressed on, determined to go over and see him. It had felt like she had hardly spent any time with him all evening and she wanted to change that.

"Let's go, let's go!" she insisted.

"Nah, he's making his move, can't you see?" he responded, his attention already turning back to the circle of friends.

Frustrated, Elena persevered. "It's *his* birthday, we should be with him as a group! He can still spend time with Kate if he wants!" she was almost sick at the thought, but retained her even tone.

"Alright, alright, guys, Buck's over that way!" Alex proclaimed to the rest of the group, motioning with his thumb in the general direction as he was being whisked away by Elena. They meandered through the crowd as one, stepping on feet, bumping into shoulders and pushing and shoving.

"Yes Buck!" Evan exclaimed, greeting John with a smile and yet another drink, which he clumsily fumbled into John's grip.

"Alright mate," Henry interjected, his large arm reaching around John's neck, pulling him closer for a manly embrace. The welcomes continued and the drinks flowed as they all toasted something arbitrary. John and Kate drifted away from each other and Elena smiled, satisfied that her job was complete. It wasn't that she wanted John for herself (although this was probably true, she wouldn't allow herself to admit it) rather she wanted someone *for* John who wanted him like he deserved.

"Alright, alright, alright. Listen up, listen up!" The DJ had stopped the music, much to the surprise of many, annoyance of some and indifference of others.

"Right now, I'm gonna need everyone up to the dancefloor, we're holding a competition up in here!" With a click of a button, klaxon horns blared out from the gigantic speakers, shaking the foundations of the club.

"The fuck is this about?" Henry asked, to nobody in particular.

"Dunno, worth checking out though. John, you game?" Dom asked.

"Yeah, fuck it, why not," he replied. "Come on then, up we go," he ordered, taking Kate's hand as they began their ascent up the spiral stairs to the floor above. Elena glowered behind them, walking separately from Alex.

"Gather round, gather round, we have ourselves a competition, unlimited drinks to the winners!" This announcement by the DJ was met with a roar of approval from the crowd.

"We need to see the *best* dance moves you have, so step up if you think you have what it takes. You got one minute per couple," he bellowed, and immediately there was a buzz of excited chatter. "We only have space for five couples, so get yourselves to my booth if you want to be in," he finished, dropping the microphone and resuming the music.

"Buck, you absolutely have to do this, it's your birthday and you're actually good!" Evan immediately insisted.

"Yeah, come on Buck, do it!" Freddie provoked, giving John a gentle dig in the stomach.

"Yeah, do it!" the chorus of encouragement rose from each person until finally John answered, "Alright, fine! But I need a partner." He scanned his friends, his eyes landing on Kate, who looked away, shaking her head.

"I'll do it!" he heard Elena announce, and it caused his heart to leap into his throat. "Yeah, let's go Buck, we need to win these losers some free drinks!" She smiled as she said it and a ripple of laughter went through the group.

"If you say so," John replied, raising his eyebrow quizzically. "Lead the way." He motioned for her to go first, which she did. She could feel his eyes on her as she walked, and her stomach flipped. They approached the booth and Elena was clearly nervous.

John suddenly asked, "Can you actually dance well?"

She was almost insulted by the question; of course she could. Confident in her own ability, she simply stated, "You'll see," a mischievous smile accompanying the response.

"Names?" the DJ asked.

"John and Elena," replied John.

"It's his birthday today!" Elena added.

"Well, well well, happy birthday my man," the DJ responded, flashing a grin revealing his gold tooth in the upper right corner of his mouth. "You two are on next, go and smash it!"

"Thanks, we will," John confidently replied, looking down at Elena with a smile that made her go slightly weak at the knees.

"Alright ladies and gents, last up we have birthday boy John!" The crowd applauded and cheered at this announcement, as John walked towards the dance floor. "And Elenaaaaaa!" he let the "a" hang as he began to spin the music amidst the cheers and applause.

John and Elena locked eyes and then the music started. Elena danced like a professional. She moved and adjusted her body so fluidly in time with every drop of the beat, the rhythm of the music pulsating through her. John, who had taken a passing interest in dancing for the last few years based purely on various music videos on MTV, unleashed all that he had learned. He wasn't quite keeping pace, but was certainly holding his own. They locked eyes as they moved, staring at each other and learning more and more as each beat thumped in the background. The electricity between them was palpable, igniting more fires within them as they continued to dance, oblivious to the cheers, the appreciative eyes and clapping, they kept moving in their own bubble, laughing the whole time. The track finished as John and Elena timed their final flurry to perfection, coming to a halt inches away from each other. They both flushed a scarlet red and turned back towards their friends, beaming huge smiles.

"I think we have our winners!" the DJ announced, the crowd clearly in agreement. "Go get your drinks and have a great night!"

As the evening went on, Freddie disappeared, Leo made his excuse to leave and the club became busier. John, who had entirely given up on Kate, was now content to dance and have fun with his friends. Dom, Henry and Evan joined him and they moved without much passion, just enjoying the evening and sipping their drinks. Elena and Alex were approaching them clutching drinks and suddenly Elena stumbled, spilling some of the contents of her glass onto a large man standing next to Dom.

"Oh my god I'm so sorry!" she exclaimed, mortified by her momentary clumsiness. The man looked down at his ruined shirt, which was untucked and now soaked through. He was with two girls and three other men.

"You fucking clumsy bitch!" he spat, flicking ice and liquid off his hands. John heard this and stared with wild eyes in disbelief, as Alex stood there motionless.

"I'm sorry, I'm sorry," Elena repeated, becoming visibly upset.

"You're a fucking idiot!" the man continued.

John didn't hesitate. With a powerful right punch, he shattered the man's nose and dislodged a few of his teeth.

"DON'T YOU FUCKING DARE TALK TO HER LIKE THAT!" he screamed, as a fist impacted John's right cheek. Henry and Dom pounced on the offender, swiftly bringing him down and continuing the assault.

Alex took Elena out of harm's way and they moved towards the exit. Behind them, the brawl continued and John, momentarily stunned, did not lose focus on his prey. The man was standing groggily to his feet and John swiftly punched him precisely on his jaw, making him back away. By now, bouncers had arrived and John received a punch in the stomach and was in a tight headlock as he was hauled outside. Dom and Henry soon followed, escorted in a similar fashion. Blood was flowing freely from Dom's nose as the trio collected themselves in the street outside.

"Where's Elena?" John asked, clutching his ribs as he did.

"No idea, let's move before any old bill come," Henry answered.

~

Elena and Alex were joined by Kate as they fled the scene. "Oh my God, I can't believe that, we should go back!" Elena cried.

"No, no, we need to go and get home safely," Alex responded, hailing down a cab as he did so.

"What happened in there?" Kate asked.

"Big fight," Alex responded, checking uneasily behind him as he did. "We need to leave and get away from here, let's share a cab, come on." The three of them clambered in the back of the London taxi and gave the appropriate instructions to the driver to take them to their respective homes.

"That's a shame," Kate began. "It was a great night up until then," she finished.

With adrenaline coursing through her, Elena decided to act.

"So, what's actually happening with you and John?" she probed. "Do you like him?" she added, before she had even received a response.

"Yeah, I like John. He's great, but we're just friends, you know?" she said bluntly.

Elena began to shift in her seat, uncomfortable with Kate's attitude. "Well, he really likes you."

"Oh, well you know, I do like him, but..." Kate responded, trailing off.

"You just like the attention, don't you?" Elena pressed, her temperature and anger rising together.

"I don't know what you mean?" Kate responded in ignorance, whether genuine or otherwise.

"You like the fact that he wants you, pays for your meals and drinks, but don't want him back. You need to let him move on and stop stringing him along," Elena insisted.

"No, it's not like that," she replied, dismissive of the insinuation.

"I'm going to tell him then, I have to. It's not fair," Elena answered, barely containing her anger.

"Leave it," Alex opined.

Elena had completely forgotten he was there. The silence descended on the passengers like a heavy weight as they continued their journey home in complete silence.

In a separate taxi, John was simmering with frustration, a tissue dabbing the cut that was open just below his eye. Dom had what looked like an entire Kleenex box up his nose and Henry nursed his bruised and cut knuckles. Despite their injuries, the three boys were fare better off than the group they were fighting with in the club. John reached for his phone, a tornado of thoughts circulating in his mind. *Why didn't Alex defend Elena?* Frustrated, he opened up his contacts and found Elena, firing off a quick message that read:

R u ok?

Elena's phone chirped noisily in the cab, cutting through the tense silence. She jumped a little in her seat, which went unnoticed by anyone else, and delved into her clutch, emerging with her phone in her grasp. She had received a text. From John. *Ohmygodohmygodohmygod.* Four letters and a question mark were all it took for her heart to flutter a little. Despite all of the unpleasantness in the air and the events they had just left behind, she allowed a small smile to herself. Her fingers danced rapidly across her phone's keyboard as she responded:

```
Yes are you? You didn't have to stick up for
   me like that. I hope he didn't hurt you?
```

Elena had typed out "X" denoting a kiss, but quickly backpedalled, deleting that singular important letter. She sent the message and waited, looking out into the murky depths of London through the window of the taxi, noticing people clearly intoxicated and basically falling into the road, watching the abnormally long queues for a cheap kebab at 2AM. Her phone buzzed (she had silenced the ringtone so as not to draw attention to herself) and she opened John's reply.

```
Ye. In a cab wiv Dom n Henry. We're ok. You
                going home?
```

She was relieved to learn that he was fine, but was desperate to tend to him and longed to be sitting beside John, comforting him where she could. A flash of anger wobbled her mind and she remembered how smugly Kate had dismissed John's feelings in their earlier chat. She glared at her and began typing her response to John.

```
Yes, just sharing a cab. She doesn't like
              you by the way.
```

Send. A moment elapsed and John responded with just one word:

Who?

Elena paused, biting her lip. How to say it? Honesty would be the best policy here. Again, her fingers rapidly punched in the message which read:

Kate. She likes you as a friend.

A longer delay this time, but eventually John replied:

Oh. How do u know?

This time Elena didn't hesitate:

I asked her. I didn't want to see you wasting your time. You can do so much better.

Send. A faster response this time:

Oh yeah, can I? Like who?

Elena caught herself from smiling too broadly. "ME!" she had wanted to scream and send, but she couldn't.

How about a clone of me? Haha.

Send. She anxiously played with her hair, the wait agonising. Her phone at last buzzed and she nearly dropped it on the floor in her desperation to read what he had said:

Wouldn't that be nice :)

Her heart skipped a beat and her excitement grew, but it was immediately punctured like a balloon being stabbed with a pin when the cab driver announced that she had reached her destination. Reluctantly, she left with Alex, unlocked her door and made her excuses to immediately shower. Her heart was racing as she sat on her toilet still fully clothed, reading John's message over and over again. The shower was turned on and was thudding away gently against the base of her bath, but she made no attempt to get in. She just kept reading.

John, Dom and Henry quietly entered the Buckston residence with relative success, the sound of their arrival going unnoticed by John's parents.

"Right boys, showers and bed, let's just get our nut down and try and look forward to a greasy fry up in the morning," John proclaimed.

He allowed Dom and Henry to shower first, making use of the bathrooms on the ground and first floor. John sank into his usual position on the sofa, pulling his phone out from his pocket and noticing that there was another text from Elena.

Going to bed now. Thanks for sticking up for me. Goodnight x

Woah. A kiss. John was happier than he should have been with this and was glad to be alone in this moment, for it would have been impossible to suppress the enormous grin on his face. He realised he hadn't responded yet, so hastily input:

Anytime. Goodnight you x

Satisfied, he leaned further into the comforting embrace of the sofa and allowed the swirling thoughts of the evening to circle and settle. One by one, images flashed by his mind's eye as he reflected on the night and then the best part of all came swimming into vision; the dance competition. Not the fact that he had won, he didn't care about that. What he did care about was dancing with Elena. Her moves were intoxicating, her body's curves were perfectly highlighted with every single deliberate motion and he was completely under her spell. The way she had looked at him with that sensual look in her eyes only got him more excited and as the dance drew to a close, he felt like he'd been on a rollercoaster of passion.

"Shower's free," Dom whispered, yet to John it had been as though he had shouted it through a megaphone, such was the magnitude of the interruption to his private thoughts.

"Sweet, thanks mate, see you in the morning. Nose is bleeding again by the way," he said casually as he brushed past his friend.

"Oh shi-" he said, rushing to stem the flow with a tissue. "Oh by the way, did you get anywhere with Kate in the end?"

John paused as he was climbing the steps and turned back to face Dom. Smiling, he replied, "Nah, but it's okay. She isn't the one for me anyway."

CHAPTER SEVEN

J ohn sat scrolling mindlessly through his phone when he stopped upon his final message to Kate three months ago:

Hey, I know that you don't like me the way I like you, but it would've been nice if you'd told me. I know now that you only kept me around to make yourself feel better and have someone buy you dinner. Take care and have a nice life.

It had been a much-needed release for John in that he could put his focus elsewhere; namely on himself, his friends and his family. When he wasn't working at the garage, he was at the gym. At home he was cooking more frequently and making a conscious effort to learn some decorating skills from his dad. Essentially, John was throwing himself into everything and anything to keep himself busy, for if he wasn't involved in some sort of task, his mind would seize the opportunity to remind him that he was very much single and seeking the woman of his dreams. He knew exactly the sort of girl he wanted; beautiful, intelligent, independent and with a wonderful sense of humour. Just like Elena. He had admitted as much to her boyfriend, Alex, disclosing the fact that he wished he had a girl just like his.

Alex was very quick to then criticise John's life choices and blamed his inability to "bag a girl like Elena" on the fact that he "kept pissing around at the gym".

However, John knew that deep down he didn't want a girl just *like* her, he wanted *her*. Equally, John knew that he couldn't dare allow such a thought to blossom and develop, so he channelled a lot of energy into burying those ideas by involving himself in the aforementioned activities. So, John and Elena hardly exchanged more than a few words since his birthday, save for the occasional piece of small talk. There were far more important words they wanted to say, yet they would need to remain unspoken.

Presently, John slammed the passenger door of the Audi he was working on, satisfied that he had successfully installed the radio the customer had requested.

"Just taking a break, boss, be back in fifteen," John announced to his manager Neil, who simply nodded in acknowledgement from his seat. Walking through the office, John collected his phone and plastic tub containing chicken and broccoli. He looked down and saw four new notifications. One, a message from his mum, which simply asked if he would like spaghetti bolognese tonight. Another was an enquiry from an unknown number about a car service, which he ignored for now. The third was a flurry of messages from the group chat he shared with his friends, again to be read later. Lastly, and most importantly, a message from Elena. John's adrenaline spiked momentarily, the mere sight of her name got him excited and slightly anxious.

He swiped the message open and it read:

Hey Buck, hope you're okay? Alex and I are wondering if you fancied bowling this weekend?

John paused to consider the proposal. Was it just the three of them? Maybe not, that would explain the onslaught of messages in the group chat. He decided to venture there and scroll through the lines of unread text. Carter apparently had been drinking for three days straight, an accompanying photo showed the state he was in. John chuckled as he read on, shaking his head at some of the comments from his friends. Freddie and Henry were particularly jovial today. Most of the exchanges had actually been between those two with Alex chipping in now and then, but there was no mention of bowling. John stuffed some cold chicken in his mouth as he again reflected on the text from Elena. It occurred to him that he was probably making more of a big deal out of this than was merited. For one, he was almost certain he liked her more than she did him, especially in a romantic way. He closed his eyes, picturing for a second her face and her smile, again wistfully thinking that he could be her man. Shaking himself free of such thoughts, he finally summoned the courage to respond:

Yea sounds good, who else is coming?

He felt his pulse quicken and a few moments later, the reply came:

Just us 3 so far, can ask others?

John was surprised by this, firstly that it was indeed an occasion reserved just for the three of them and secondly that such an invitation would be extended his way.

. . .

John and Alex were friends certainly, but one wouldn't go as far as to say close. John had a far deeper connection with Dom and Evan for example. This caused John to wonder then if bowling had been an idea floated by Elena rather than Alex, which posed even further questions. Or was John simply reading far too much into this and instead, he should just accept that perhaps they thought he might need something to do at the weekend, seeing as he wasn't romantically involved with anyone. With renewed clarity, John sent the last text before returning to work. It simply said:

```
Can do, I'll see if anyone is free, speak
                    later
```

With a final bite of chicken, John put his phone away and went back to the workshop, where he was greeted by a beaming Dom.

"What's got you so happy?" John asked.

"Mate, this absolute rocket has just walked in, proper worldy have a look. "

John rolled his eyes before responding, "Yeah just like that last one, real head-turner mate!" Dom looked puzzled momentarily, before his eyes widened in recollection, followed by a bellowing laugh. "She was a good time mate. If you weren't so picky, you could have just as much fun."

"I'll pass, thanks," John said, grinning as he brushed past Dom to inspect the alleged beauty waiting to be seen. For once, Dom had been accurate in his assessment. Her ginger hair stood out against the dull interior of the garage, which was contrasted by her porcelain skin. Dressed in a hot pink velvet tracksuit accessorised by large gold hoop earrings, she certainly cut a striking image. She was standing unattended, with an impatient tilt in her stance. John looked around. Neil was still fussing over an old Jaguar in the corner, Dom was preparing an invoice for a customer, leaving John to deal with what was a potentially volatile interaction, judging by her demeanour.

He approached her and as he got closer, saw her eyes were heavily caked in mascara and liner, making their green tones pop unnaturally. She was short, coming up to John's chin (he guessed) and her arms were crossed, signalling further impatience.

"Hey, are you okay?" John inquired.

"No, I'm in deep trouble," she replied with a heavy Scottish accent.

"Oh, what's the problem?"

"Well, I've got no idea, that's why I'm here," she said in an aggravated tone, and John couldn't tell if she was joking or serious.

"Okay, well, let's take a look and see what we can do," he said, flashing a smile and hoping it would disarm her. It appeared to work somewhat and her arms unfolded as she pointed to her grey Vauxhall Astra that was about fifteen years old.

"It's over there," she directed, leading the way. John stole a glance at her bum which moved freely in the tracksuit. He idly wondered if she might be the sort of girl he should be going for, she certainly had the right body for him, but her personality might be a challenge. She unlocked the car and John turned the ignition on to see if any error signs came on. The dashboard lit up like a Christmas tree, the engine management light caught his eye first, but there were plenty of others that needed attention as well. He let out a low whistle which caught her attention and she asked, irritated, "What? What is it?"

"Well, I'm going to check the engine out for you, there's a lot here that could need work."

"Oh great, just what I need." She sighed heavily, once again folding her arms and looking towards the sky.

"It might not be that bad," John suggested hopefully. "Maybe just some loose wires causing the warning lights to appear, I've seen it plenty of times," he finished, again flashing a grin to disarm her.

"I really hope so," she said earnestly, John's smile again seeming to work its charm. "It's just I have to go back home tomorrow and I'm taking this," she gestured to the car in front of her, a slight look of dismay on her face.

"We'll get it right, don't worry. How far is home?"

"Glasgow."

"Woah, some journey, you by yourself?"

She opened her arms wide and looked around, somewhat mockingly. "Do you see anyone else?" she responded sarcastically.

John laughed, taking this in good humour and giving her leeway due to the situation. The car would likely need a lot of work done, so it was better to be overly polite at this stage.

"Okay, stupid question I know. Let me see then." He opened the bonnet and peered inside at the mess of components that had never been cleaned and likely sporadically serviced. Surveying the landscape, John noticed the air filter was clogged with all sorts of particles. He checked the oil and saw there was barely anything there, coolant levels were also well below minimum and to top it all, the spark plugs needed replacing.

"Well.." he began, scratching his head, thinking it was a miracle the car was even running. "We're going to have to get this in now and do a full service as a minimum. Then we can look at individual parts and see what you want to do, okay?"

"Oh God this is a nightmare," the woman exclaimed, her hands on her head. "How much is this all going to cost?"

"I'd estimate anywhere from three hundred and fifty pounds to a thousand, depending on what needs to be done."

"What!" she cried. "I can't afford that! Can't you just do the minimum so I can leave?"

"Believe me, the three fifty is the minimum, I can't in all good conscience let you drive out of here as it is," John replied, softening his tone and empathizing with her situation. This apparently placated her and she calmed down.

"Okay, will it be ready for tomorrow morning?" she glanced at her watch as she said this, noticing that the time was four in the afternoon, an hour before closing.

"I'll make sure of it, don't worry," John replied, with a kind smile. "Let me get this inside and we'll start right away." John drove the vehicle into the garage and whistled for Dom.

"Hey man, we got a real doozy here. She's gonna need work all night."

"Yeah that's my boy, so you taking her out then?" Dom replied with a cheesy smile.

"I meant the car, you dick, God, get your mind out of the gutter," John answered with an equal smile.

"Fine, but this better be worth it. At least offer to take her home or something."

"Her home is Glasgow, which is where she's headed tomorrow morning, hence the urgent need to fix this tonight."

"Ah," Dom mused. "Alright well in that case, offer her a ride to wherever she's staying. Come on man, you need to get back out there, Kate was months ago! This is a perfect opportunity!" Dom was right, John did need to expose himself to the world of dating again, he just didn't expect the opportunity to arrive in this package. He glanced over at the woman again. His first impressions of her? Bit rude, clearly high maintenance, but wasn't bad to look at. On closer examination, she

65

could just be stressed out with her car problems. She probably just needed someone to help her, assuming of course she was indeed single. *Fuck it, why not?* John thought. *I'll ask her if she wants a lift and see if she fancies going out later.* As he arrived at this decision, he was already briskly marching over to her.

"I've pulled some strings and we'll make sure this is done tonight. Can I offer you a lift somewhere?"

"Oh...erm. Yeah, thank you. I'm staying at a hotel not far from here, I just wanted to go out for some snacks, you know?"

"Sure thing, give me two minutes and I'll get my car."

John turned out of the street and headed towards *The Bridge*; the hotel around fifteen minutes away where the woman was staying. He looked across at her and decided to break the ice, "Sorry, I didn't catch your name earlier?"

"It's Chelsea," she responded staring blankly ahead.

"I'm John, in case you're wondering," he said with a laugh.

"Who said I was?" she replied flatly. Again he wasn't sure if she was joking or not, so breathed out a minute laugh that was more of a cough.

"So what's your story, Chelsea? How does someone from Glasgow end up down in Dagenham?"

"What's your story?" she repeated. "You sound like a cop in one of those American shows," she laughed as she did, the first time she had so far, John noted. "Well, John, if you must know, I was down here to see a friend."

"Oh yeah? Boyfriend or..." his voice trailed off as he asked.

"Nah, just a wee hook-up from the internet," she said.

"Oh, I see" John replied, his gaze fixed on the road.

"I'm joking ya dafty," she replied, lightly tapping John's arm as she did. "Is that the sort of girl ya think I am?"

"Ha, no, of course not!" he recovered, now smiling as well. "Just that you know, you're a pretty girl so I figured you'd have a boyfriend, that's all," he suggested, stealing a glance at her as he did.

"Oh you think I'm pretty then?" she said, smiling again and revealing row upon row of whitened teeth, which glinted almost menacingly, like those of a tiger about to feast on its prey.

"Did I say that? Must have been a slip of the tongue," he replied, smiling mischievously as he did.

"Does that happen to you a lot then, aye?" Chelsea asked.

"Only when I'm nervous," he said, laughing.

"So I make ya nervous then do I?" she inquired. "I think you're trouble, I'm gonnae have to watch you aren't I?"

"You can watch me this evening if you like," John blurted out, seemingly from nowhere. Where had that come from? He didn't really know, but he went with it.

"Is that a proposition then?"

"Yeah, let's have dinner. Seeing as I'm fixing your car for you, it's the least you could do."

She laughed again. "Oh aye, and the small matter of a massive fuckin' bill you're lumping me with. But as it happens I'm free tonight and without a car, so you can come and pick me up at seven."

"It's a date," John agreed, just as his car arrived at the entrance to *The Bridge*.

"See ya tonight Johnny boy," she said as she exited, winking at John.

"Can't wait," he replied.

~

John woke up the next morning and for a few seconds had no idea where he was, but as the hotel decor started to fill his vision, he was immediately aware of his surroundings. He looked over to his left at sleeping Chelsea, her ginger hair messily covering half of her face. He noticed one of her false eyelashes beginning to peel off so John slipped out of the bed and made use of the utilities. Stretching and yawning he clambered back into the bed. Reaching for his phone, he saw two notifications: messages from Elena. His heart skipped a beat. He flicked open the first message, which had been sent the night before and was left unanswered. A pang of guilt flared up within him at this.

The message said:

> Hey, booked bowling for 2pm. Where do you want to eat?

John then opened the next message which had been sent a few hours after the first:

> Buuuck, don't ignore me!

Suddenly, John felt a pair of arms wrap around him like a cobra. "Who's Elena?" came Chelsea's voice. "Something you're not telling me?"

John felt an inexplicable wave of panic, like a child who had been caught stealing sweets from the shop. With a sharp intake of breath, John replied, "No, no, that's my mate's girlfriend." He immediately felt absolved of the crime, not that there was one.

"Oh, tryin' to make me jealous are ya?" Chelsea quipped. John turned to face her and was relieved to see she was smiling and clearly joking.

"Wouldn't dream of it," he said, smiling and kissing her on the lips.

"Good, 'cos that's a game ya wouldn't win," she answered.

"Is that a threat?" John asked.

"No," Chelsea replied, her eyes flashing with malice for the briefest of seconds. "It's a promise," she kissed him firmly on the mouth, before whispering in his ear, "Just remember, you're mine now," as she did so, she dug her nails deep into John's back. John cried out in shock, but swiftly laughed it off, embracing the momentary pain.

"Come on you, let's get you back to your car."

CHAPTER EIGHT

E lena and Alex arrived at *Watford Bowls* just before 7pm as planned. Alex was over-dressed for the occasion, but that could be forgiven as he had just left his shift at *The Fallen Oak*, the pub that his parents owned. His job there was very fluid, in that he didn't have a defined role and simply managed the day-to-day operations, whenever he did actually work. To his credit, he made sure to clock in at least forty hours a week and didn't mind opening on Sundays. His parents had owned the pub, which was a mere ten minutes from *Watford Bowls*, for the last twenty-five years, curating a firm following from the locals and even achieving notoriety from local media outlets, who praised Sharon's "Wicks' Wicked Wings" in particular.

"Buck! Dom!" Elena shouted, noticing John first as soon as she entered the arcade-cum-bowling alley. He spun around, looking left then right, before finally fixing his gaze on her and vigorously waving, that beaming smile of his etched on his face. Dom looked up from tying his bowling shoes.

"How are you both?" she asked, greeting John with a faint

hug, being overly cautious not to linger too long. As she pulled away from him, she could smell his aftershave, that familiar, peppery scent that had remained on her skin the first night she met him. It had stayed with her as she slept, despite her shower that night.

"Hey, what about me!" Dom quipped as he emerged behind John.

Elena rolled her eyes, feigning disapproval, "Hello Dom," she said, embracing him.

"Hello gorgeous," he replied with a cheeky grin. "Yes Alex! All good?" he asked, shaking Alex's hand as he did.

"Yeah good, just finished up at work," said Alex.

"I can tell, my man looking dapper tonight! Hope you two are ready for some mad bowling skills!" John proclaimed, knowing full well he was rather awful at the activity.

"Oh yeah same here!" Alex replied, laughing as he did.

"You seem well really happy tonight, Buck!" Elena remarked.

"Do I?" he answered nonchalantly, with a small smile. Elena felt the familiar tingle of butterflies floating around her stomach as she hoped it was because he was with her.

"Yeah can't imagine why, mate," Alex said, grinning, nudging Dom as he did.

The butterflies suddenly dropped with the weight of a thousand tonnes. Did Alex know that she liked John? Thinking on her feet, she interjected, "Yeah, what's wrong? You're normally really grumpy!" again with a sweet smile to hide her inner turmoil.

"Must be because of Chelsea," Dom answered on John's behalf.

Thank God. Football. Elena thought. "Oh did they win? I didn't know you supported Chelsea?" she asked, her nerves settling finally.

John laughed heartily, Alex and Dom joined in as well. "No, not quite."

"Oh shit didn't I tell you?" Alex suddenly asked, facing Elena, who was now struggling to keep her smile from fading.

"No... what, what, tell me, tell me!" she asked excitedly, albeit now realising with horror what the answer would be.

"Chelsea is a girl. Long story short, she came down to the garage needing a lot of work and it turns out she wanted much more than her car fixing," Dom said, beaming.

Alex laughed jovially at this description and Elena was stunned into silence. She felt a lump rise in her throat as she struggled to get her voice out. The words never came and she swallowed hard, feeling the familiar sting of tears welling up in her eyes. She realised that the smile she thought he had reserved for her at the start of the evening was because he was thinking about someone else. A million questions stormed into her mind all at once.

Was it true? What did he do? Why? How? Who is she? At the climax of this barrage she settled on a solitary answer in her mind; *He doesn't like me.*

John had seemingly not noticed any of this internal dialogue Elena was having even though she seemed forlorn all of a sudden, and instead displayed his phone. "Here, take a look, a couple of pictures of us from when we met on Wednesday."

On Wednesday? He was this smitten and it had only been four days? She silently took the phone and stared intensely at the image that was before her. John, looking his handsome self, had his face next to a woman who Elena presumed was Chelsea. Her eyes seemed to gloat as they stared back up at Elena, her smile contorted in a mocking grin of ownership. Her hair fell lankly around her freckled skin. She was the complete antithesis of Elena in almost every conceivable way.

"She looks nice," was all Elena managed to squeeze out, her

lips were almost locked shut in an effort to keep her cool. She wanted to grab John, shake him and scream in his face, "WHAT ON EARTH ARE YOU DOING? I'M RIGHT HERE!" She wasn't though and she could never be. She looked from John to Alex to Dom and heavily sighed, resigned to the destiny that awaited her. Finally regaining her composure, she briskly smiled before announcing, "Let's bowl!"

～

The three boys were in discussion about something as Elena stood up to retrieve her ball. They were one game in with one to go and Elena was acutely aware that she wanted John to notice her more than she should have allowed. She deliberately slowed her walk and put a slight twist in her hips as she did so, bending just that bit more carefully to pick her ball up.

It seemed John noticed as said, "Try and hit the pins this time, yeah!"

"Oh you just watch me Bucky," she answered back, not even looking in his direction and instead, walked determinedly towards the bowling lane. She could feel his eyes on her and she smiled to herself, satisfied that her plan was in motion. Elena bowled and managed to score six pins.

"Ooo not bad, but just not *quite* good enough," John quipped, standing up as he did so.

"Maybe you can show me how to do it then, Buck," she replied, brushing past him.

He eventually tore his gaze away from her, grabbing his ball and announced, "Watch and learn." John hit a strike. He turned around to the group with his arms wide in celebration and then Alex looked up from his phone to see John gloating, "You see? You need to stick with me and learn something."

His words were not really aimed at anyone in particular, but she knew that they were for her. Alex was next and Elena and John had a moment to themselves as Dom excused himself to go and get another drink.

"So, tell me more about Chelsea," Elena asked, wishing she hadn't.

"Well, she lives in Glasgow," John began.

"What? So she's not even from down here?" Elena was now getting angry rather than upset. *What was he even doing entertaining this idea? Why do I care so much?*

"Nah, she was just down visiting a friend, but her car was busted so she needed it fixed before going back home," John was avoiding eye contact whilst recounting the events of how he and Chelsea had met. "Then we went out for dinner that night and, y'know…" he trailed off, not wanting to go into further detail, and Elena noticed colour flushing in his face.

As if to acknowledge it, she suddenly took off her white jumper, revealing a black strappy top. John's eyes were drawn immediately to Elena's chest and the fine, long gold necklace which rested just above her cleavage.

"It is hot in here, isn't it?" she said, justifying the move. She didn't allow John time to respond, for Alex had returned and she was now getting up to take her turn. Alex didn't seem to notice she had removed her jumper and went immediately to his phone, leaving John to stare in bewilderment at Elena as she stepped up to take her turn. She struck out again and John went over to her immediately.

"Look, you need to just take your time, go nice and slow, you know?"

"Oh do I?" she answered, a playful look across her face.

"Yeah," he answered, smiling just as much. "You can either be fast and hit it hard, or take your time. Enjoy it, make it last longer." With that he reached across her, his arm lightly brushing across her stomach in order to pick up his bowling ball.

"*Mira*, just like this," he said, making Elena laugh at his poor Spanish accent. He gently rolled the ball down the lane, toppling several pins.

"Looks easy," she answered, "Let me see what I can do, *amigo*," she replied, deliberately emphasising the Spanish. Elena mimicked John's style and her ball gently rolled into the first two pins, not making any further progress.

"Ah you know why?" John began. "It's because I've got these and you don't," he finished, flexing both of his biceps.

Elena was fixated on his strong arms, barely contained by his white t-shirt.

Clearing her throat, she said, "Guess I'd better hit the gym then!"

John merely smiled and turned his attention to Dom as they struck up a conversation about football.

Elena knew that he was trying hard not to look at her for too long, especially in the presence of Alex, who was shaking his head and laughing.

"You two, bickering like brother and sister again!"

Elena was unusually quiet on the way home. She had driven over halfway when she found her voice again.

"I can't believe you didn't tell me about Buck and Chelsea."

"It genuinely slipped my mind," Alex replied. "I think it's good for him, he's been alone for a while, you know? Especially after the Kate thing."

Yeah, the Kate thing, Elena remembered, a fresh wave of anger washing over her for the briefest of moments.

"I think he's making a mistake," she said flatly.

"What do you mean?" Alex inquired.

"She lives too far away, for one. Secondly, she just seems...dunno, not right for him," she finished, her eyes never leaving the road.

"Well, he's big enough to make up his own mind, we'll just have to see."

"Yeah, I guess," Elena replied, the conversation finishing as they arrived at Alex's home.

That night, she dreamt entirely of John.

CHAPTER NINE

"THE 10:55 VIRGIN EXPRESS TO GLASGOW IS NOW BOARDING, PLATFORM 2!" came the instruction blaring from the PA system in Euston. John hoisted his bag over his shoulder and marched towards the nominated platform for his departure. It had been just over a week since he had met Chelsea and in that time, there had been an untold amount of text messages, phone calls and the occasional video chat. Eventually, they had settled on John coming up to Glasgow to visit her for the weekend as she didn't have the money to come to London, a fact which he had declined to share with any of his friends for now. His feet carried him robotically towards the barriers, where he flashed his ticket. John opted for First Class, which was fifty pounds more expensive, but he preferred the space and quiet. He sat on the train and before he knew it, was being whisked away to his destination, caught up in the scenery flying past his window as he gazed out.

~

"Bloody hell!" John blurted, as the refreshments trolley hit his elbow, shocking him both physically and mentally from his hypnotic state as he realised what he was doing. The roller-coaster that had been the last week had uplifted John from his mundane routine; he felt liberated and excited and was throwing caution to the wind. He didn't mind making the long journey up to Scotland, *you only live once right?* Yet as the train rolled into Manchester, one of the stops on the way, he questioned why he was doing this. *Was she the one for him, truly? Was this just a bit of fun? If the latter, then why go to this expense and effort?* He didn't know the answer to any of these questions and he decided he didn't care. He simply wanted to see where this went, and with that, he found some uplifting music to listen to for the remainder of his journey.

∿

Chelsea's phone buzzed ferociously and almost fell right off her dining table before she could grab it and answer.

"Hello?"

"Chelsea, hey, it's John. I'm at the station!"

"Oh shit, is it already there, aye?" Chelsea responded with some alarm, noticing she was still in her pyjamas despite it being well past 2:30pm.

"Yeah!" John said laughing. "Don't worry, I can grab a coffee or something, take your time."

"I'll be there soon baby, sorry, bye!" she said, clicking the phone off and frantically moving to get some acceptable clothing on for the outside world. She hastily stubbed out her half-consumed cigarette and made her move.

John pocketed his phone and, with a sigh, moved to leave the station and grab a coffee from the nearest kiosk. Ripping open two sachets of sugar, he was mildly annoyed that she wasn't here to pick him up, but this wouldn't be the first time he had made a long journey somewhere to meet a girl who never showed.

John had then floundered in a sea of one-night stands, dead-end relationships and as seen more recently with Kate Bradstock, friend-zone situations with no romantic developments possible. All the while, he had seen his closest friends start to pair off and settle down, seemingly able to pluck their dream girl from obscurity at a whim. Take Alex, for example. He had met Elena by chance at his workplace where he spotted her eating alone. *What did they even have in common? What do they even talk about? He's only interested in Formula One and inheriting his parents' pub, for God's sake.*

Focussing on the here and now, John attempted to banish thoughts of Elena to the confines of his mind, yet as he did, one final flurry of Elena flashed through his head; when he had accidentally touched her body at bowling for the first time. He could almost feel it again as though it were happening right now. Finally (and with a great effort) John buried those thoughts, consciously deciding to shift his attention to a woman who was available. John wasn't envious, but he was starting to get anxious, as the growing dread of being left behind was creeping up on him. So, when opportunity arrived at his door in the literal sense with Chelsea, it was not exactly hard to see why he flung himself at it once he knew there was a possibility it could be something that he was yearning for; a relationship. The fact that she seemed keen on him from the first night as well was unique to John, he was usually the one chasing the girls and having to make the effort, yet Chelsea seemed to be on his wavelength. But she wasn't here and he did start to feel the familiar sense of rejection brewing within him.

John had finished the contents of his overpriced coffee when Chelsea's grey Vauxhall rumbled into view. He relaxed and smiled, relieved that she had actually turned up. She seemed somewhat flustered and was throwing things that were apparently occupying the front seat into the back. Her hair was tied up in a bun, but her makeup was very much as it had been when they had met. She was wearing a baggy t-shirt which had something illegible scrawled across it and John presumed she would be wearing tracksuit bottoms. Finally looking up, she smiled when she saw him and ushered him over, yelling, "Quick, before some bastard gives me a ticket!" She was parked in a yellow cross section which clearly stated, "No Parking." John hurried a little, opened her boot and flung his bag in carelessly, eager to get in the passenger seat.

"Hi," John greeted her, smiling. They kissed on the lips briefly, Chelsea keen to move off and get home.

"Sorry, I thought you were coming at 3:30!" she exclaimed, weaving in and out of traffic as she did.

"Ah that's alright, had my music and my coffee, it's all good," John answered, looking her up and down again. She was indeed wearing tracksuit bottoms as he had guessed, which was good to know, because he was too.

"Been up to much today?" John asked, assuming she must have been busy.

"Not really," she said laughing, clearly with a degree of guilt. "But I just thought you were coming later that's all," she explained, reaching out a hand to squeeze his. "Sorry if I seem a little bit up-tight or on edge," she began. "It's just, I haven't had a man in my car for... God knows how long," she finished.

Before John could answer she continued, "And, I haven't had anyone spend time with me over a weekend for as long as I can remember. I'm just used to being by myself you know?" she explained as she pulled into a side street of Glasgow's clever grid system of roads.

"Well, you have someone now, so get used to it," John said, smiling earnestly and looking directly into her eyes, which didn't seem to be as emerald as he remembered, but he was sure that was a figment of his imagination.

"Let's see shall we," she replied, smiling back. "We're here!" she announced, as they turned into Pickering Street and pulled up outside number twenty-two.

"Nice road," John remarked, noticing that the neighbourhood seemed quiet, the houses were similar to his own road in Dagenham and in all honesty, it felt like home.

"It's not bad, aye, but it's no mansion in Beverly Hills," Chelsea answered, her keys jangling as she fumbled with them, searching for the right one to get them inside.

"Honey, I'm home!" Chelsea announced to the empty house, dropping her keys into a Rangers FC bowl.

"Football fan, then?" John inquired, taking his hoodie off and hanging it with the other coats absentmindedly, not paying attention to the contents on the stand as he studied the key bowl.

"What? Oh, nah," Chelsea replied, noticing John's gaze. "My dad, *big* Rangers fan. Always makes sure to get me some sort of memorabilia every year around birthdays, Christmas and that."

"Oh I see, well I won't bore you to death with football talk this weekend then," John answered, smiling as he did.

"Nae bother. Fancy a drink?" Chelsea asked, moving into her kitchen, which was in desperate need of a clean and had plates, pots and pans scattered about the worktop requiring attention. John mused that his mother would be going insane right now, she liked to wash plates up almost as soon as she dished the dinner on them, such was her desire to keep a clean house. John didn't mind as much, again presuming Chelsea had been too busy to see to them right away. He realised he hadn't actually answered her question and replied, "Sure, whatever you're having."

"Okay, vodka and coke then," Chelsea announced, reaching into a full drinks cabinet and extracting the alcohol of choice.

"Ha, bit early ain't it?" John replied, presuming he would be offered some water or similar.

"What? Nah, we're here now, may as well just get into it, we're going into town later so pace yourself." She finished pouring their glasses. "Cheers!" she said, striking John's glass and taking a sip, John pausing for a brief moment but mimicking her actions.

Chelsea exited the taxi first, her mini skirt not leaving much room for the imagination as she clambered out. Adjusting her red top, she was satisfied that enough cleavage was on display before clicking her way onto the pavement in her heels, waiting for John to pay for the cab. He was dressed in black fitted jeans accompanied by a long-sleeved dark blue Ralph Lauren top. Payment made, he joined Chelsea and they linked arms, beginning their slow march towards the club.

"Christ, look at that queue," John said, pointing at the snaking throng of people that were waiting patiently to enter *Steam Room*, their fairground for the evening.

"Don't worry about that," Chelsea answered, as she moved confidently ahead to the bouncers on the door, by-passing the queue.

"Hi Dave," she said, greeting the bouncer with a kiss on the cheek.

"Alright there Chels," Dave the bouncer replied, eyeing John with suspicion, which Chelsea noticed.

"He's wi' me tonight, Dave," she explained, offering her hand out for John to grab, which he did.

"Aye, nee bother big man," Dave said, eyeing John up and

down. "Have a good night, won't ya?" he said with a menacing grin.

John, unfazed yet cautious, replied with a polite smile and a nod, careful not to let his obvious London accent out just yet.

"Come on, the girls are already here!" Chelsea said excitedly, as she led the couple inside, booming music being their greeting the moment the steel doors were opened by two more bouncers.

"You a regular here then?" John asked, shouting over the thump of the beat.

"Aye, well, not really, but I come here a bit," Chelsea answered, her head turning to face forward, ginger hair flicking about her as she did.

John wasn't really convinced that "coming here a bit" would have been enough to skip the queue, but he didn't mind too much, they had after all just entered one of Glasgow's top nightclubs without a wait.

"That's them, come on!" she squealed with delight, almost yanking John's arm out of his socket as she hurried over towards three girls who John assumed were her friends.

"Girls!" Chelsea screamed and they screamed back in unison a mangled garble of vowels and syllables as they all embraced.

John simply stood back a bit, somewhat awkwardly, smiling but not sure what to do with himself. After an excruciating few seconds, Chelsea seemed to remember John was there, her eyes widened as she grabbed him, pulling him centre of attention.

"Girls, this is John, the man I told ye about," she proudly proclaimed, displaying John like a medal she'd won at a sports event.

"Hi John," one of them said, smiling flirtatiously, her dark hair up in a ponytail that revealed a gaunt face and sunken eyes.

"Oh, he's handsome, Chels!" came the remark from the second, who was sipping her drink provocatively, her blonde hair, framing her slim face like curtains.

"Aye, I'll say," came the final appraisal from the brown-haired girl whose eyes hungrily studied him.

"Well, tough, 'cos he's all mine," Chelsea said, yanking John close to her in an embrace before landing a sloppy kiss on him. "Oops, bit of lippy, babe," she said, wiping the red lipstick she had left on him with her thumb. "There, all gone. Right, drinks, girls, John's round!" she said, turning towards John and winking, who reluctantly smiled back thinking of his tumbling assets in his bank account.

Oh well, got to live for the moment, right? Finding his voice and confidence, John announced, "Time to show you girls how we drink down South, come on then," which was greeted with whoops and cheers.

The drinks were flowing generously from that point forward and the tipsier John became, the more his wallet loosened and the more his bank balance depleted further towards empty. But he didn't care, *you can't buy experiences like this*, he thought.

"Johnny boy," Chelsea said, slurring her words as she slumped into John, her arms draped around his neck.

"Yes, my love," John answered, unsure where that turn of phrase came from, but saying it all the same.

"Do you want something?" Chelsea asked, smiling in a devilish way.

"Yeah, what do you have in mind?" John asked, misreading the situation and firmly grabbing her bum.

"Some of these," Chelsea replied, revealing five pills in a small, clear packet.

John was taken aback and asked, "What are those?"

"Just some pills, have ye never had one?"

"No, I er… no I haven't," John answered, the effects of the alcohol he'd consumed suddenly losing their grip on his mental clarity, as he focussed more sharply on the offering Chelsea had presented to him.

"Oh well, you've got to! You'll feel *amazing*! They just make you feel all happy, ya know?"

"I feel happy now," John answered, smiling and pulling Chelsea in for a kiss, which she blocked by talking some more.

"Go on! Just try half, I'm only having half to start so you can have the other." She looked around briefly before extracting a pill from her bag and biting one in half with practice and speed that only someone who had clearly been doing this for a while could manage, before swallowing her half down with a sip of her vodka and coke.

"I'm good babe, honestly, but thanks. Just going to go to the toilet, be right back," John finished, releasing his grip and walking with pace to the men's toilet. He secured a cubicle and locked the door behind him. Breathing hard he muttered to himself, "What the fuck was that?" John had never taken drugs in his life, he wasn't ignorant of their existence of course, but he hadn't been around them in such an intimate way; namely someone dropping a pill right in front of him. *Should I do it?* He thought. *What for? You're having fun anyway, what's the point?* The internal dialogue continued for a moment and rather than answer the question, he wondered what Elena was doing this very moment. Taking his phone out with such haste that he almost dropped it in the open toilet, he fumbled to the letter 'E' in his contacts and typed a simple message to her:

```
Hey, hope ur having a good evening, what u
                    doing?
```

The time was half past midnight, so it was unlikely he would get a response and he felt ridiculous for even sending it. Sighing, he left the cubicle and returned to the dance floor, where he would spend the rest of the night turning down more offers for drugs he didn't want and switching his drinks from vodka and coke to just coke.

~

The next morning, John awoke with a clear head, but in desperate need of sleep. Chelsea, who had consumed a total of one and a half pills, hadn't wanted to sleep at all and instead demanded John lay down and be used as some sort of sex object for her own gratification. He left Chelsea snoring on her side of the bed, her make-up had stained the pillow a little and she had nothing to cover her dignity.

John washed his face and moved to the kitchen, hopeful of finding some bacon, eggs and sausage to make a quick fry up for the pair of them. He found a fridge that had various opened packets of processed meat, some cheese, milk and a solitary packet of chicken. *Guess we'll have to eat out then.*

He looked at his phone and saw three notifications; one from Dom, one from Evan and one from his dad. The time was 8:30AM, so perhaps Elena hadn't seen his message yet. *Probably enjoying a nice lie in with Alex, with a hearty breakfast lined up.* He chuckled to himself as he contrasted that image with the scene before him. Clothes scattered messily around the floor of the bedroom, his new flame passed out in her bed and the room in desperate need of airing. He opened some windows and began tidying up when Chelsea stirred, stretching and yawning noisily.

"Morning babe," she croaked, her voice hoarse from the drinking and shouting. "What time is it?" she muttered, one eye welded shut either because of her glued eyelashes, or lack of sleep.

"It's just gone half eight," John answered, glancing briefly at his watch.

"Oh, shit!" Chelsea exclaimed, her eyes firing open and widening. "Oh no, I need to get ready, just, can you help?" she asked, wildly dashing out from the bed and scrambling to pick up their clothes.

"Erm, yeah, sure. What's happening?" John asked, moving to assist.

"Just stuff these in here. Oh, and put that on the table for me would you?" Chelsea asked, giving no real answer. "I'm just going to shower, we'll get breakfast soon," she said, rushing to the door adjacent to the bedroom, blowing John a kiss as she did.

As the door slammed shut and the shower fired on, John was left alone again, pondering the sudden rush.

A few minutes elapsed and Chelsea emerged from the bedroom, dressed this time and looking anxious.

"Everything alright?" John asked, when suddenly the doorbell chimed, not allowing Chelsea to respond. She hurried to the door and pulled it open, greeted by a small voice exclaiming "Mummy!"

John was frozen in place on the sofa. *Did he just hear that right?*

"Oh my sweetheart," Chelsea said, sweeping the boy up and into her arms, bringing him into John's view for the first time. He had black hair and fair skin and looked to be around seven years old. Following in close proximity was a tall, slender man, with tattoos on his neck and the exposed parts of his arms.

"Alright Chels," he said, entering and looking around the house, before his eyes settled on John.

The beady brown eyes narrowed as he saw him and he looked sideways at Chelsea who had suddenly remembered John's presence and said, "Oh, shit. Yeah, Gary, this is John."

"How's it goin' mate," he said, extending a skinny arm out for John to shake.

"Yeah, good thanks pal, you alright?" John answered, matching Gary's firm grip.

"Oh a wee southerner, eh Chels?" Gary said, smiling. His tone took on a hint of mockery and John felt his adrenaline flare up.

"Ah shuddup Gary," Chelsea answered, rolling her eyes, now letting the child down. "Liam, I want you to meet someone. This is my friend John, go ahead, say hello."

The child cautiously approached John, waving as he did and saying "Hello" with a small voice. John crouched onto his knees to be at eye level with Liam and smiled kindly at the boy.

"Hey mate, how are you?" he asked with a softer infliction in his voice than normal.

"I'm okay," Liam answered shyly.

"You like Spider-Man?" John asked, pointing at the Marvel character emblazoned on Liam's top.

"Yeah, he's my favourite," Liam answered, suddenly finding his confidence. "One time, I saw a cartoon with him and he beat up this lizard man!"

"Oh really? That's so cool! Do you have any toys you can show me?" John replied earnestly, smiling as he did.

"Yeah, I'll go and get them," Liam said, thundering off suddenly to a door John didn't seem to notice before, which must have led to Liam's bedroom.

"Right, well, I'll leave you all to it," Gary said, looking from Liam to Chelsea, ignoring John.

"Okay great, we'll see you on Wednesday," Chelsea answered. "Liam! Say goodbye to Daddy!" she cried out.

Liam came thumping back around to his dad, gave him a hug and then went running back to his bedroom, presumably still looking for toys.

"Bye, have fun!" Gary said, now looking at John and smiling, a flash of menace dancing across his face.

John had sat back on the sofa and Chelsea made her way over, seemingly unaware of the gigantic elephant in the room.

"So, you have a son?" John asked, laughter creeping into his voice, out of disbelief more than anything.

"Yeah, didn't I tell you? I'm sure I did," she remarked, not meeting John's eyes.

"Erm, no, you didn't," John replied, trying to process this sudden bombshell.

"Well, I do. Is there a problem?" she replied, rounding on John and looking like a wolf about to devour her prey.

"No, not at all. It's just... well, a heads up would have been nice, ya know?" John answered as diplomatically as he could.

"Well *sorry*," Chelsea answered, clearly annoyed.

What has she got to be upset about? John thought.

"Let's go for breakfast shall we, the three of us? My treat?" John proclaimed, trying to swiftly alleviate the tension, Liam now rushing back into the living room with Spider-Man toys clasped in each hand. Chelsea's eyes lit up at the thought of some hot food she wouldn't have to pay for and she returned to her usual self.

"Okay, sounds great. Liam, come on, we're getting food, put those down," she instructed. As they headed out of the door, John suddenly noticed the small coats hanging on the rack and the tiny shoes underneath. What he didn't notice was his phone flashing as he picked it up and placed it directly into his pocket.

CHAPTER TEN

E lena finished typing her text and pressed send. She put her phone away as Alex returned from the toilet, joining her on the terrace. A gentle breeze whistled through the air as Alex rested his arms on the railing, taking in the surroundings. This was the first time Alex had been to visit Elena's family and indeed crossing the invisible barrier between cultures of England and Spain. He wasn't sure what to expect, but as he allowed the sun's rays to bathe him, he was pleased to be there. Elena was completely content in that moment, for she adored her home country of Spain. Her eyes closed as she felt a wave of relaxation wash over her, which had been a long time coming.

"What are you thinking?" Alex asked, breaking the peace between them.

"Nothing really, just love being here, you know?"

"Yeah, I can see why," Alex mused, again staring out across the landscape of Seville. He had rarely ventured abroad, having only been outside of the United Kingdom on two occasions; once to France with his secondary school on an educational trip, and once to Germany with his parents to celebrate

Oktoberfest. By contrast, Elena was quite the globetrotter, having visited most of Europe either alone, with her sister or with her ex.

Elena's previous relationship had been one of passion, intensity and an unmitigated disaster overall. For five years she had been embroiled in a toxic on-again off-again pairing with Simon Gravesly, whom she had met whilst working as a waitress at the Hard Rock Cafe in London during her studies. She had suffered abuse (both physical and mental) with Simon and felt unable to break the cycle. However, Alex had unexpectedly come into her life and made her realise that not all relationships had to be difficult. Where Simon was a ball of ferocious energy, which often exploded in either rage or animalistic sex, Alex was a quiet wallflower, gentle and kind. Elena had found solace in Alex, who was the polar opposite of Simon, and had attached herself to him, deciding rather quickly that this was in fact what she wanted in a boyfriend. Easy, no stress, no arguments and no problems. Yet, it would become clear that there were large gaps within their relationship that would forever be unfulfilled. The sexual chemistry was non-existent between them and Elena had resigned herself to this aspect of her life being incomplete within the first few months of being with Alex. She didn't mind so much, for Alex had other qualities that shined through. He was able to offer rational advice for Elena at times where she would need to hear it, normally to do with overspending on something she didn't really need. He was steady and would be someone with whom she could settle down and raise a family.

Elena looked up at Alex from her chair, noticing that he was going a slight shade of red under the sun's intensity.

"Alex, shall we go inside for a bit?" she asked, giving more of a command than a suggestion.

"Yeah, good idea, I should probably grab the factor fifty cream as well," he said, laughing. Elena chuckled along brightly, collecting her book and phone and sweeping inside the apartment, her dress flowing gracefully as she did.

"Are you looking forward to tonight?" Elena asked, trying not to sound too excited. She didn't want to put pressure on Alex, for it was the first time he would meet her family in person. There had been video calls, but obviously it wasn't quite the same.

"Yeah, should be good. How many people will be there?" Alex responded, trepidation creeping into his voice.

"I'm not too sure, maybe fifteen? Depends if my aunts, uncles and cousins are there too." Elena said casually, as she plugged her phone in to charge, missing the expression of terror that formed on Alex's face as he heard the number of potential attendees for the evening.

"Will we be staying long, do you think?" he asked, attempting to sound casual, but instead coming across just as agitated as he was. Elena sensed this and felt her own sense of annoyance rise to match his.

"I don't know, probably." She didn't turn to face him for this answer, pretending to be busy with her phone, but as each second ticked by, she felt more and more upset at his insensitivity. She hadn't seen her family in over a year and what's more, she was bringing him to her childhood home, which should be a joyful occasion that they could both enjoy. Instead, it seemed to her that Alex wanted to be anywhere else except with her visiting her family.

"Well not too long, I hope," Alex muttered, unpacking his sun cream from the suitcase.

"Excuse me?" Elena said, now rounding on him.

"Well, I just mean, you know, it's a lot isn't it, we'll be there from four-ish so it's going to be a long evening."

Elena was speechless and her mouth hung open in disbelief.

"Are you kidding me?" she asked, genuinely not sure if he

was being serious. "I haven't been home to see my family in over a year because of work, I'm not going to cut the evening short!"

"No, no, I'm just saying," Alex stammered, his words tumbling out of his mouth quickly as he fumbled carelessly for the right thing to say. "Just, I don't want to be a burden," he finally said weakly, Elena not fooled by the false sincerity in his tone.

"Don't worry we won't be there long." She brushed past him and slammed the door of the toilet.

Meanwhile, her phone buzzed on the table with a new notification.

Later that afternoon, Elena and Alex were taking a stroll through the neighbourhood, Elena thinking it might be a good idea in order to take Alex's mind off the upcoming event that evening, which he was clearly fussing over still since their earlier argument. She had suggested going for a walk in an effort to clear the air between them and try and expose Alex to more of her upbringing so he could learn more about her in a meaningful way. She had never brought any other boyfriend home to her parents, so this was a massive deal, not only for them but for her as well. She had chosen to omit this fact from Alex, for she guessed he would feel even more pressured by the whole affair. Instead, she linked her arm with Alex's as they meandered their way through Seville's narrow streets at a gentle pace.

"Here's the best place for tapas," Elena pointed excitedly, her eyes lighting up as she took a literal walk down memory lane.

"And here you can buy churros for dessert. Have you had

them before?" she pointed again at a nearby diner before turning to Alex for his answer.

"No, I haven't, what are they?"

"Oh my God, what! They're so good! Basically, they're like doughnut things you dip in chocolate, but they're so nice! Let's get some now!" Elena said with a flurry, her enthusiasm infectious and passers-by swivelled their necks to see what the fuss was about, much to Alex's discomfort.

"Okay, okay," he said, hurrying Elena along inside. He felt the eyes of the strangers on him and he hated it, he just wanted to have a quiet evening and go about his day in peace, what was wrong with that? Instead, here was Elena causing a scene over some random treat. His embarrassment was turning into anger. "Can you not be as loud? Everyone's looking," Alex aggressively whispered.

Elena looked around her, barely noticing anybody in the street, let alone anyone looking at her or at him.

"What are you talking about? Get off me!" she cried, moving her arm away from Alex as he attempted to placate her in a hurry, in order to control her alleged outburst. "Forget it, I'll see you back at the apartment," Elena stormed off up the winding street back towards their holiday abode, tears emerging at the corners of her eyes.

"Oh come on, don't be like that, you're causing a scene," Alex protested, still cemented to the spot, allowing Elena to walk away.

The door swung open forcefully as Elena marched in, and sweeping her phone up in a single motion she retreated to the bathroom, locking the door behind her. A few moments later, Alex arrived.

"Elena, come on, I'm sorry," he whined.

"Just get ready please, we have to go soon," Elena replied, struggling to keep her voice even. Alex did as he was told and produced his attire for the evening from his suitcase, a smart pair of light chino trousers accompanied by a light blue buttoned shirt. He undressed in silence, allowing Elena to stew and presumably come out soon to forgive him.

Elena, however, was now noticing the two notifications she had received from John, both messages. The first one read:

Hey, sorry for late reply, was caught up in a lot of shit. Just on train home now, what you up to? Sorry as well for the late text the other night.

Elena wondered what he could have meant by that, *wasn't he supposed to be with his new girlfriend?* She read on:

Soz to spam you with messages ha. But yeah, be good to talk to you if you can, speak soon.

Elena bit her lip. She wanted to confide in him; tell all about this weekend break with a phone call and knew for certain she would feel instantly better upon hearing his voice. Yet with Alex just a few inches away on the other side of the door, she knew this wasn't possible. Her fingers danced across her phone's keypad and she hammered out word after word, spilling her all about how she just wanted to be back home in London, possibly even sharing a coffee with John and having a catch up. She deleted those lines and instead replied with:

All good thanks, just about to go and see my family, can't wait! How was your trip, all ok?

She hit send and waited anxiously for a few moments, hoping John would be on the other end of the line and replying instantly. A few seconds later, she got her wish as John's reply came:

```
Glad ur ok. Yeah it was nice, but there's
        something I need to tell you...
```

John replied, making Elena desperate to know more:

```
Omg what is it, tell me!
```

She sent, all of a sudden feeling giddy and excited. *Maybe he had realised that this Chelsea woman was no good for him at all and that actually what he needed was her!* She waited with baited breath as his reply suddenly burst up on her screen:

```
Chelsea has a kid.. He's 7…
```

Elena was utterly dumbfounded. *Had she read that right? A child?* She quickly began typing her response:

```
Wow, did she not tell you? That's a bit odd.
    Are you not seeing her again then?
```

The last line was in hope more than anything, but she sent the text regardless. Again, biting her lip, Elena mulled over this information. She was sure that Chelsea didn't mention to John that she had a child, which was deceitful and really untrustworthy. Hopefully John thought the same and would swiftly end this fling and return back to London permanently. A new notification arrived:

```
Nah she didn't. Probably just slipped her
```

mind I guess. Nah, I'll see how it goes,
planning on going up again in a couple of
weeks.

Elena's heart sank. "Probably just slipped her mind" was John making excuses for her, she had no doubt about that. And seeing her again in a few weeks? It didn't compute with Elena at all. She had quite blatantly lied to him and yet John was already making plans to see her again. Elena let her phone dangle loosely in her hand before it tumbled to the floor with a loud thump. She felt utterly hopeless and could have cried for hours. Here she was, locked away in a small bathroom in Seville, whilst John was in another country, seemingly jumping head-first into a long-term relationship. She knew it shouldn't bother her as much as it did, but she couldn't help the jealous waves washing over her.

"I'm ready," Alex called out, snapping Elena back into the present.

"Okay, let's get going," she said, swinging the door of the bathroom open and making her way out of the apartment, her head bowed as she swallowed hard the disappointment she felt.

CHAPTER ELEVEN

"Oh mi amor!" Maria Viegas exclaimed, wrapping her daughter Elena in a loving embrace that was warm and long-lasting. Stepping back, her hands cupped Elena's face. "Look at you, you need some good food, you're so skinny!"

"Mami, por favor! I'm always eating, ask Alex!"

Maria's eyes looked over her daughter's shoulder to Alex, who looked forlorn, standing just outside of the wooden door.

"Come in, come in, let me see you!" Maria waved Alex in before extending her hand in greeting.

"Hello," Alex said, his English accent much more amplified in the Mediterranean household.

"So, you're the one who's making my daughter stay away all this time, huh?" Maria said, jokingly. Alex looked panic-stricken for a moment, believing himself to be in trouble, but it dawned on him that she was joking.

"Oh," he laughed, "yes, well I suppose I am," he answered nervously, not really sure of what to say.

"Mira, both of you, come and see what we have," Maria ushered the couple into the kitchen, which was a narrow space adorned with beautiful patterned tiles on the wall and an exposed copper pipe running along the roof line. Spread across the worktop were rows of traditional Spanish dishes, all lovingly prepared by Elena's mother.

Elena instantly felt the weight of the day fall off her shoulders the moment she stepped into her family home. Thus far, the trip had been a bit of a disaster; Alex had been controlling and showed a side of himself she hadn't yet experienced. She knew immediately that it was something that she didn't like. Yet within the bubble of her home, such thoughts were banished and instead, she was excited for Alex to meet her family, a milestone in any relationship, but particularly this one.

"Alex!" she yelled, waving him through the kitchen, which was situated in the centre of the house. "Come through, meet my Dad and everyone!"

Alex squeezed past Maria, who was now busy chopping vegetables that were to be offloaded into an enormous bowl ready to be drizzled in olive oil and dressing, completing the salad. He smiled politely as he shimmied past, Maria's squat form not noticing his skinny frame as it slid by her. Alex joined Elena, his eyes wider than usual and a fearful grin on his face, making him look as though he was on the edge of madness.

"Hola!" Elena shouted into the din of chatter that occupied the living room, which was full to the brim with her relatives. They all simultaneously turned their attention to her, beaming and throwing out their arms in welcome. Her father, Carlos, leapt to his feet and rushed over to his daughter, moving with the agility of someone half his age.

"My sweetheart," he said, a tear rolling down his cheek, landing gracefully into his bushy black beard, speckled with flecks of grey.

"Papa!" Elena replied, now welling up herself and embracing her father, almost clinging on to him.

"Too long, my daughter, too long."

"I know Papa, I'm sorry," whispered Elena into his shoulder, as the father and daughter embraced for several moments longer. A weathered hand gently grasped Elena's shoulder and she turned to see her grandfather's face, tanned and lined with wrinkles, but the eyes blazed with a sharpness that belied his age. All of Elena's family were young at heart, it was this same joy and love of life that John had noticed and been drawn into when he had first met Elena.

"Abuelo!" Elena cried out, removing herself from her father's arms as she moved into her grandfather's embrace.

The greetings continued; uncles, cousins, aunts, until everyone had said hello. By the end of it, Elena was dizzy, her head spinning with emotion that threatened to overspill into further tears of joy. She looked around at bright faces, happy smiles and her loving family, before suddenly remembering Alex, who had simply faded into the background. Rushing to his side, Elena quickly put her arm around Alex's waist and said, "Everyone, this is my boyfriend Alex." Her relatives seemed just as surprised as she was that he was standing there, nobody having noticed him enter the room.

He allowed a hand to pop up in a wave and slightly inclined his head before saying, "Hello, nice to meet you all." No further effort was made on his part to interact with the family.

Elena nudged him slightly and used her eyes to direct him to her father, affirming the need to make the first move and introduce himself officially to him. At first, Alex didn't get the hint and looked at Elena with confusion, contorting his features as though he'd suddenly smelt something foul. She again made the same motion with her eyes, deliberately slower this time, and the lightbulb moment happened as Alex realised what he should do.

He moved towards Carlos with his hand extended, "Hello. Alex Wickerman, it's a pleasure to meet you."

Carlos took his hand and his eyes rapidly took Alex in, scanning him from head to toe. "So, this is the man, huh?" Carlos said, cocking an eyebrow skywards as he continued to shake Alex's hand, which was limp and held no authority.

"Si, Papa," Elena said, guiding her boyfriend towards other family members for further introductions.

"I hope you know she's a wild one," Carlos said jokingly to Alex, who could only offer a polite grin in return. Carlos raised both his eyebrows and looked to the side as if to say, "well, he must have *something* about him that Elena likes."

The feast was served up with thunderous applause. Maria took her seat, smiling and linking hands with her husband, who sat at the head of the table. Carlos warmly returned the gesture and took up his daughter's hand and bowed his head, signalling for the other attendees to copy. Alex looked around with confusion, not sure what was going on. Elena squeezed his hand and met his gaze, firmly declining her head down to the table just as Carlos began to speak.

"Father, we thank you for providing this wonderful food for us today, for our blessed family. Thank you for returning my little girl to me. We pray for those less fortunate than us, that they may experience the same joy and blessings that I feel right now. Amen," he finished, raising his head and opening his eyes. "Let's eat!" he exclaimed, beaming and throwing his hands in the air.

There was an immediate rush as the guests clamoured for the biggest pieces of chicken, the largest portion of paella and the most amount of salad. Everyone was happily dining, speaking loudly and gesturing with exaggerated movements. Alex helped himself to a modest portion of chicken, combining the poultry with a meagre amount of salad and a single potato. He ate timidly, careful not to drop anything, and refrained from talking. Maria noticed and kindly offered him more food. "Alex, do you want something else?"

"Oh, no thank you, this is lovely," he said, smiling and delicately cutting apart the chicken drumstick.

By contrast, Carlos held a chicken leg to his mouth, tearing at the meat with authority. Through a mouthful of food, Carlos used the aforementioned chicken appendage as a pointer, highlighting the rapidly disappearing paella. "You want to try some of this?"

"Oh it's fine, thank you, I'm quite full," Alex said, smiling and patting his stomach.

"Suit yourself. Sweetheart?" he enquired of Elena, his hand already halfway to dishing some on her plate.

"Yes please, Papa," she gratefully accepted, holding her plate closer to accept the offering.

"Ha! That's my girl! If only your sister were here, this is her favourite!" Carlos exclaimed, pleased to see Elena eating with such enthusiasm.

Elena had missed the home cooking of her mother and father more than she realised.

The meal had finished, and the women rose from the table to tend to the dishes. Carlos led the contingent of men away to the living room, immediately turning the television on and finding the football match.

"Alex, cerveza?" one of Elena's cousin's asked, two bottles of beer in his hand in anticipation.

"Er, yes, please," Alex responded, accepting the offer. Alex cracked off the lid, "thank you."

"De nada."

Alex wasn't sure what that meant, so he nodded politely and took a sip of his drink.

"So, Alex, which team do you support?" Carlos asked, gesturing to the television.

"Oh, I don't really like football," Alex said, taking another drink.

"I see," Carlos said. "Tell me, what is it you do? You know, for a job?" Carlos finished.

"Well my parents own a pub, so I work there, managing and...stuff," Alex said, not able to quite put into words what he *did* do.

"So, it's a nice living?" Carlos pressed, taking another sip of beer.

"Pardon me?" Alex said, the noise in the living room escalating as one of the teams scored.

"You make good money?" Carlos said, raising his voice a level and becoming more direct with the question.

"Oh, erm, well, yes, not bad," Alex fumbled, flabbergasted that someone would ask that. The noise was getting to him and he could feel a headache forming across his brow.

"Good. Well, *salud!*" Carlos finished, clinking his bottle with Alex's.

"Cheers," he copied and the two drank in silence, their conversation over.

Elena washed the dishes with a tranquillity she hadn't felt in a long time. Through the open window, the warm night air swept in, swirling around her hair and shoulders before moving on.

"Mi amor," her mother said, approaching from her left side.

"Si, Mama," Elena replied, looking down to her mother and meeting her dark eyes, which matched her own.

"How to say, how to say..." she began, seemingly talking to herself more than Elena.

"What is it, Mama?" Elena asked, a tone of worry in her voice.

"This man. Are you sure about him?" Maria said, looking into Elena's eyes and grasping her arm tightly.

"What do you mean?" Elena asked, taken aback somewhat.

"He just doesn't seem... right for you, you know?" Maria pressed on, concern in her face. "I can tell, he's too quiet, he doesn't seem like a man who can look after you," she finished, pleased to have got this off her chest but at the same time worried how her daughter would react.

"Well, no, yes, he's quiet, but..." Elena spluttered, unusually lost for words as she scrambled around trying to justify the choice of man she had brought to meet her family and into their home. "Mama, he loves me and I love him. It's just easy with him, *sabes*? No arguments, nothing like what I've known with previous boyfriends. He's safe. He's good for me, don't worry," she said, a reassuring touch to her mother's arm letting her know all was well.

Extending her own hand to her daughter's face, Maria simply smiled and said, "Easy and safe? Where is the passion Elena? You seem so different when you're around him, like your flame is less...is smaller, you know?"

"It's not like that Mama. When you get older the passion dies and you're just companions, I've seen it on TV. I need someone who will be my partner, not someone whose clothes I want to rip off every second or someone who makes me excited all the time!"

"No, my daughter. It's not like that with your father and I. We still have passion, we still want each other, that side of things doesn't have to die. And you're so young, you shouldn't think this way right now, there should be some spark there."

"Mama, I had passion before and look where it got me;

bruised ribs and a broken heart. I need to be with someone who doesn't play games or want to hurt me or mess me around. He will be a good father and a good husband one day."

Unbeknownst to the Viegas women, Carlos had entered the kitchen to get another beer and heard this conversation. A look of concern crossing his face, he looked his daughter in the eyes, "Elena, don't settle. Don't change to try to fit in with someone who we all know isn't the right match for you. You need someone with *pasión*, someone who will look after you; a man!"

"Papa, he is a man. He is kind and he makes me laugh. Yes, at times I need to tell him what to do and help him do things but...it doesn't matter, he's nice."

Carlos gently took his daughter's arm. "Por favor. Just think carefully before any big decisions, no?"

"Papa, of course," Elena smiled reassuringly.

It was midnight and Elena and Alex were lingering at the door, about to take their leave. Elena and her father had exchanged heartfelt goodbyes and now it was the turn of Maria to say farewell. She embraced her daughter in a tight squeeze, finally letting her go.

"So, when will you be back for good, huh?" she asked, some degree of seriousness in her voice.

"Ay, Mama, I don't know, but I'll be back soon now, especially as you've all met Alex!" she finished, cosying up to Alex, who stood there, processing what Maria had just said.

"Okay you two, be good and travel safe!" Maria said, waving, as echoes of farewell followed Alex and Elena out the door. Alex waited until they were out of sight and earshot of the house before rounding on Elena.

"Go back for good?" he blurted out.

"Sorry?" Elena responded, the sudden question catching her off guard.

"Go back for good, that's what she said, what does that mean?" Alex spat, his anger rising and his eyes widening as fear led his voice and emotion.

"It means nothing, what is wrong with you?" Elena questioned, furrowing her brow and pulling away from him.

"You've never mentioned coming back here, has that been your plan all along?" Alex continued, his voice beginning to tremor, either with fear or anger.

"I-I don't know, maybe? One day?" Elena answered, shrugging.

"You didn't think to maybe consult ME?" Alex said, aggressively jabbing a finger to his chest.

"It's a nightmare, it's so loud in there! And jobs! What would I do over here?" he cried out, lurching suddenly from one topic to another.

Elena, however, was too sharp to let the first statement fly under the radar.

"What do you mean *a nightmare?*" she asked, her own anger beginning to boil over as she felt tears forming in her eyes. She had taken Alex into her family home to meet her parents and his first comment was that it was a nightmare?

"Oh, you know what I mean, everyone was so loud and it's hard to talk and..." his voice trailed off as he finally realised the mistake he had made. "No, I didn't mean it like that, it was great to meet your family," he backpedalled desperately, his own anger having now faded and been replaced with concern that he had made a serious error.

Elena stopped dead in her tracks, tears now falling from her eyes as she wrestled with the decision to stay at her parents or go back to their rented apartment. If she stayed here, that would be the end of her relationship, her parents simply wouldn't allow her to stay with him.

"Elena?" Alex asked, timidly approaching her, as her silence extended.

"Just, forget it. We'll talk in the morning, it's late," Elena decided, trudging off through the narrow streets that were dimly lit by the pale lamps.

～

That night, Elena didn't sleep. She instead read through her text conversation with John, wishing he were with her instead. Wishing she had told him by now how she felt and if he would like to come with her to Seville for a weekend or maybe forever. She typed a text at 1:30am that read:

Missing you, hope everything is okay.x

before deleting it and shutting her phone down, turning away from Alex and finally attempting to rest.

CHAPTER TWELVE

"What do you mean he slept in your bed?!"

"Oh, where else was he supposed to go?"

"I don't know, the sofa or something?"

"Oh please!" Chelsea said dismissively. "He's the father of my son, he deserves more than the sofa if he's staying over!"

"Sorry, but can we just backtrack a bit? Why was he staying over anyway?" John responded, his anger rising with his confusion.

"We had a night in, just the three of us, and he had a bit too much to drink, so I wasn't going to let him drive home. Is that what you'd prefer, John? To have him drink-driving?" Chelsea asked, incredulous and shifting the true topic of discussion.

"Are you fucking kidding me? You're making me out to be wrong here?"

"Oh, you're just being so insecure. Nothing happened!" Chelsea said dismissively.

John was standing alone in the car park, just outside of the church. His polished black shoes crunched on the loose pebbles as he paced around in a circle speaking to Chelsea over the phone. He had spent virtually every weekend in

111

Glasgow since the first time he went three months ago and this was the first time he couldn't be present.

"I'm not there for one weekend and you have that...that guy, jump straight back into bed with you?" John asked, careful not to be too insulting to her ex-boyfriend. He was the father of her son after all. Chelsea was quiet on the phone and John started to feel his stomach churning.

"Chelsea?"

"Yeah, yeah sorry. John, you know he comes and stays during the week sometimes, right?" *There it was.* Chelsea had managed to drop another bombshell on him, expecting him to either know the detail already, or simply not react to some big news. John's head was spinning, his thoughts leaping to the conclusions one would make upon hearing this information. He doubted very much that she was being loyal to him and he couldn't quite find the appropriate way to tell her that it was over between them. He was spared from having to do this at this moment in time, as he suddenly saw Elena's car rolling up to the church. John promptly clicked his phone off and tucked it away into his suit jacket.

Elena could see John standing by himself next to his BMW. *God, he looks so good in a suit,* she thought to herself. John also noticed her and was waving her over, signalling for her to park next to him. He pretended to be an air traffic controller, guiding Elena's vehicle into the generously spaced parking spot with exaggerated movements, making her laugh. He noticed that Alex wasn't with her, much to his satisfaction. As she opened the car door, he was able to see her and for a moment he was glued to the spot, unable to say or do anything.

"Can you help me get out, Buck? My dress is so tight I might just fall out and land face first onto the gravel!"

She was wearing a skin-tight gold dress which stopped just above her knee, the colour complimenting her olive skin and dark features perfectly. As he held her hand and bag and she climbed out of her Fiat, her hair fell in loose waves past her shoulders; it had grown quite a lot since the last time he saw her, he noted, and had little flecks of blonde in it; honey coloured from the sun. Her makeup was perfect; not too much, yet glamorous enough to show she had made an effort. She was quite simply a work of art, he mused. She adjusted herself and bent to remove her fluffy pink slippers.

"What the hell are those?" John laughed as he pointed to her footwear.

"Oh, there's no way I can drive in heels, I'd crash! So, why not be comfortable? I'd wear them to the wedding if I could!"

John laughed again as Elena slipped her perfectly painted toes into a pair of heels so high he thought she might topple over. They were covered in glitter and had red soles.

"There! How do I look?"

What a fucking ridiculous question, you look like a fucking goddess, John thought.

"Yeah, you look great!" he said weakly, disgusted with himself that he wasn't brave enough to say or do more.

"Thanks!" Elena responded, smiling, her eyes now level with his thanks to the added height from the stilettos. "You don't look so bad yourself!" she said, winking as she did.

"Ha, thanks. Shall we?" John said, motioning Elena inside, resisting with all of his might to not take her by the hand. As they walked, John glanced back over his shoulder and chuckled softly at the sight of his and Elena's cars side by side, noting that they would look good together on a driveway of their shared house someday.

"What's funny Bucky?" Elena asked, her light tone accompanied with a gorgeous smile.

"Nothing, nothing," John said, still smiling.

The ceremony came and went in a most unremarkable fashion. John didn't really enjoy weddings as the ones he'd been to were usually rather boring affairs that all merged into one. The crowd moved from the church to the adjacent field, the convenience of having the giant marquee right next door was a pleasant surprise; typically, you'd be forced to drive for a while down stupid country lanes to get to the next venue. Elena was walking by his side, a distant and pleasant smile on her face as she sighed deeply.

"What is it?" John asked. This seemed to rouse Elena from her trance as she dreamily looked at John.

"I just love weddings. They're so romantic and special. They just fill me with feelings of love and happiness!"

"Yeah?" John said quizzically, raising an eyebrow.

"Of course, but this one's been rather boring so far," she finished, smiling as she did and they both laughed in tandem.

"Where's the rest of our lot?" John asked, scanning the crowd.

"Who cares?" Elena blurted out, her eyes momentarily widening as she realised what she'd said.

Thankfully, John simply laughed, but had he realised the true meaning behind her words? She wasn't sure. She was about to change the topic when John announced, "I hope we're next to each other."

She almost toppled over in shock and was stunned into silence before John carried on. "There's never enough food at these things, so I know I could nick yours and you wouldn't be able to fight me," he finished, grinning as he did.

Elena breathed out a sigh of relief, her nerves calming and allowing her to respond with her typical wit, "Oh yeah? I'd hit your hand with my bread roll before you get near it!"

"Charming!" they both laughed again, the conversation coming so easily and enjoying each other's company fully. It dawned on Elena that this was probably the most amount of time they'd spent together alone and she was grateful for every second.

"Right, moment of truth. Excuse me," John said as he moved between two people, one was a short girl with closely cropped hair, whose eyes lingered on John a moment longer than needed, thought Elena. John studied the seating plan for a few moments and then came away, looking dejected.

Oh no, Elena thought, panic suddenly gripping her.

"I'm afraid..." John started, his words trapping Elena with a vice-like hold. "We're on the same table!" he finished, suddenly beaming and unable to contain his delight.

"Oh no, that's awful!" Elena replied, equally as ecstatic and almost throwing her arms around John's neck, instead settling on a playful slap to his arm.

"Yeah, Tom has done a decent job to be fair, we have a few people on our table we know like Freddie, Henry and Leo."

She didn't care, as long as they were on the same table and next to each other, they could continue to enjoy this time together, uninterrupted.

The two of them walked into the marquee, which was bigger than Elena thought it would be. At the top table she saw Tom Bentley, beside him his now wife Beth, who Elena hadn't met before. Her gaze ran along the length of the table and she finally saw Alex perched at the end, making small talk with Beth's mother, she presumed. There was a distinct chill that swirled through the air and Elena suddenly shivered.

John noticed immediately, "Do you want my jacket?"

Elena was stunned. She had never been offered a man's

jacket before, usually if she was cold she had to tell Alex several times before he got the hint and even then, he wouldn't do anything about it except shrug his shoulders uselessly and tell her she needed to wear more layers.

"Actually, hold that thought, take a seat, I'll be right back," John instructed, leaving Elena at the table to talk to Leo, who was asking how she had been. She listened to Leo talk about his next travelling adventure, which was to take place in Iceland, yet her eyes were watching John, almost in awe as she saw him converse with the staff and come to some sort of arrangement, before he made his way back over.

"Sorted," John proclaimed, grinning and satisfied with himself.

"Sorted what?" Elena replied.

"You'll see - ah, here we go," John finished, motioning to the two members of staff who were dragging a portable heater across to their table.

"Right here please, fellas," John instructed, pointing to a spot adjacent to Elena so she could reap the entire benefit of the heater.

"Will that be all, sir?"

"Yes, thank you chaps, much obliged," John coolly replied, flashing that winning grin of his, before turning in his chair to meet Elena's face. "Told you I'd sort it," he said, pouring himself a glass of water.

Elena still hadn't replied, she was utterly transfixed by him, astounded that he was able to resolve her issue with minimal fuss, without instruction and with pleasure. She had never experienced that before and it was becoming more and more clear that this was the man she needed in her life.

Leo split her thoughts wide open by announcing, "Your love is waving at you," to Elena and for a moment she was baffled, with John sitting right beside her she would have noticed if he was waving. It then dawned on her that it was

Alex waving from the head table. The three of them waved back, none as guilty as Elena who was now embroiled in an internal battle of how to gently end this relationship, move on with John and keep all of their friendships intact. The more time she found herself spending with John and getting to know him, the more she felt that they were indeed a perfect match. Truth be told, things at home had not been great with Alex. She had been gradually noticing how little they had in common, how he was unable to do anything for himself and how he depended on her, like a child does its mother. However, he was kind to her and things were easy – there were no real arguments or disagreements bar those about Seville, and it was all very safe, but rather boring.

I'm getting ahead of myself, thinking that I could be with John instead – what if he doesn't like me like that and anyway, what about Chelsea?

As far as she was aware, John was visiting her every weekend and things were seemingly progressing at a steady rate. Her heart sank a bit as she realised that John was out of reach, but she would always keep a little bit of hope inside her heart that something could happen between them some day. With that renewed sense of vigour, she asked John, "So, how's Chelsea, you guys okay?" praying that he would announce that they had split up.

John looked around before answering, noticing Leo now engaged in conversation with Freddie and Henry. "Well between you and I," John began, leaning tantalisingly closer to Elena so that she could now smell that familiar fragrance of his that she adored, "I don't think we'll be together much longer," he admitted quietly, causing a chain reaction of joy that erupted inside Elena like an explosion of happiness.

Her outward demeanour was sheer calm and gave nothing away as she asked, feigning concern, "Oh no, what's happened?"

John began to recount the events of the phone call he had with Chelsea just before Elena arrived at the church.

John finished his story and Elena offered a hand on his shoulder, "You know what, Buck? Everything happens for a reason, so it might be a bit rubbish right now, but you don't know what or who is around the corner," Elena finished and actually would remember those words for when she spoke to Alex, as she wanted to gently let him down and assure him that he would move on.

"That's really nice of you to say, thank you. How are you guys doing?" John replied, the question catching Elena off-guard as she remembered the horrendous events of their recent holiday.

"Well, to be honest Buck, not great," the words left her lips and she felt immediately lighter. She had taken her first step towards Buck and there was surely no going back now.

"Oh no, really?" John asked, his eyes opening wider in surprise, or maybe it was hope? Anticipation?

"Yeah, did he say much to you about our trip back home?"

"Not really," John pondered. "Just that it was warm, he met your family and they were all nice, that was about it."

Elena bit her lip, cautious in how to respond. "Well there was more to it, then that," she was able to begin, John now waiting with bated breath on her next words. He silently nodded, allowing her to continue at her own pace, which she did. "We had arguments, Buck. So many. We don't really argue over here but when I talk about going back home to visit or anything like that…well, let's just say, he doesn't like it."

She was trying to get the words out and John was patient in letting her finish, suddenly feeling the urge to just pull her in for an enormous hug, but resisting.

"He was so passive aggressive over there; he hated me being loud and complained about my family being noisy and me potentially living there again, oh it was just so bad," Elena finally said, her words rolling out in rapid succession, finally free of the cage they had been in for months. "It just made me really think, you know?" Elena said.

"Yeah," John began, "I do know," as he kindly squeezed her hand on the table. Their arms had been in constant contact throughout the conversation.

CHAPTER THIRTEEN

John pushed the bathroom doors open with such force that he caused a thunderous crash as they impacted on the wall. He winced as it happened, clearly overestimating the amount of strength needed. He was also more nervous than he'd ever been; he could feel that he was on the verge of something important and life-altering and that it would happen tonight. It would be the beginning of embarking on a relationship with Elena, he felt sure of it. John strode across to the mirrors lining the adjacent wall and stared at himself. His hair was now shaved entirely, he had given up trying to cling on to the last remnants the follicles had to offer and instead diverted his efforts to maintaining a clean beard, which had been freshly trimmed the day before.

His eyes were focussed and he began an internal dialogue: *Tonight is the night. You got this. Alex will be upset, of course, but he's a good guy, he'll recover. Dom and the guys will understand. What's important is that everyone is happy. Clearly I'm not happy with Chelsea and she's not happy with Alex. Let's change all that.*

Satisfied, he washed his hands and checked his teeth for

unwanted remnants of food. Taking a deep breath, he moved away from the taps and made his exit, almost knocking over a petite girl who was about to make her way into the women's toilets.

"Oh my God, I'm so sorry!" John exclaimed, barely stopping his momentum.

"It's fine, don't worry! Hey, you're John, right?" she said, looking up at him as she did so.

"Yeah, that's right, do I know you?" John remarked pleasantly, smiling as he did.

"Well, no, but I work at the garage close to you, I've seen you around," she admitted, blushing slightly as she did.

"Oh I see, so *you're* that stalker everybody warned me about?" John playfully replied, which earned him a scowl and a flirtatious slap of the arm.

"Hey! That's out of order," she said, pouting as though offended.

"Oh, I can only apologise, Miss?"

"Black. Josie Black," she answered.

"Oh!" John slapped his head in realisation. "I have heard of you!" he exclaimed.

"You have?" she asked, involuntarily standing on her tiptoes for a brief second.

"Yeah, you're that weirdo who works at the garage near me!" he finished, laughing as he did.

"You're so rude!" Josie replied, laughing fully and placing her hand on his chest as she contained her hysterics. "You're a funny guy, John," she said, her eyes locked on his with hungry intent.

"Am I? Well come by the garage some time, we can hang out for lunch," John said, oblivious to Josie's flirtatious nature.

"That would be great, do you think I could take your number? Maybe you can send me some jokes, funny man."

"Well clearly that's why I'm here. Sure, pass me your phone, I'll type it in."

Elena was watching this developing situation with keen interest. John had been talking to this girl, the same one that had been drooling over him back at the seating arrangement, and she noticed plenty of things she didn't like. For a start, they seemed to be laughing a lot and she was touching him far too frequently. *Did they know each other?* Elena decided she would find out. She got up out of her seat and paced towards the bathroom where this mystery woman had gone. Elena passed John and flashed him a smile, which he returned earnestly. Maybe it would be nothing, she was probably overthinking things right now, such was the dilemma she found herself in. She was on the precipice of ending one relationship and starting another, so naturally things would be of a heightened exaggeration in her mind. Calming her panic, she walked into the toilet and saw the woman there, chatting with two of her friends by the sinks. Elena slid into an empty cubicle in order to eavesdrop on the conversation.

"I'm so excited for you, Josie! You've been wanting this guy for months!" the first voice announced.

"I know! What are the odds that he's ACTUALLY at the wedding I'm at? It's like fate is bringing us together! Well, I mean, if fate were only interested in a shag!" Josie (Elena presumed) answered.

"What's your next move then?" came a third voice. "Maybe a slow dance and a smooch? Then back to your room?"

Elena heard exaggerated kissing noises, and a chorus of cackles accompanying it.

"Do you think he likes you?" said the first voice.

"Well, he gave me his number, so he must do!" said Josie,

excitement clear in her tone.

The words hit Elena like a lightning bolt and she held her head in her hands. *He gave her his number?* She repeated in her head, as her inner voice was squashed by the piercing tones of the third woman.

"What about that girl he's sat next to? The pretty one in the gold dress?"

"I actually asked him if he was with her and he said they were just friends! This could be it girls! I've wanted to add him to my little black book for ages! God, imagine what it would be like to have him pushing me around the bedroom!"

Upon hearing this, Elena gagged a little. She heard the girls leaving the bathroom, giggling and laughing as they did, their chatter now unable to be heard properly. Elena sat in silence and allowed a single tear of betrayal to roll down her cheek. In a few short hours she had gone from planning on leaving Alex in order to be with John to now finding herself in no-man's-land. She suddenly stood up, a pulse of dignity sparking through her and she brushed her dress down. Elena marched to the mirrors to check her make-up was okay, did the necessary touch ups and clicked her pocket mirror shut with authority. If John didn't like her, that was fine. At least she knew. Alex was out there and he was a good boyfriend to her, on the whole. Yes, the answer was clear. With renewed purpose, Elena strode out of the bathroom to go and make a statement of intent.

John watched Elena leave the bathroom, smiling to himself as he admired her elegant walk. She carried herself with such authority and confidence, he mused, appreciative of every inch of her as she flicked her hair carelessly away from her face. It dawned on him that she wasn't returning to their table but was instead making a beeline straight for the dancefloor. He followed the direction her eyes were looking and saw Alex, surrounded by Tom, Henry, Dom and Leo, dancing in typical goofy fashion. John suddenly grasped what was happening and almost choked on his water; she was going straight for Alex, presumably for an intimate dance. It made John's adrenaline spike, but he calmed himself as he realised what was happening; keeping up appearances. Surely, she would have a dance with Alex, maybe ask him for a private word outside and then that would be it. Break-up, they part ways, John would be free to move in. He relaxed back into his chair, content with the plan that he had formulated and watched the reality unfold.

As predicted, Elena did tug Alex aside for a dance. John smiled, slightly sad for his friend, but after what he had heard about the way Alex treated her, he wasn't all that sympathetic. He continued to watch, absentmindedly, as thoughts drifted away to the future. His parents would absolutely love her, she would fit right in. It's going to work so well, they get on like a house on fire, always comfortable with each other and to be honest, he couldn't wait to see her naked and the thought of kissing her...He dreamed idly about how he imagined the first time with her would be, beginning by lifting her dress over her hea-...

John's thoughts were interrupted as though he had been shot. His eyes bulged in amazement and disbelief at what he was witnessing. Elena had pulled Alex in for a deep and passionate kiss, their lips locked and John saw his fantasy crumble in real time. His mouth was wide open and his surprise turned to despair. What had happened? It looked almost certain that they were on the same wavelength, he thought they both wanted the same thing. How could he have misread the situation so badly? Disgusted with himself, John pushed his chair back and abruptly stood up, making his way over to the bar. Josie Black was watching his every move and followed him.

~

Elena removed herself from Alex and her gaze went over his shoulder, finding John's back as he moved to the bar. Looking around, she also saw Josie making her way over as well. *Probably orchestrated*, she thought, bitterly. *He probably text her: "hey, let's get a drink and then have sex all night,"* she imagined, her face darkening with displeasure.

"I wish you wouldn't do that in public. Kiss me like that. That kind of thing shouldn't really happen in front of other people, it's embarrassing - I've told you before," Alex said, snapping Elena out of her hateful thoughts.

"Sorry, I forgot," she answered, looking down at her feet to hide her sorrow.

Alex smiled with satisfaction, and the pair continued their dance, which was now serving just one purpose, to allow Elena a vantage point for watching John.

~

John let his elbows rest on the bar as he patiently waited to be served. His thoughts were swirling, he felt so stupid for allowing himself to dream of something more, when there was nothing concrete to base it on, just a gut feeling.

"What can I get you?" the bartender asked.

"Vodka and coke, please," John reluctantly replied. He didn't really enjoy drinking and he knew he could only have one as he was driving, but what else could he do?

"How about you make that two?" came a voice beside him.

"Josie! Hey!" John said, forcing himself to sound more enthusiastic than he felt. "Two please, mate," he said.

"Having a good evening?" Josie asked, dangling her leg suggestively as she perched on her bar stool.

"I've had better," John remarked, flatly. "Yours?" he asked, turning his attention to the bartender to collect the drinks.

"Oh, you know, the day has been fine, hoping the night will be better."

They both laughed. John understood the suggestion, but didn't think much of it, his mind preoccupied on other matters.

"Cheers," John said as they clinked glasses, Josie seductively sipping through her straw to try and entice him.

Elena continued to dance, though more alone now than with Alex, who had drifted back to his friends. They were engaged in some sort of comedy routine, which normally would have amused her greatly, but not tonight. She felt so crushed by what had happened, she truly thought John liked her. She realised though that he saw her as a sister or just a friend and now he was single, was intent on being with as many girls as possible. Elena looked over to Tom and Beth, dancing closely with their eyes closed, Beth's head resting on his shoulder as they seemed in complete happiness and in a world of their own. Elena then looked at Alex. *Could she have that same level of joy with him?* She thought she could, maybe. He was a solid choice for a husband, she supposed. Steady job, family business. That was good. He would likely make a good father as well, as she had reasoned before with her own parents a few months ago. *Sure, I can marry him*, Elena concluded as she walked back into the group, dancing her way over. She merrily moved with the boys, all of whom were a little bit in awe of how she looked tonight. She allowed a smile to herself as she looked down at her feet, her feelings beginning to normalise somewhat. As she looked up, she chanced a glance over to the bar and she saw Josie and John kissing. Her heart nearly stopped and she immediately looked away and up at the disco ball, fighting back tears as she did so. The lights danced on the ceiling in a maddening frenzy as her thoughts spiralled down towards total despair.

∼

"What the- Josie?!" John pulled away from Josie who had pulled him in for a kiss.

"What, don't you like me?" she asked, somewhat offended.

"No, it's not that, no..." John started.

"What is it then?" Josie pressed, her hands on John's thighs as she began to lean in again.

"Josie, I've got a girlfriend," John exclaimed suddenly, realising that it was indeed still true.

"Huh? I thought she was just your friend?" Josie replied, removing her hands from John.

"What? What are you talking about?" John answered.

"That girl at your table, I thought you were just friends?" Josie explained.

"Well, yeah, we are, but, that's not who I'm talking about. Look, I have to go, okay?" John finished, taking his leave and pulling his phone out of his pocket. He noticed that he had two missed calls and three unanswered texts from Chelsea which he quickly read in order:

I miss you.
Please call me.
John where are you?

He inhaled deeply, unsure of whether his next move was the right one. He dialled Chelsea's number.

~

By the time Elena had recovered, she dared to glance back at the location where John had been. She noticed that Josie was now by herself, idly sipping her drink and clearly waiting for him to return. Her turmoil raged on and she found herself now with one last moment of hope flaring up inside of her. It was only a kiss, nothing else had happened yet. There was still a chance. She began a dialogue with herself: *But you kissed Alex in front of him. But that was because he was moving on with Josie, clearly,* she reasoned. *Fine, that's all in the past. Mistakes have been made by both parties, but there's no reason to throw this all away over some silly misunderstanding.*

She had to speak to John to tell him how she felt and pray that he felt the same, and she had to do it now. Elena departed from the group of boys and hurried outside, where she presumed John would be. She pushed open the doors and frantically looked around for him. Should she shout his name? She refrained for now and continued into the car park, perhaps he was there. She saw him and almost ran over to him but this time, she did let her voice escape, "John!" she cried out.

John looked around to the source of the sound, noticed it was Elena and opened his car door, getting inside, apparently ready to leave.

"John?" Elena said, a bit softer this time as she was near enough to be heard at normal speaking volumes. "John, where are you going?" she asked, her heart thumping in her chest, afraid of the answer but at the same time, the inevitability of it hitting her before he even spoke.

"To my girlfriend's," he said flatly, slamming the car door and turning the ignition, his gaze fixed straight ahead. John's car roared away, scattering pebbles, and in the blink of an eye Elena was left in the cold, dark night, all alone.

CHAPTER FOURTEEN

SIX MONTHS LATER

It was Elena's birthday, and Alex had organised a celebration to take place at *The Fallen Oak* with his family and the familiar group of friends. John was invited and had accepted the virtual invitation on Facebook, speaking directly with Alex as opposed to Elena. John would ask after Elena in a casual way on the rare occasion he would speak to Alex, phrasing the question to be "how are you both?" when in reality he meant, "how is Elena?" John himself was now much harder to get in touch with, for all his efforts were concentrated on Chelsea and his new responsibilities; namely looking after her and her son. John put on a brave face, but in reality, he was drowning under an increasing amount of debt. It had crept up on him slowly and on the fateful night where he left Elena alone at the wedding, John had been in a relatively healthy situation financially.

On that night, John had driven directly to Glasgow from Suffolk, which took him into the early hours of the morning before he arrived. Chelsea didn't answer for a good twenty minutes as she wasn't awake yet and her phone kept ringing out. John had time to reflect on his decision in that space and regretted leaving Elena. The moment he arrived in Scotland, he desperately wanted to leave and drive to Notting Hill, grab Elena by her hand and flee to god-knows-where, but just anywhere with her. Instead, he was shivering in the cold air, waiting to be let into Chelsea's house. When she did finally answer, she forced John to sleep on the sofa, as punishment for ignoring her all evening and making her beg for him to answer his phone. John fell asleep soundly and didn't see Chelsea sneak her ex-boyfriend out of the front door at 5am.

Elena awoke on her birthday to sunshine pouring in through the curtains. She squinted and rolled over to see Alex still asleep. She slipped out of bed quietly and slotted her feet into her slippers that allowed her to pad around noiselessly, so as not to disturb her boyfriend. She silently closed the door, descended her twisting staircase to the kitchen and began preparations for their breakfast; poached eggs with avocado and bacon. Making a coffee and having a moment to herself, Elena reflected on the last three months; the time she and Alex had officially been living together. What had happened in that period? Nothing, really, it was all very sterile and easy. Elena knew she was coasting along and she also knew it wasn't sustainable. As far as the physicality of their relationship, they hadn't even kissed on the lips in that time, let alone had sex. She sighed as her thoughts drifted back to John, who she missed dearly but was too afraid to reach out to. She checked her phone as the first of the birthday wishes began to trickle through, she smiling appreciatively but admittedly looking for one name in particular, and he had not sent anything yet.

"Happy Birthday!" came Alex's groggy voice from the top of the stairs.

"Thank you babe!" Elena called back up, rising from her chair and checking the eggs.

She heard Alex shifting some items around and dropping something, causing him to swear in frustration.

Elena giggled quietly. He hated when things went wrong and felt embarrassment at times like this. Elena always found clumsy mishaps to be funny (as long as nobody was hurt, of course) and had to always control her urge to burst out laughing whenever Alex dropped something. She had once laughed loudly when he had tripped over a slightly raised piece of concrete in the street and he had rounded on her with fury in his eyes and snarled at her to shut up immediately as it was drawing more attention to it and embarrassing him. Elena remembered how startled she was by this outburst and it took her back to that ill-fated trip in Seville. She shook these dark thoughts from her mind as she flipped the bacon, which sizzled satisfyingly in the pan.

"Here you go, my love," Alex said, now downstairs and with a bag of presents in one hand and a card in the other. They hugged and he kissed her cheek, presenting his offerings as he did so.

"Oh wow, thank you! Hold on, let me sort breakfast, go and sit, I'll be in soon."

Alex dutifully obliged, slouching comfortably on the grey sofa in the living room. He then buried his head in his phone, scrolling for an eternity as he caught up on social media platforms and news outlets.

"Here you are," Elena said as she presented their plates.

"Thanks," Alex said, digging in immediately. "Open your presents," he said with a mouthful of food.

"Okay, I will!" Elena said excitedly. She began unwrapping her gifts, of which there were three. One was a pale blue top which she loved, another was a bracelet from Tiffany's and the final present was again from Tiffany's, a set of silver earrings.

"Thank you so much!" she said gratefully, hugging Alex and kissing his cheek.

"That's okay, there could be more coming as well," Alex replied, looking down at his food and smiling subtly.

"Oh, what is it, what is it!" Elena pestered, prodding Alex's arm.

"Ow! Well just wait and see," he said, smiling still.

"Man of mystery today aren't you!" Elena joked, beaming.

"Yep, that's me," Alex replied, looking back at her and smiling.

Elena relaxed back into the sofa, a wave of contentment washing over her as she looked at Alex. *He's good to me*, she thought.

"I love you," Elena said, like a sister would to a brother.

"I love you too," Alex replied, the words sounding unnatural coming from his mouth, such was the rarity in which he uttered them.

John finished zipping his travel bag shut as he was ready to depart for his train back home. "Right Chels, I'll see you Sunday, okay?"

"Alright. Liam, how will we cope for two whole days without John?" Chelsea replied, directing the question to her son who was sitting in the back of Chelsea's car.

"I don't know, Mummy, John please come back quick," said the child, earnestly.

"Oh, bless you little man, don't worry you won't even know I'm gone!" John replied, holding his fist out for Liam to touch with his own. John made an explosion sound which Liam mimicked and they both laughed.

"Be good for your mum, yeah?" John said with instruction, winking at Liam.

Chelsea got out of the car and gave John a hug and a kiss on the lips, biting hard on his bottom lip.

"Don't do anything stupid, okay?" she warned, her eyes flashing like sharpened daggers.

"Like what?" John laughed back.

"We just need you, okay?" she said, burying her head in John's chest.

"That's sweet. Oh, I almost forgot, here's some money for this month - one thousand one hundred, should help."

"Thanks babe," Chelsea said, quickly grabbing the envelope John held out for her. "It's an expensive month for me, I hate not having a job but I have to pay for the travel to these interviews somehow, you know?" she said.

"Hey, I know. It's fine. I'm responsible for you both now," John said with determination.

"Thank you, really, I've never been so well looked after," Chelsea responded.

"I love you, Chels. Of course I'll do what I can to help, even though it's from a distance for now."

"I love you too," Chelsea replied and with a final kiss, they parted.

John boarded the train and let his mind drift off into thoughts of no consequence as he sank into the chair, content that he was doing as much as he could for Chelsea and of course Liam.

That night, Chelsea accumulated a two-hundred-and-fifty-pound bar tab at *The Works* and was escorted home by Gary at one in the morning.

"Happy Birthday!"

The chorus of greeting hit Elena like a tidal wave as poppers were let off and balloons released from their restraints. Elena screamed briefly, actually surprised. She looked around the function room, which was upstairs from the main bar and seating area at *The Fallen Oak* and admired the effort Alex and his family had put in. Long tables were arranged so people could sit spaciously and enjoy the buffet of food, yet there was a massive space for dancing, which was occupied by the usual suspects; Carter and Dom, along with Dom's girlfriend, Annabelle, who was making her first appearance to the group en masse.

"Hi everyone!" Elena grinned, saying individual greetings to the people she passed on her way over to her reserved seat at the head of the table. She thanked Alex's parents and finally settled in her chair, the whirlwind of the initial greeting over and the dust now settling. She scanned the room again, this time taking in everything more carefully. She spotted Leo engaged in conversation with Beth and Tom, next to them was Henry and Freddie, laughing at something Evan had said and then there were some of Alex's uncles and aunts, now talking with Alex's parents and Alex. There was a very obvious missing element, and that was John. Elena started to get nervous for two reasons; one being that it had been half a year since she had seen him and the second was the question of whether or not he would actually show up.

"Looking good, girl!" Dom announced, appearing to her left out of nowhere.

"Thanks Dom, you look nice!"

"Well, I do try, you know."

"I can see! Hey, do you know if Buck is coming?" Elena asked, trying as hard as she could to make her voice as even as possible.

"Er, yeah I think so. He's been up north again, so haven't spoken to him since last week at work."

"Oh, I see, so he's still with Chelsea then?" Elena asked, again trying to be as carefree as possible with her question but waiting on tenterhooks for Dom's answer.

"Ha, yeah, just a bit! He's up there every weekend and any holiday time he takes, it's spent in Glasgow as well. Hardly see him except for down the garage."

Elena felt flat and it was apparent in her voice. "Right, so pretty serious then."

"Yeah, I guess so. Although none of us have met her yet, don't think she's been down here once come to think of it."

"Really? Wow, that's... strange," Elena remarked, genuinely believing it to be abnormal.

"Yeah, anyway, let me go grab Annabelle a drink, I'll speak to you in a sec," Dom said, making his way back over to his girlfriend.

"Sure, speak soon!" Elena said, as cheerfully as she could manage. Alone again and with new information, she had a swirl of thoughts bombarding her as she digested what Dom had told her. Critically, John was going to be here, which was good, and bad. She was nervous again, now purely because she was going to see him, and she had no idea what she would say to him. Elena suspected that she would keep it friendly and casual, especially as it seemed he was getting more and more involved with Chelsea, going by Dom's words.

"EY, here he is!" Henry suddenly exclaimed, throwing his arms in the air in welcome.

Elena whipped her head around to the entrance and there he was, John Buckston had arrived. Her heart leapt into her mouth and she was completely transfixed. John's beard had grown a little, but his head was still shaved. His face looked leaner, but he filled out his black polo t-shirt more than before; he had clearly added some muscle to his frame. He walked towards the huddle of friends who had raced towards him to say hello and an enormous grin split across John's face.

He shook Alex's hand and handed over a card, presumably her birthday card. Elena was watching this all unfold, her heart beating faster and faster as he carried on conversing with the others.

John then suddenly looked across to where Elena was sitting, her pale blue top standing out against the dark backdrop, with disco lights streaking across her body in sporadic fashion, keeping her hidden, yet revealing just enough now and again for John to be drawn in.

Elena shifted uncomfortably in her seat and adjusted her skirt as well as her top, to ensure her appearance was as flawless as possible. John was making his way over and he was alone. His steps seemed to cover ground at an extraordinary rate and she was running out of time before he would be right in front of her. Elena quickly plumped her hair and as she looked up, John was there.

"Hi," he said, and Elena gasped audibly. "Sorry, did I scare you?" John asked, a small grin forming from the corner of his mouth as the ice was broken.

"No, not at all. H-how are you?" Elena stumbled, her composure still not with her, resulting in her eyes not meeting John's.

"I'm good, thanks. How are you?" came his reply.

The conversation was stilted and there was still a notice-able tension between them, yet still a spark of attraction bubbling away under the surface.

"Yeah, fine, thanks," Elena replied, now meeting John's eyes. They looked different from last time, the sparkle that was there on Tom's wedding night was gone and he looked tired and a little bit lost. He smiled back and though it appeared to be just as it was, there was an undeniable sadness lurking behind it. Elena smiled and to John, she looked just as beautiful as ever, if not more, yet there was something there; a pain, a longing. The two stood in silence and continued to look at each other, unsure of what to say and drowning in their thoughts, and then it was as though they both came to the same conclusion in their mind; that their fates had been sealed and that was the end of it.

"Aren't you going to wish me a happy birthday?"

John slapped his head comically. "Oh, yeah! That's why I'm here! Happy birthday, you," John began to turn away and said, "It's good to see you again, Elena."

Elena reached out and touched his arm, causing John to turn back around, expectation and hope rising in his face. Elena was frozen and couldn't find the words so simply said, "It's nice to see you, too."

John smiled, walking back to his friends and again Elena was left by herself.

The evening continued on and was mostly a jovial affair, however John and Elena kept their distance from one another, either through design or coincidence as both of them were socialising with different groups of people at different times. Elena was all too aware of the divide and would occasionally glance over at John to steal a look at him without him realising. She was successful every time and noticed more and more that he wasn't as lively or carrying as much infectious energy as before and she wondered if the reason was because of her, or the situation he was in with Chelsea. Her thoughts were interrupted when Sharon Wicks made her voice heard above the din of the crowd as the music was abruptly cut.

"Thank you, thank you, sorry everyone, sorry!" she said

merrily, pointing at Dom who was throwing up arms in exaggerated exasperation.

"We do hope you've been enjoying yourselves," (this was met with loud approval from everyone present), "but there's something now that must be done. Alex?" She motioned for her son to join her in the middle of the dancefloor. He shuffled over, spurred on by cheers and whoops from his friends.

"And of course, Elena, dear, who we're all here to celebrate with!" Louder cheers and Elena twirled her way to Alex and Sharon, her heart racing at this spontaneous action.

"Alex, over to you," Sharon said and departed, melting back into the crowd, her eyes shining as she looked at her son.

"Elena," Alex began, "remember when I said there would be more surprises?" he was stammering with nerves and Elena was suddenly acutely aware of all eyes being on her and she felt overwhelmed. She knew what was coming and she was dreading it.

"Well…" Alex began, as he slowly descended onto one knee. Gasps emitted from the onlooking crowd with a few muffled cries of joy from some of the women, who instantly snuffed out the noise by clasping their hands over their mouths.

"Elena," Alex began, now withdrawing a small box, opening it and revealing a diamond engagement ring, "Will you marry me?"

Time stood still and Elena was in utter disbelief. She again could feel every pair of eyes boring into her, waiting for the expected answer, but she couldn't give it. She looked down at Alex, her expression one of pity, knowing that she couldn't say yes.

"Don't embarrass me," Alex mumbled through gritted teeth.

Elena dared to take a look at John and she saw his blank expression, his eyes dead and his mind easy to read. He was the only one there who wasn't smiling or excited, his look simply said "don't" and Elena was fighting back tears.

"Elena!" Alex hissed. Beads of sweat began to appear on his upper lip and his eyes were looking at her with increasing urgency.

"Yes," she said, out loud, and the guests erupted, Sharon hugging everyone within a few inches of her and crying, friends rushing towards the newly engaged couple and the colours of happiness exploding everywhere except around Elena, who was feeling nothing but darkness and dread.

CHAPTER FIFTEEN

"Thank you for shopping with us, have a nice day," John smiled pleasantly as he handed over the woman's change and her receipt. That was the last customer of the evening and John allowed a long, slow sigh to escape from his body. Exhaustion was taking a firm grip on him and it showed. He had dark circles under his eyes, his hair was growing and his beard was unkempt. Yet, his smile never wavered, he was always cheerful when speaking to customers and made sure to shield Chelsea and Liam from the signs of his tiredness. John removed his green jacket and stuffed it into his arms in an untidy bundle. Saying his goodbyes to work colleagues, he hopped into his car and accelerated off to his second job; night security at the university.

John arrived just before eleven at night, a minute before his shift was due to start. He clocked in and hurriedly changed his clothes from the supermarket attire to the uniform of the night guard. He slumped into his chair which creaked under the weight and he again let out an enormous sigh. The job was fairly simple and in the two months he had been working it, he hadn't encountered one incident. However, the accumulated hours he now worked were long and he wouldn't be home until six in the morning, where he may be able to sneak an hour of sleep, before having to wake up and get Liam ready for school. Tonight though, he would get a reprieve, as it was Friday and therefore, no school tomorrow. John relished the weekends as it gave him time to catch up on his sleep and enjoy some family time with Chelsea and Liam. Just then, his phone rang and he saw it was Chelsea.

"Hey babe," he answered and was immediately met with a garbled reception and a muffled response. "Babe?" he repeated, furrowing his brow and putting a finger against his opposite ear in a futile attempt to hear more clearly.

"Hello? Hellooo? John? Johnny boy?" finally came Chelsea's voice.

"Hey! Chelsea!"

"Ah, there you are! John! How are you?" she exclaimed, her words slurred.

John sighed once again in exasperation; she was drunk already. "I'm fine love, you having a good night?"

"Yeah, yeah, listen John? You gonnae be okay to pick me and the girls up?" she said, her Glaswegian accent strengthening with each syllable. John paused before responding, he hadn't remembered agreeing to being a taxi service tonight but supposed it would be for the best.

"Erm, yeah, what time?"

"Ahh I dunno, maybes 3 or 4? Anyway, got te go, byee!" She hung up making kissing noises down the receiver and John was suddenly alone with his thoughts. He put his phone away and buried his head in his hands. After a few moments, he re-emerged, his eyes slightly bloodshot and looking even more haggard than before. John returned to his phone and began scrolling through social media, not taking much interest or paying attention until he saw a post from Elena. His heart stopped almost as quickly as his finger did in the endless sea of images and he exhaled heavily, his eyes wide as he saw the picture. It was nothing remarkable in all honesty; Elena was holding the camera in order to take the "selfie" and Alex was standing next to her, pointing at the ring with his mouth open in faux surprise. His heart sank again, as he remembered the events of her birthday three months ago. She had agreed to marry Alex and that had been the last time they had spoken to or seen each other. John knew he had to be away from her for his own sanity and had finally made the decision to move in with Chelsea. That meant leaving the garage, his family, his friends and firmly dedicating himself to his girlfriend and her son. Chelsea didn't work, not really. She got the occasional temping job as a secretary, which would typically allow her to pay the rent and put food on the table, but that was it. It wasn't that Chelsea had bad luck with job interviews, she just flat out refused to apply for anything she deemed was beneath her, which, as it turned out, was quite a lot.

John therefore took charge of the situation and immediately got a job at a local supermarket which was swiftly followed by this night job at the university, allowing them a stronger financial position with a combined income. At first, it was manageable, and the rewards were well worth it. He was able to get toys for Liam, take Chelsea out for romantic dinners and most importantly, provide for his new family.

John's phone again buzzed as the hours tumbled away, it was now two in the morning and he had just received a text from Chelsea:

Miss you, can't wait 2 see u.

John smiled broadly at this, it was unusual for Chelsea to send an affectionate text like this, especially on a night out.

Miss you too x

John replied, just as a new text came in from his bank, HSBC:

YOU ARE CURRENTLY IN AN UNARRANGED OVERDRAFT, PLEASE RECTIFY THIS BEFORE 11:59 TONIGHT TO AVOID FURTHER CHARGES.

John's heart sank and he suddenly felt nervous, a bead of sweat trickled off his forehead. He tentatively opened up his mobile banking app on his phone, hesitated and then hit *View Balance* which unleashed a fresh wave of terror. His eyes bulged and then he squinted, making sure that he hadn't read the figures wrong. His balance read:

Current Account £-3,312
Available Balance £0

He swallowed hard. The room seemed to suddenly close in on him and he felt the air beginning to thin as he struggled to breathe. His chest heaved up and down in laboured rhythm and he clutched his left side as he sat in utter despair. He was three thousand pounds overdrawn and earned roughly one thousand, eight hundred pounds a month. It didn't add up. He was in big trouble and he had known it was coming; he had ignored the warning signs for far too long. John had extended his arranged overdraft limit steadily over the past year, for the costs of travelling up to Scotland every week, as well as sending Chelsea money every month had now tallied up to an unmanageable amount. He was breathing heavily still but was regaining control. *What the hell should I do? Take out a loan? Maybe something to get me through until payday.* John frantically searched the web and found what he was looking for: a money lending service which would quickly send funds to his account right away, repayable over three months. *Great!* John didn't stall and immediately applied. Within minutes, his account was topped up. Although still not exactly healthy, his balance was now back within his arranged borrowing limit. He exhaled with relief, ignorant to the small-print of this credit arrangement which came with enormous rates of interest.

John's phone rang at 2:30AM, but only for a second at most. He took that as his signal to leave and paused. He wasn't supposed to clock off for another three and a half hours and should he be caught, that would surely mean getting sacked. "Fuck it," John said and swept his car keys up in one motion, reasoning that the club was only ten minutes away and that he would be back within an hour. John made it to the club in just under ten minutes and waited patiently across the street, scanning the doors for Chelsea's exit. After a further fifteen minutes, he saw her stumble out, her vivid ginger hair proving a beacon of visibility in the darkness. She was flanked by two of her friends and they were giggling and falling over each other, clearly very drunk. They started walking down the road and John got out of the car, ready to shepherd his flock into the vehicle. He cupped his hands to call Chelsea's name, but his voice caught in his throat as he suddenly saw where they were headed. Gary emerged from his black Mini and was grinning broadly. He opened his passenger door for Chelsea's friends to clamber into and then kissed Chelsea deeply on the lips. He released her and they drove off into the distance. John stood there forlorn, his hands slowly descending to his side. He was utterly perplexed by what he saw and knew what he had to do. Engaging first gear, John sped off towards Chelsea's house.

John switched off the engine and waited. He was outside of the place he now called home and that description of the bland, lifeless brick and mortar he now saw couldn't have felt further away from the truth. He already knew that he would be leaving tonight for London, he didn't care. His jobs here in Scotland would have to find someone else for the role. He had to escape, he had to get out. But first, he had to deal with this betrayal. He didn't care about Gary, he wasn't here for a fight. He did care about Liam and he was sad that he would have to leave this little boy behind with someone who clearly didn't put her son first. But enough was enough. This relationship had sucked the life out of John and buried him under a mountain of debt, bringing stress and putting a strain on friendships that were now fraying and held together by a thin strand. Just then, he saw headlights swing into view, as Gary's car rounded the corner lazily, driving past John's car which remained undetected, John ducked anyway. Gary pulled up outside Chelsea's house and he flung open the passenger side door, collecting a laughing Chelsea up in his arms and gingerly putting her on her feet. She continued to giggle and her arms lazily slid down his top as she allowed herself to fall completely into Gary's embrace. *She looks almost asleep*, John mused. *Time to wake up.*

"OI!" John bellowed, slamming his car door and striding over to Gary, who was visibly surprised and Chelsea who took a second to realise what was happening before suddenly regaining her wits.

"N-n-no, no John, no, it's not what you thi-"

"Shut up," John said, an accusatory finger pointing at Chelsea. "Gary, would you mind fucking off for a minute while we sort this? Cheers pal." John said, before turning back to Chelsea.

"So, how long then?"

"How long, what? What's long?" Chelsea replied, her hand on her head and her eyes shut in confusion.

"How long have you been sleeping with Gary?" The question hung in the air like a bad smell and lingered until the accused finally spoke.

"I never stopped." Chelsea said meekly, her voice like a mouse squeaking in the darkness.

"Right then," John said, now moving to the house, removing the keys which jingled happily in the silence.

"Where are you going, don't touch my boy!"

"Oh, please. You know I adore him. I'm getting my things and I'm off," John replied tersely. He left Chelsea and Gary in the cold night and swiftly moved into the house, putting his belongings into the one suitcase he had, stuffing them in carelessly and quickly. The entire process took minutes and John had swept the entire house of his contents. He sighed, moving to the last room; Liam's.

John gently opened Liam's bedroom door, which creaked in protest. John winced and hoped he hadn't woken Liam up; he hadn't and was blissfully snoring away. John smiled, taking a moment to look around the little boy's room one last time. Posters that they had purchased hung, the corners folding slightly through age, but the sheen still very much there. Toys which they had spent hours playing with together were strewn across the floor, ready to be picked up and the activities resumed. Then he looked at the photograph on the wall. Chelsea, Liam and John together at the park, Liam holding his fingers up behind John's head in mock bunny ears, Chelsea and John smiling with carefree happiness. It was only one month old, *yet look at where we are now,* John thought bitterly. With a great effort, he moved towards Liam and gave him a soft kiss on his jet-black hair. "Goodbye mate. I'll never forget you. It was the best time ever playing with you. Take care of your mum yeah?" John whispered and felt a single tear roll down his cheek. He had truly bonded with Chelsea's son and this was the one true loss of the entire relationship. Puffing out his chest, John returned to the living room, where Chelsea was now sitting on the sofa, silent tears streaming down her face. John ignored her and picked his suitcase up, moving towards the front door where he paused.

"You know, it's funny. The one night you say you miss me, and then I find out..." He shook his head and laughed.

"That text was for Gary, not you," Chelsea answered coldly.

"Well, that does explain things. Good luck with everything, I hope I never see you again." With that, John closed the door and unlocked his car, finally breaking free and vowing never to return.

CHAPTER SIXTEEN

The plane touched down with a squeal as the rubber from the tyres shed upon landing. Elena sighed in relief and relaxed her grip on the armrests. She actually hated flying, particularly the landing, so was thrilled when the captain announced that they had arrived safely. She gathered her belongings and turned on her phone. No new notifications. She sent a quick text to her dad informing him of her arrival and stowed her phone away again. Elena normally felt at ease and calm when she arrived back in her hometown, however this visit was laced with a more serious undertone; she was due to plan details of her wedding with her family. What should have been a happy occasion was causing her to feel anxious and have palpitations every now and again. As she exited through the sliding doors into the Arrivals hall, she spotted her family waiting for her and her fears momentarily melted away.

"Hola mi amor," her mother sighed, embracing her tightly.

"Hola Mama," Elena replied, on the brink of tears. "I've missed you so much. Hola Papa, it's so good to see you," she said, embracing her father now too.

"Hola my girl. Come, let's go home."

～

"ELEEEENNNAAAAAA!!!!!!" shouted Rosa, "Let me see that ring!"

"Your sister has been talking about your ring for weeks and weeks, I thought she'd never stop!" said Elena's mum, smiling and shaking her head in faux dismay.

Elena pushed her hand forward towards her sister's face, brandishing the small diamond ring.

"It's small, but perfecto! I love it!" her sister enthusiastically commented. "Anyway, I have a full weekend planned for us; first, we go and look for venues with Mama and Papa, then tomorrow you will come to my shop and we will design your dress. Whatever you want, my treat!"

"Wait, what do you mean venues? Unless we're flying back to London I don't know what you're expecting us to do!" Elena replied, confused.

"Aren't you getting married here, in Seville?" her father asked, equally as confused as his daughter.

"Papa, I told you, Alex wants to get married in London, I tried to explain that our family can't all afford to come over to the UK but he said that having a wedding in Spain was 'tacky'," Elena admitted, trying to mask her disappointment.

"But the family...your grandparents can't make the trip, they're not well enough. And your Aunt Lucia, she cannot come because she has to visit your Uncle in the hospital every day, you know this!" Elena's mother protested. "These people practically raised you, Elena!"

"Mama, I know, I tried. I begged him, I even suggested two ceremonies, one here and one in London, so we could have the whole family there, but he said it was a waste of money and he won't do it. What more can I do?" Elena implored.

"Elena, I think there is something not right here, no?"

"Papa, por favor, I can't handle the stress of this right now. I'm trying to balance everything, I'm trying to do the right thing and make sure everyone is...happy. It's hard," Elena gulped, struggling to hold back tears.

"But what about your happiness, Elena? What do you feel?" asked her mother.

"Mama, he loves me, he does. It may not seem it. I know I have to do a lot for him and yes, he drinks too much and doesn't make an effort with you but that doesn't mean he's a bad person, only that he's...different. He's not like the other men I have dated. He's a safe choice for my future. I need consistency. Security. I'm getting older, I need to settle down and make a home like you and Papa, I want to have a child and live happily ever after, like you and Papa." With this, Elena started to cry. Her sister rushed over and put her arms around her, but Elena could not be comforted. She sobbed and whispered, "Lo siento, Rosa. I need a moment alone."

Elena walked to her childhood bedroom, closing the door behind her. She looked around and was overwhelmed with happier memories when she had put her family first and was able to spend all her time with them. She resolved that no matter what, she would visit them more going forward, whether Alex liked it or not. She could hear her parents and sister talking about Alex and the impending wedding which they didn't approve of, but she didn't care and she didn't bother straining to try and catch what it was they were saying.

She sat on her bed, removed her shoes and looked out of her window. She could see the Spanish sun bathing the cobbled streets in golden light, the orange trees blooming and releasing their sweet fragrance into the air, the gentle breeze blowing the scent into her bedroom through the open window. Suddenly, she felt an urgent need to speak to John.

153

She took her phone from her bag and found WhatsApp. Scrolling down to find their chat, she saw that she had changed his profile picture; he was standing on a beach, with nothing but blue sky, white sand and turquoise water behind him. He was wearing a vest and shorts and looked nothing short of god-like. His strong shoulders looked more pronounced than the last time she had seen him at her birthday, his back broader and his arms significantly more sculpted. *Where was he?* Her curiosity getting the better of her, she decided to investigate in order to strike up conversation easily. She went to Facebook and immediately wished she hadn't. Dom had posted an album:

BALI BITCH!!!!!!!!!!!

As though she were watching a car crash happen in front of her eyes, she couldn't avert her gaze and step away from her phone, although she knew she should have. The first photo was of Dom and John, surrounded by about seven girls, looking as though they were having the time of their lives at a club. The next photo showed John at a table, empty bottles of beer all around him, a blonde girl's arm wrapped around his shoulders as they both smiled into the camera. Photos of beautiful scenery followed, which Elena hurriedly scrolled past, desperately searching for more fuel to add to the raging fire inside of her. The final photo of the album was one of Dom and John, standing outside a strip club, Dom pointing to it and grinning. John was standing outside, seemingly about to go in, with the same group of girls flocked around him.

Well. That was it. Elena made a list in her head of things to be mad about:

1. *Obviously blondes are his type*

2. *He's a womaniser, judging by the amount of girls around him*
3. *He clearly frequented strip clubs*
4. *He had forgotten about her*

"Rosa!" Elena yelped, "Let's go to your shop. I want to make my dress!"

"Yes! OK Sis, let's go!" Rosa burst into her room, hugging her with joy, "You're going to be the most beautiful bride ever!"

On the way to Rosa's bridal shop, the sisters caught up on each other's news. They were very close and spoke numerous times a day via various platforms whilst they were away from each other, but when together, they were like a perfect dessert; one the icing and one the cake, both pleasant on their own but better together.

"I'm annoyed," Elena said, out of nowhere.

"Why? Because of Mama and Papa? Don't worry, they'll come around," reassured Rosa.

"No. It's not that. There's this man, one of my friends, and I've seen that he's on holiday with loads of girls around and he's going to strip clubs and it's all just. So weird! I didn't think he was like that, I thought...well, I don't know what I thought," Elena finished, looking down into her lap, again choking back tears.

"Hold on, why do you care what one of your *friends* is doing? Do you like him or something?" Rosa probed.

Elena paused for a moment, debating on whether to tell her sister the truth or to yet again mask her true feelings. "Yes. I think I more than like him," Elena sighed, holding her head in her hands.

"What?? What do you mean Elena?"

"It's one of Alex's friends. I can't explain. The first time we met it was like...I just felt like he was my match. Then, every time we met after that, it was just always electric. I thought he liked me at this wedding we went to. I thought he was going to tell me how he felt. But then he kissed a girl, right in front of me, and then he went back to his girlfriend's! When he said he was going to break up with her!"

"He sounds like a bit of a *cabrón*!" spat Rosa.

"I've made it sound worse than it is. He's not. He's lovely. He's so handsome and....he's a man, you know? He is so kind and once he offered me his jacket when I was cold and he helped me out of my car and…"

"Elena," Rosa cut her off, "he obviously doesn't like you if he has done all this stuff in front of you. And now these photos? He's just a *Don Juan*, a player. Forget him!"

"I didn't think he was like that, Rosa. I thought he was The One. He's like the other half of me."

"Chica, look, you had a crush on him, that's fine! But move on, you're getting married! It's natural to have doubts but you need to realise that everything you said to Mama and Papa was how you felt about Alex, no? You want to marry him and live happily ever after like you said. Surely that means that you're happy with him?"

"I guess. But John…"

"Enough of this John. Let me see him,"

Elena produced her phone and showed Rosa John's profile picture.

"Ufff, well, I can see why you fancy him, but he's clearly a ladies' man. Anyone who looks THAT good in a vest is dangerous!"

"That doesn't help!" Elena playfully hit her sister on the arm. "What do you think I should do?"

"It doesn't matter what I think. As always, you will do what you think is best and I will support you no matter what. I know *who* I think you should do though!" Rosa said.

"Stop! I'm not just after his body! I really like him!"

156

"Claro. So do all the girls in that photo you talked about. Stop wasting your time lusting after him and focus on the task at hand. Now, let me work and make you the best dress that ever existed!"

Elena smiled half-heartedly and followed her sister into her shop, leaving thoughts of John behind her at the door.

CHAPTER SEVENTEEN

"My word, it is hot," Dom concluded as he disembarked from the aircraft, wiping sweat that had already formed on his brow.

"Yeah no shit, this ain't England is it?" John said as the wave of humidity hit him.

"Welcome to Bali, have a nice stay!" a friendly steward remarked as they both departed.

"Thanks," they replied in unison.

"Two weeks mate, here we go. Just what we both needed!" Dom exclaimed, grinning broadly and grabbing John around his neck with one chunky arm.

"You can say that again," John answered, smiling weakly.

"Hey, come on mate, I know it sucks that you had to dump her, but at least you're free from that nightmare situation. We were all wondering what you were playing at to be honest."

"I don't even know, pal," John answered glumly, ashamed of his recently finished relationship with Chelsea. Yet it wasn't the reason he was feeling low. The truth of the matter was that he still couldn't quite get over the fact that Alex and Elena were engaged, when it had looked almost impossible for them to be together much longer just a few months prior.

"Besides, look at us now, both newly single and ready to mingle on a lovely island, full of cheap booze and birds!" Dom cheerfully proclaimed, slapping John's back enthusiastically.

"Yeah, just what we needed," John repeated, though in truth he was looking forward to spending time as far away from England and therefore the memory of Elena as possible; Bali just happened to be the one destination that was cheap enough and distant enough. John wasn't quite as determined as Dom to chase women, in fact he suspected that he would simply sit back and watch Dom tear around like a Tasmanian devil in his effort to entice as many women as possible with his unique style of charm.

"Cab should be waiting for us, then it's off to the hotel and straight out!" Dom said gleefully, his thought process following the outline John had assumed he would take.

"Great, you feel fine, no jet lag?"

"Nah, nothing a few drinks won't sort anyway."

The duo continued the lengthy walk to baggage reclaim, Dom with a spring in his step and John lacking his usual spark, which he hid well enough.

"This place is bloody wicked!" Dom surmised as he looked in awe around the massive club they were in.

"I gotta admit, somewhere that has an all you can eat buffet that turns into a club is pretty spectacular," John agreed.

They both piled mountains of various meat onto their plates, John neglecting to indulge in any salad for fear of experiencing a bad stomach the next day. Dom however threw on some lettuce, tomatoes and cabbage onto his growing heap, which was now precariously balancing on his arm as he collected two beers for himself.

"Over there, looks like a seat or two," Dom pointed with his head to a gap in the seating area, which were simply long tables and benches arranged in uniform fashion, which encouraged mingling and conversation. John noticed the gap Dom had spotted was situated between two groups, one was a mix of men and women and another were all women. John felt nervous, he wasn't inclined in any way to force conversation with strangers, let alone attempt to flirt when his heart simply wasn't in it.

"Do you mind if we sit here?" Dom said politely to one of the girls, a blonde who had a deep tan and had likely been travelling for a while.

"Sure, go for it," she replied with a smile, her Australian twang very pronounced.

"Thanks! From Australia then?" Dom said smoothly as he sat down carefully, holding his mountain of food and his two jars of beer.

"Yeah, what gave it away?" she answered sarcastically but playfully.

"Probably the tiny shorts and sandals," Dom replied, getting into his groove.

John turned his attention to his food, smiling as their conversation continued. *Good for Dom*, he thought. He surveyed the scene before him, a large contingent of mostly white faces dominated the area, many of whom had dreadlocks and tans and were likely all travelling around the world on "gap years." He spotted many couples who had arms interlocked and were either kissing each other or just engaging in pleasant conversation. Despite himself, John sighed and immediately wondered what Elena would make of it. *Probably hate how busy it was and be scared shitless of all the flies and other wildlife buzzing around*, he concluded with a laugh.

"And this is my best mate John," he suddenly heard as he felt Dom's hand rest on his shoulder.

John looked to the expectant faces surveying him, three women sat across from him who were apparently with the blonde girl Dom was talking to. John sat in silence for what felt like an eternity before he finally remembered how to talk.

"Hi, this guy getting on your nerves yet?" he remarked coolly, flashing his trademark smile and getting a laugh from everyone.

"No, he's alright, just saying you guys are here for two weeks, you staying just in Kuta or going elsewhere?" a girl with a lip ring and black hair answered and she was looking at John with interest.

"Well, he wanted to take me on a romantic getaway to Ubud, but I said no," John answered, again with a smile and starting to feel a bit more comfortable with the situation as the laughter increased in volume.

"So we're getting some culture here first," Dom answered, getting more laughs as Kuta wasn't exactly famed for that.

"Then we'll probably head to Lovina, see the dolphins and stuff," John interjected, which drew nods of interest, probably feigned in all likelihood.

"What about you girls, what's your story?" Dom asked.

They began recounting their plans and John's phone buzzed, signalling a notification. He glanced down and saw it was from HSBC. Fresh panic took hold of John and he tentatively tapped on the message:

YOU ARE NOW IN AN UNARRANGED OVERDRAFT. TO AVOID ANY CHARGES, PLEASE ENSURE YOUR BALANCE IS IN CREDIT BY MIDNIGHT TONIGHT.

"Shit," John whispered as he opened his banking app to survey the damage. The screen glared back at him with the result:

Your Balance; - £3,728
Available Balance; £0

John's heart sank, he poured through his statement as the conversation around him continued normally. He was sweating (not from the heat), his nerves were frayed beyond all belief and he felt as though the world was closing in, despite the open-air rooftop location. He spotted the culprit. Payment for the emergency loan he had taken out in Scotland. £2983.

"Fuck me!" John exclaimed. Everyone around him looked.

"Everything alright bud?" Dom asked, genuinely concerned.

"Yeah, sorry guys, just something my Dad sent me, nothing to see here," he smiled as he took a swig of beer, his hand trembling somewhat.

"Lunatic, your old man," Dom grinned as he resumed his discussion, unaware that John was on the verge of a breakdown.

"Well, I'd call that night a success, wouldn't you?" Dom proudly proclaimed the next morning as he joined John by the luxurious pool at the hotel.

"I guess, yeah, you brought her home then, the blonde?"

"Course I did. How about you? Any luck with the one with the lip ring?"

"Nah," John said, looking down. "Wasn't really feeling it mate."

"Ah, better luck next time," Dom said with a broad smile.

"Yeah."

"Hey, there's more good news as well. The girls are here for a few more nights, then they're off to somewhere called the Gili Islands? Anyway, sounds right up our street, white sand, clear sea, sun, drinks, and more cheap booze."

"Oh, sounds cool, how do we get there?"

"Well, there's a boat that leaves from Ubud, of all

places. So we could get a bus or cab there and then hop on the ferry, what do you think?"

John paused, mulling over the proposition, which did appeal. Then the reality of his financial situation crashed into his thought process like a wrecking ball and the enthusiasm was suddenly gone.

"I dunno mate, won't it be expensive?"

"Expensive? Here? Gotta be joking haven't you? Probably about a hundred quid extra on top of everything else?" Dom guessed.

John swallowed hard at this revelation, fear gripping him as his woeful bank balance flashed before him in his mind's eye.

"Dom, I..." he started, before letting his head hang in shame.

"What is it mate?" Dom asked, a look of concern spreading across his face as he sank into the sun lounger beside John.

"I-I'm in trouble," John admitted.

"What happened? Something last night?" Dom asked gently.

"No mate, nothing like that. Look, it's all my own fault," John began, swallowing hard. "I'm skint mate. Not mucking about, proper, nothing in my bank and I'm in trouble," he finally admitted, feeling some relief at confiding in his friend.

"What do you mean, what happened?"

John produced his phone, accessed his finances and revealed the extent of his situation. He showed the phone to Dom and witnessed his friend's eyes grow wide in recognition.

"Fuck me, how?" Dom asked, confused by the extent of the debt and increasingly concerned for his friend.

"Chelsea. I was giving her money every month, paying for everything, all the trips up there as well. All so she could just fuck some other bloke while I wasn't there and take me for a ride," John explained, laughing at his own plight.

"Mate..." Dom said quietly, looking quickly at John and then at the pool. "I-I dunno what to say, I had no idea," he finished.

"It's okay mate, it's my own stupid fault," John admitted.

"No, listen, listen," Dom said quietly, his hand resting on John's shoulder. "We all make mistakes, right? This isn't impossible to get out of. You hear of people in much worse financial positions and they survive. You can too. Do your parents know?"

"No way, they'd kill me. They hated how much I was going up there anyway, they felt as if all my energy and concentration was on her and I was abandoning my real family. At the time I was angry with them for saying that, you know? But now, bloody hell, they were right," John concluded.

"Well alright, we keep this between us then. And as for this trip? Don't worry mate, I got you."

"What do you mean?" John asked, confused.

"You can forget about your troubles for a few weeks at least mate, you deserve it. I've got enough to see us both over, we'll be alright mate don't worry."

"Dom... I can't let you do that, it's too much!"

"Sod that. You can pay me back whenever you can, but it's really not an issue. I got some good results on some accumulators this season ain't I, had a nice bit of wedge tucked away for something like this, so fuck it, let's just enjoy it, what else am I going to do with it?" he finished, smiling.

"Thank you, I don't know what to say," John timidly responded, hugging his friend.

"Don't worry mate, this trip is for both of us, time we had a laugh."

"Yeah you're right," John paused, feeling liberated. He bit

his lip in hesitation, feeling on the verge of spilling another secret, this one far more personal and important.

"There's something else..." John began.

"Sure, what is it?" Dom answered.

"It's about Elena..." John said, his heart thumping as he formulated the words in his mouth. "I..."

"Hi boys!" came a shrill Australian voice from the gated entrance to the pool.

"Blimey, didn't think they'd show up! Alright girls!" Dom called back. "Tell me later, yeah mate?" Dom said, nudging John.

"Sure, it can wait," he replied, fairly certain an opportunity like this would arise again.

~

Thanks to Dom's act of kindness, John was able to relax a little in regard to his finances, but now the bigger challenge of admitting his feelings for Elena was dominating his thoughts, precisely what he had tried to avoid in the first place. Though there were moments of distraction, thanks to the idyllic scenery provided by the island of Bali, coupled with more than a few nights out, John's thoughts would always drift back to Elena and about what she might be doing right at that moment. Presently, John was sat awake at 3AM staring at his bedroom ceiling, imagining what Elena might be up to. He couldn't take it any longer, he was desperate to talk to her, so he turned his phone on and began to load up his contacts when a notification buzzed from Facebook, announcing that Elena had uploaded a new photo album. John scrambled to find the source of this information and quickly discovered the origin:

Wedding Planning <3

John felt that familiar wave of disappointment as he was reminded of the fact that she was marrying his friend. However, he committed to looking through the pictures regardless, out of curiosity, likely doing his mental health no favours but he didn't care, he had to see her. The first picture was of Elena and her sister. John soaked in the image for over a minute, studying every pixel and admiring every pore. Her dark eyes were bright and full of joy, her smile illuminated the frame and her long hair flowed effortlessly down to her shoulders. John didn't really pay attention to her sister, a fleeting glance informed him that she too was pretty, but couldn't match Elena's beauty. He touched her face with his finger, longing to be with her and resigned himself to simply admiring her from a distance. For now.

"Hey," came Dom's voice out of the darkness, startling John so much that he dropped his phone.

"Jesus, you made me shit myself, I didn't know you were awake!"

"Yeah, too hot really ain't it?"

"Yeah, just a bit," John agreed, returning his phone to the pedestal next to his bed.

"Hey, remember the other day, by the pool?" Dom began.

"Yeah?"

"You had something you wanted to say about Elena?"

"Did I?" John lied, pretending to have forgotten.

"Yeah, what was it?"

John paused, mulling over the decision in his head of whether to reveal his deepest, most well-kept secret.

"Buck?"

"Sorry mate, can't remember."

"Mustn't be important then! Goodnight," Dom answered, turning over in his bed.

"Night mate," John replied, keeping the most important thing to him hidden from the outside world for another day.

John's alarm on his phone rang for a solid two minutes before either of the boys stirred from their sweat-drenched slumber. Dom grunted as he took hold of the situation, John seemingly passed out for the time being. Dom fumbled with John's phone and managed to switch the alarm off, but as he did, the screen reverted to the last thing John had open; Elena's Facebook photo album she had recently uploaded. Dom looked carefully behind him at the still-snoring John, a sudden awareness coming to him. He smiled and put the phone back on the desk, returning to his bed and making an exaggerated yawning sound in an attempt to wake his friend.

"Blimey, is that the time?" Dom asked into the room.

"Urgh, what?" John groggily replied, sitting up in his bed and wiping sleep away from his eyes.

"Hello sleeping beauty," Dom grinned. "Come on, we gotta be off soon, ferry leaves at ten thirty."

"Shit, does it? What's the time?"

"Nine forty-five," Dom answered.

"Christ, best get a move on, you showering first?"

"Nah, can't be arsed."

"Disgusting, right give me five minutes."

"Okay, cool," Dom said, waiting until he heard the water running before leaping back over to John's phone to confirm his suspicions. He decided that he would speak to John about his *Elena Situation* as soon as possible.

The ferry tumbled over the waves as it began to slow its speed as the island of Gili Trawangan came into view.

"Here we are lad, you can put your head up now," John said to Dom, gently patting his back as he did.

"That was fucking awful," Dom responded, his face paler than usual. "Didn't realise how violent this poxy boat trip was," he summarised.

"Yeah, wait until the disembarking," John said, witnessing

other passengers leaving the transport, having to throw their luggage as far as possible in an attempt to make it to dry land and then launching themselves in the same way.

"Fuck me, health and safety or what," Dom remarked, craning his neck to see past the rest of the crowd.

"Ah, makes a change doesn't it from our sterile way of living. It'll be fun!" John said enthusiastically.

Dom put on a sarcastic smile in response as he hoisted his rucksack over his shoulder in preparation for the landing. Despite his best intentions, he hadn't had a chance to talk to John about Elena, due to his priorities being elsewhere; namely on stifling a wave of vomit from spewing out every time he opened his mouth to speak.

"Right, here we go!" John said as he threw his own bag as far as possible, it coming to a thud in the white sand, safely away from the water which lapped gently against the boat. John followed this up with a forceful leap, landing successfully but his sandal getting caught on a small rock.

"Bugger it," John swore, shaking his now sandy foot.

Dom laughed and pointed, before throwing his luggage in the same way. He was rather unfortunate in that his bag decided to roll back a little, allowing one of the straps to dangle carelessly in the water.

"Oh shit," he said, making his own leap and landing a little short, splashing water up to his vest.

"Brilliant."

"Haha! Not as easy as it looks is it?" John said with good nature, lightly punching Dom's arm.

"Yeah, yeah, let's find our huts and go get settled."

The pair walked for a mere ten minutes until they came to their living quarters for the next few nights. It was as Dom had described, a hut right near the beachfront that had room for four people, giving the duo lots of space. They unloaded their luggage, Dom took a shower and headed out to get some lunch from the communal eating area, which had a multitude of cuisines to choose from and everyone was congregated around the familiar bench and table set up as seen in other parts of Bali. They both picked a chicken with rice dish and found a quiet area to sit in and enjoy their meals.

"This is good!" John said through mouthfuls of food.

"Yeah, best meal we've had I reckon," Dom agreed. They continued to eat in silence for a few minutes before Dom finally broke the quiet in the most abrupt way.

"So, you gonna tell me about how you fancy Elena then?"

John almost choked on his food in surprise. "Come again?" he exclaimed, rapidly putting more food into his mouth through nerves.

"You had something to tell me about her a few days back, remember? In Kuta?"

"Did I?" John feigned a lapse in memory, putting more food on his fork.

"Yeah, you did. You fancy her don't you?" Dom pressed, his own cutlery abandoned and his hands folded together. John however was very interested in his food and continued to pile rice onto his fork.

Dom reached out a hand to stop John's manic eating and looked him in the eyes. John's panic was clear, but at last he relented and put down his utensils.

"Fine, fine," John at last admitted with a sigh.

"Shit, so it's true!" Dom almost shouted, his eyes bulging in alarm.

"Well, I dunno. Yeah, yeah I guess it is," John said, owning the statement and feeling that familiar sense of relief wash over him at having told Dom another personal secret.

"Oh man, does she know?"

"No."

"Do you think she likes you as well?"

"Honestly? I thought she did, but clearly not right?" John grimaced.

"Yeah that is true, the sparkling ring on her finger would suggest not," Dom said unhelpfully.

"Cheers mate."

"Sorry, just trying to be realistic here. Shit Buck, this is big news. What are you going to do?"

"I don't think there's anything I can do, is there?" John asked.

"Well, not really. Especially if you're not convinced she likes you. I mean if you tell her and she doesn't feel the same way, that's going to be *so* awkward. Plus, she'll obviously tell Alex and then that's you two likely no longer mates."

John pondered all of this in silence, looking at Dom and feeling grateful that he was at least having this debate with him in a friendly way, it could have been much worse, he realised.

"I think..." John began.

"That you're a twat?" Dom interrupted, smiling.

"Piss off," John answered, with a matching grin. "No, I think that if I say something now, it wouldn't look genuine? Like it's a last-minute decision and I'm panicking 'cos I'm single and she's getting married."

"Perhaps," Dom pondered as he finally allowed himself to eat a slice of chicken. "But if you don't say anything, it's going to be too late, isn't it?"

"That's true. You think I should text her?" John asked, his fingers already reaching for his phone.

"Couldn't hurt just to see what she's up to?"

"Yeah, maybe, let's give it a go. Been ages since we spoke though." John opened up his contact lists and found Elena and began a new message:

Hey, hope you're ok? Just wanted to see how you are?

John continued to eat while he waited for the response, glancing at his phone nervously as no response was sent.

"Shit, reckon she's pissed off at me as it goes," John said with worry in his voice.

"What for?" Dom said, clattering his knife and fork onto the now empty plate.

"Well, probably because she doesn't know I'm single, she thinks I'm with Chelsea still and just purely because I haven't said a word to her in months."

"Keep the faith mate, you never know," Dom offered reassuringly.

"Yeah, I guess," John said flatly as he returned to the final portion of his lunch.

Hi Buck, yes I'm good thanks, you?

"Oh shit she's replied!" John informed Dom, grateful for the Wi-Fi present in their living quarters.

"Good! Get on it! I'm gonna go grab some supplies for later, you stay here with the Wi-Fi and crack on!"

"Nice one, cheers, see you in a bit," John paused before replying, wondering how he could steer the conversation in the direction he wanted it to go and if that was actually the right decision.

John: Yeah good! Just chillin' at the moment by myself.

Elena: Cool. How's Chelsea?

John: Guess you haven't heard, we broke up.

172

I'm out in Bali with Dom at the moment in celebration lol

There was a longer delay here and John was getting worried, *why was there a pause? Oh shit, she probably thinks I'm here chasing girls like some kind of desperado,* John thought to himself. He started sweating from his forehead, possibly due to the heat, but more than likely down to the nerves he was suddenly feeling. Just then his phone buzzed with a new notification and he frantically opened the message:

Oh, didn't know you'd broken up. Sorry to hear. Say hi to Dom for me

John stared at the message for a moment and let the coldness of it sink in. Elena really didn't seem in the mood for talking. "Fuck it. I'll call her out on it," John said aloud to nobody in particular.

John: *Nothing to be sorry for, best decision I've made. Everything ok with u?*

Elena: *Good, she wasn't right for you. But I'm sure you knew that in the end. Yes fine, just been a long day and I'm feeling tired.*

Of course, it was probably late at night in Spain. That made John feel better, but only slightly, he was still wishing that the tension between them could be cut. He sighed in defeat, knowing that this wouldn't be resolved today, especially not over text and committed to simply keeping the message on an even keel.

John: *Ah fair enough, time delay,*

it's early here. Hope you get some rest,
talk soon.

Elena: *Yh speak to you soon.*

"Hey lover man, how did it go?" came Dom's voice from the dirt track that wrapped around the rear of the hut.

"Oh mate, shocking."

"Why what happened?" Dom said, hoisting a leg over the short fencing and joining John at the front of the hut, throwing him a can of beer.

"Cheers," John said cracking the can open. "Nothing really, it was very... awkward?" he continued, sipping his beverage.

"Well, you haven't spoken in an age, give it time?"

"Yeah I guess. I'm just anxious, mate."

"Why's that?"

"Because it's more than just liking some fit girl in a club. This is real, this is really real," John admitted, pausing and letting the bitter taste of his beer sit on his tongue for a second.

"Shit me," Dom replied in amazement.

"Tell me about it. So yeah, not a great conversation but what can you do?"

"Baby steps mate. Keep at it."

"Yeah I guess."

"Though the bigger question," Dom began, pausing to swat a bug on his arm, "Is the whole you know, her getting married thing? Like, if you feel as strongly as you do about her, are you going to try and stop the wedding?"

John didn't respond immediately, he hadn't thought that far ahead to the wedding as it turned out.

"I don't know. What I do know is that the second we're all back in England, I need to talk to her, face to face," John finished, sitting back and taking a deep glug of beer, looking into the distance.

174

CHAPTER EIGHTEEN

It was three months before the wedding and Elena was starting to get incredibly anxious about the entire event. There were warning signs everywhere, telling her to stop, to call the whole thing off and start over with someone else, or better yet be single for a little while. Her mum and dad were concerned, her sister had given her plenty of words of warning to heed, yet here she was, back at her home with Alex smiling over breakfast.

"Doing much today?" Alex asked, some milk dribbling onto his chin from the half-chewed cereal in his mouth, causing Elena to visibly shudder, which he missed.

"Nothing, just housework, call my parents and maybe watch a romantic film on TV."

"Nice, you should try and find something for us to watch for when I get home."

"Yeah good idea, but we're FaceTiming my sister tonight aren't we? What time will you be finished?"

"Not sure," Alex began, swallowing another mouthful. "Probably about ten?"

"Wow, that late?" Elena asked, taking a delicate bite out of her toast.

"Well yeah, I have to stay a bit longer and see people, you know."

"What? What time does your shift actually finish?"

"Six."

"Six!" Elena exclaimed, "So why will you stay for *four* more hours?"

"I just told you, I need to show my face, be around. Sometimes it's nice to have a beer after work."

"Right okay. Come back whenever you want," Elena said, getting up and putting her plate in the dishwasher.

"Oh don't be like that," Alex moaned, which Elena ignored.

"I'm going for a walk, see you tonight at some point," Elena responded, stepping into her trainers and exiting the house in a fluid, swift movement. She sighed as she walked. Another warning sign; Alex putting his socialising before a family commitment. She turned around, not expecting to see Alex chasing after her, as he never had the initiative to do such a thing and as usual, wasn't surprised to see that he wasn't there. Trying not to think about how intoxicated Alex would be when he got home, she shook her head to avoid thinking about what she always did whenever she was around anyone who was drunk.

Years ago, while living in Spain, Elena had been staying at her friend Teresa's house after school. They had been friends since primary school and frequently slept over at each other's houses. However, on this occasion it was different, as Teresa's father had just returned to the family home after being stationed in some remote place with the army. The girls were getting ready to go out for the evening. Teresa and a few of her friends from Madrid had decided to

join a "botellón"; a traditional Spanish ritual of young people getting together in the evenings to drink in a square in town. Groups of different people will converge with their respective friends and have a gathering en masse. Contrary to popular belief, these nights hardly ever got out of hand, with the majority of participants merely enjoying being with their friends. No music is played, everyone chats and catches up. Teresa and Elena had been at the "botellón" for a few hours and were ready to go back to Teresa's as they both had to get up early for their Saturday job; teaching English at a local youth club. They walked the short twelve-minute journey through the cobbled streets of Seville, enjoying the sweet smell of the air as its coolness washed over them. Upon unlocking the door, Elena had a strange foreboding feeling as she heard a glass bottle being opened in the living room.

"Mama must be asleep. I'm exhausted, let's get to bed," said Teresa as she made her way upstairs.

"OK, I'll just get a drink," replied Elena, walking to the kitchen to get some cold water to take up to bed with her.

"Hola Elena," came a voice which seemed to slur the vowels of her name into one.

"Ay! Hola Señor Trevino," replied Elena politely, "You scared me!"

"Ay chica, I didn't mean to. You look very nice," he said, as Elena felt his eyes travel up and down her body.

"Gracias Señor. Well, I must be going to bed now, I have to be up early for my job," she said hastily, trying to make her way to the door, his big frame blocking her from leaving.

"Not so fast. Aren't you going to kiss me goodnight?" he said, edging closer to her.

"Sorry, Señor Trevino. I really must be going now," she gulped, wishing she could disappear.

Teresa's father stumbled towards Elena and pressed up against her. Elena tried to scream and felt his hand reach across and cover her mouth, muffling the sound completely before she could even

177

make it. His other hand brushed her shoulders and moved down to her chest. She tried to move away from him with all her might, but to no avail. She could smell the strong stench of alcohol coming from his body in waves and she wanted to be sick. Her eyes searched frantically for something to help her escape, and she managed to use her leg to kick over a kitchen chair. The noise startled her friend's father to the point where he released her for the briefest of moments, giving Elena enough freedom to knee him swiftly in the stomach and flee.

Elena ran out of the house and into the street, crying hysterically. She didn't realise that she was barefoot when she banged on the door of her own house at 1am. Her father answered the door and would never forget the look on his daughter's face, which still haunted him to this day. He immediately called the police and within the hour, Jacinto Trevino was arrested and locked in a prison cell where he belonged. Whilst this gave the Viegas family some peace, Elena now associated alcohol with this traumatising event and every time she smelled it, she was automatically and unwillingly transported back to that night.

As she walked, Elena remembered how she had shared all of this with Alex on one of their early dates. She wanted to make him aware early on that she had intimacy issues and also that she didn't like drinking excessively. She made Alex swear not to tell anyone, as this was something she didn't want to bring up ever again. He simply agreed and gave her some rather non-committal and reassuring pats on the hand while she told her story (hardly the reaction she had wanted or needed) and made no effort to curb his drinking habits.

Elena looked at her smart watch to check how far she had walked, when suddenly it flashed up with a new notification; a text message. Elena paused and sat on a nearby bench, retrieving her phone from her pocket, expecting to see something from Alex. It was from John:

Hey, hope ur ok? Just wondering if ur free today for a late lunch?

Elena's eyes grew wide, she was completely taken aback by this. John had never asked to meet her for a one-to-one engagement before, was something wrong? She pondered the request and whether to tell Alex or not. *Well why should I? It's just two people meeting up for food*, she rationalised.

Elena: *Sure, how does 2 sound?*

John: *Sounds good, Covent Garden work for you?*

Elena: *Yes, that's great, meet at the station?*

John: *Perfect, cu there at 2.*

Elena: *Cool, see you soon Buck*

For the first time since leaving her house, a big smile appeared on Elena's face and she felt a surge of excitement rise up from her belly. She got up from the seat and began to make her way back home, Alex would have left for the pub by now so she had plenty of time to get ready and ensure she looked right; she would have to strike a balance between looking good and looking like she had made no effort in. She planned her outfit on her walk back home; settling on ripped high-waisted skinny jeans with a lemon-coloured t-shirt and bright yellow Nike trainers. Matched with her beige cashmere jumper, she was sure she would look casual yet cute. She pondered her aim; she knew she shouldn't want to look cute for John, but she couldn't help it. His opinion was the only one that ever mattered to her in terms of how she looked. She always sought his approval and she valued it above all else.

She exited the underground station into the busy crowd that typified a Saturday afternoon in Covent Garden. People from all different backgrounds were meeting friends, lovers, family and all with the intention of either having some food or seeing the sights. Elena enjoyed the general hustle and bustle that London was famed for and today was particularly exhilarating in that she was about to meet John alone for the first time, just the two of them.

"Elena!" she heard her name being called by John and spun around, searching for him amongst the bobbing heads that walked past.

"John!" she said loudly as she spotted him in the distance, his arms waving frantically above the sea of people to be noticed. He said something else that was distorted by the noise and started wading his way across to her, finally squeezing through the crowd and standing in front of her.

"Blimey that was fun, hello!" he said, puffing and pulling Elena in for a tight hug which took her by surprise at first, but she allowed her arms to wrap around John, who was wearing a jumper over a polo shirt.

"You look nice," she blurted out as they released their embrace, going slightly pink at the sudden appraisal of his appearance.

"Thanks. You look great, as always. Nice trainers!" John answered with a smile and just like that Elena felt all the tension and resentment from the months prior begin to fade away. It was so good to be back in his presence, he had a way of lifting her spirits like nobody else and seemed to have an aura of positivity around him.

"I think it's this way, come on." He inclined his head forward and began to battle his way through the crowd once again, brushing past Elena gently as he led the way, blazing a clear trail for her to follow. Elena looked up and squinted at the sun which was peeking around a cloud, the first time it had appeared all day.

"This way, come on, don't want to lose you!" John shouted, grinning as he did.

"I'm coming, I'm coming!" Elena said, picking up her pace and squeezing into the gap John had made for her between two groups of people.

"Just up ahead, few more minutes," John instructed, as they continued their mazy walk through the streets of Covent Garden, becoming part of the flow of human traffic.

"Hope you're hungry," John said, as their destination came into view on the corner of a side street.

"*Bon Burgers?*" Elena read aloud from the sign which dangled elegantly above the restaurant. "Are we having burgers?" she asked.

"No, I thought we'd have some pasta at this burger place actually," John teased.

"Oh shut up!" Elena replied, laughing.

"Come on, after you," John held the door open and they were seated swiftly.

"So, how are things?" John asked nonchalantly, sipping from his glass of Coke.

How are things? Elena wondered internally. "Yeah, good," she answered lamely.

"Glad to hear it," John said, looking Elena directly in her eyes for a brief second before ducking his head back to his drink.

Unusual for John, he seems almost nervous? Elena pondered

this revelation and kept it at the back of her mind for later examination should she need it.

"What about you? Enjoying single life?" she said with the slightest hint of venom lacing her words. She recalled the photos she had seen of John in Bali, surrounded by girls and looking like he was having the time of his life.

"Well, I certainly like being away from that train wreck of a relationship I had before, if that's what you mean."

It wasn't, but she didn't feel the need to press the point, especially not at the moment.

"What happened, how did you guys break up?" Elena asked, applying a veil of carelessness to her words which hid her true desperation to find out what really did occur.

"Do you want the long or short story?"

"Everything, I've got all day," Elena said smiling.

"Okay well," John started, taking a sip of his drink and clearing his throat in preparation for his tale.

Elena leaned forward as John recounted the final moments in his relationship with Chelsea. With each revelation her eyes got a bit wider and when he announced that he had seen Chelsea kissing Gary outside the club, Elena could resist no longer and she squeezed John's hand gently.

"John...I had no idea."

"It's okay, nobody did," he said, shrugging.

"I'm sorry this happened to you, you deserve so much better," Elena said kindly, meaning every word.

"Thanks. We'll see I guess," he answered, a twinkle in his eye which made Elena feel excited for some reason.

"So that was it," he carried on, "ended it and decided to go on holiday with Dom."

"To go and pick up girls?" Elena asked, retracting her hand suddenly.

"No? What? No, not at all," John responded honestly. "I just had to get away, Dom was in a similar situation having just broken up with whatever her name was, so we both decided to get as far away as possible without spending a bomb."

"Well I know what you're like," Elena said abruptly. "The girls like you Buck, I'm not stupid."

"You can think what you want, but I didn't do more than shake a girl's hand," John said with finality, signalling an end to that particular line of questioning.

A tension now hung in the air which was awkward and not what John had in mind for this lunch at all. Elena bit her lip and admitted internally that she was probably being harsh on John, but then again he had disappointed her all those months ago at Tom's wedding by kissing that other girl right in front of her. Not that she had any right to feel that way in the first place, considering the fact that she had a fiancé and was getting married soon.

They were spared further agonising minutes of awkward silence when the burgers they had ordered arrived, which sparked fresh conversation between them.

"Oh my god, it's massive!" Elena said.

John couldn't resist, "I'll take the compliment."

"What? Oh, ha-ha! You're so rude!"

They both laughed in unison at the innuendo and the relaxed, the friendly atmosphere returning in an instant, much to their relief.

"It actually is massive. The burger, I mean," John said as he used both hands to bite into the succulent meat, expelling barbecue sauce onto his plate as he did.

"You're such a caveman, look at you, getting it every-where!" Elena mocked, as she delicately cut her burger in half and took a small square to her mouth.

"Oh, do excuse me," John said, holding a chip in his fingers with an exaggerated air of importance as he barely nibbled it.

Elena laughed loudly, "Stop it, you'll make me choke!"

John laughed himself, covering his mouth with the back of his hand to avoid any embarrassment from dropping food.

"Mmm, so," John began, swallowing the big chunk of meat he'd inhaled. "What about your trip to Seville, have a good time?"

Elena reminisced about the polarity of seeing her sister, which she loved, but having to face the reality of her wedding, which she was dreading more and more.

"Yeah, great to see my sis," she answered neutrally.

"Yeah, I saw."

"Oh did you, stalking me again?"

"Ha, you wish!" John said, going slightly crimson at the insinuation, which wasn't far from the truth as he remembered discovering these photos in the early hours of the morning back in Bali.

"So, she helped you out for the wedding?" John asked as casually as he could manage.

"Yes, she's making my dress," Elena responded, taking another bite of burger.

"You must be excited," John said, quieter this time and keeping his eyes fixed on his meal.

Not really, Elena wanted to say. "Yeah," was all she could summon from her voice box, as a fresh silence descended on them.

"There's more as well." John began, his eyes fixed on his food.

Elena's heart sank, *had he got her pregnant?* "What is it?"

"Well, I've been a bit silly."

Oh my god. He has. "Tell me, Buck." Elena said earnestly, her eyes boring into his.

"It's embarrassing, but I'm in trouble."

"Why, what have you done?" Elena said, struggling to keep her voice even.

"I've dug myself into a massive hole. I'm four thousand pounds in debt."

Relief washed over Elena, but this was momentary as she saw just how hurt and uncomfortable John was with his situation.

"But, how? You just went on holiday?"

"I know, I know. I just haven't been careful. I kept paying for everything, giving her money, buying shit for her son...it's just all got on top of me and now I'm in big trouble. I took a loan out to clear the debt, pay for the holiday and it's still not cleared what I have, plus now I have to repay this loan," John finished, the sudden admission of his burden felt good to get off his chest, but the reality of the situation was still bleak.

"So, you were in even more debt?" Elena asked, her voice soft and her gaze kind.

"It was just over ten thousand before the loan," John said quietly, biting down on a chip.

Elena bit her lip, debating with herself about what she was on the verge of saying. She made her mind up within seconds.

"John. Look at me. John, I'm going to help you."

"What? Don't be stupid," John said dismissively, the hard exterior shielding his inner gratitude as his emotions swelled.

"Listen to me, John," Elena said, taking his hand in hers and squeezing tightly. "I can help, okay? I can get you back on your feet. You don't need to worry about repaying the loan and we'll get you back to where you need to be."

"Elena, I can't. Besides, I'll just owe you then, I'm shifting the problem." John said earnestly.

"John Buckston, you can pay me back whenever you are able to. I'll transfer you the money and you'll fix this, okay? You don't deserve to have this hanging over you like a curse. You had enough of a bad time with her as it is," Elena said firmly, her hand still gripping his.

John was silent for a moment. He looked at Elena with a piercing stare that was saying a thousand words all at once, as his free hand joined their already connected palms, binding them tightly.

"Thank you," he said finally, with months of emotion that had been building up inside of him.

They continued eating quietly for the next few minutes, occasionally exchanging smiles as they looked up from their food, neither of them really knowing what to say next, as they both suspected the other person had something important to say. It was John who finally broke the silence.

"Are you sure about this?"

"What, the burger?"

"No," John laughed before pausing, knowing the next words from his mouth would be critical. "About the wedding. Marrying Alex, all of it," he said with a rush, relieved he had got it out into the open, but bracing for the impact of Elena's answer.

"What do you mean? Of course I am," she said with certainty, surprising herself at the forcefulness of the statement.

"As long as you're sure," John said, defeated.

"What makes you say that anyway?" Elena probed.

"Nothing, don't worry."

"Tell me, what is it?"

"Well, what if there was someone better for you?" asked John tentatively.

"Like who?"

John anxiously bit his lip, cautious that the words he wanted to spill from his mouth would have enormous ramifications. "Don't you just have a feeling? That there's *someone* else?"

"I did," she said flatly.

"What's that supposed to mean?" John said, feeling a

mixture of hurt and excitement at the same time that she could mean him.

"It means, I didn't realise how much you enjoyed having girls all over you and going into strip clubs!" she finished angrily.

"What? Oh, the photos. Well, we didn't go into the strip club, I just posed for the photo as a joke."

"Rubbish."

"It's true! Ah whatever, you can talk, one minute you're acting like you want me, the next you're snogging your boyfriend's face off in front of me!" John retorted, the hurt from Tom's wedding finally rising up and erupting as though from a dormant volcano.

"Oh are you talking about Tom's wedding? Really?" Elena replied, now staring at John with ice in her eyes and fire in her veins.

"I am, yeah," John said, a little less sure of himself now he'd seen the look Elena was giving him.

"When you had that GIRL all over you and you were loving it? Forgetting about me as soon as you left the table?"

"Oh my…" John hit his head with his hand, "Elena! I didn't know her, she stopped me to say that she works around the corner from me! We were just chatting!"

"Funny chat you had at the bar later on wasn't it?" Elena said, making air quotations around the word "chat" as she spoke.

"You mean when she forced a kiss on me?" John said quickly, defending himself with the truth.

"Whatever. You're a ladies' man, you just want to get in my knickers and tick off another girl you've conquered."

"That's not true at all! Anyway, you're the one that immediately got engaged when you told me you were having problems!" John spat.

"Excuse me? Everyone has problems! You went running back to Chelsea even though she was treating you badly!"

"Because you were getting all loved up with Alex!"

"Because you were kissing any girl you could find! Ugh! Just forget it! We're just going round in circles and it really doesn't even matter. Let's just move on," Elena said, hiding her face as she busied herself in her handbag, preparing to leave.

"Are you going?" John asked quietly, knowing the answer.

"Yes, here's half for the burger. Nice seeing you, Buck," and with that, Elena rose from her stool and left the building, leaving John to stare at her as she walked away. He didn't see how much she was crying on the way out.

CHAPTER NINETEEN

John's phone rang for the fourth time in as many minutes as he finally managed to force the top button of his white silky shirt closed.

"Fuck me, who's this?" he said, exasperated. John picked up his phone and saw it was Alex who had made the four calls.

"Shit," John quickly dialled the number back and pressed the phone to his ear.

"John! Thank God. Mate, we have a situation, I need your help."

"Sure, what's up?" John said, tilting his head towards his shoulder to hold his phone so he could now struggle with the task of applying his cufflinks with both hands.

"The car's broken down, Elena is stuck at her place. I know it's a lot to ask, but I think she'd love it if you could go and get her?"

John pondered the proposition for a moment and he didn't respond right away.

"John?"

"Yeah, sure, sorry was just thinking of the best way to get there, tell her I'll leave now and be there in about twenty."

"You're a lifesaver, thank you mate." The phone clicked off and Alex was gone, leaving John in silence in the hotel room. He quickly grabbed his navy suit jacket and hurriedly put it on his back, whilst digging his feet into light brown shoes. Hopping on one foot, he danced back over to the window he had left open, slammed it shut and was out of the door within thirty seconds.

"Right, yeah, of course I'll drive your bride to the wedding that I don't think you should even be having. Sure, why not?" John mumbled to himself as he unlocked his car and sat in the driving seat, put the keys in the ignition and simply waited. The rush of urgency had left him and he was now processing exactly what was going to take place. He heaved another deep sigh and put both hands on the steering wheel, his head gently resting on the horn, without making a noise. *How the fuck is this happening? I'm driving the girl of my dreams to her wedding? To someone else? Yet another prime example of my shit luck.* He shook his head and set off for Elena's house.

"Thank you girls, you've been amazing!" Elena waved goodbye to her hair and makeup team as they left her house. She looked at herself in the mirror and was thrilled with her appearance, her glittery pink eyeshadow had been perfectly applied to accentuate her large chocolate brown eyes, which were further enhanced by the subtle, slightly longer false lashes. Her eyebrows were shaped flawlessly and had little flashes of highlighter below them which caught the light when she tilted her head. Elena's lipstick was a pale shade of pink which matched her eyeshadow. Looking down at her nails, she moved her fingers as though playing an imaginary piano to examine her manicure; pink with gold glitter on top. When she had first told her soon-to-be mother-in-law what she wanted her nails and makeup to look like, she was accused of not being "bridal enough", but her idea had all come together perfectly and she loved the final look.

Her dark hair had been curled and piled atop her head in a very traditional Spanish style. Her sister had designed her wedding dress personally and it was beautiful, Elena thought. Lace straps adorned her tanned shoulders, leading down to a sweetheart neckline which showed a little, but just enough, cleavage. She had asked her makeup artist to put a bit of glitter on her collarbone and decolletage so she could shimmer in photos under the cameraman's light. The rest of the dress was fitted, full of Spanish lace, hand-stitched by her sister and her mother; a real labour of love. Elena didn't want a traditional dress and couldn't decide on a ballgown style or more fitted design, so her sister had created a lace overskirt through which Elena's silhouette could be seen. She swished from side to side, and observed the lace moving and flowing, revealing glimpses of the tighter skirt underneath. She turned to the side and noticed how her veil trailed behind her. Her sister ensured it had the same lace design as the rest of the dress and was again of the traditional style of her town. She turned back to face the mirror and took a deep breath, taking in her whole appearance. She was satisfied with what she saw, but she placed one hand on her stomach, trying to calm the nerves that had started to creep in.

In truth, Elena looked more or less as she always did, such was her natural allure, however today, her beauty was simply escalated to new heights that would ensure all the guests would be blown away. Her thoughts lingered here as she suddenly remembered one person in particular who would be attending: John. Elena hadn't spoken to or seen John for what felt like an eternity. She suddenly got nervous and began to fiddle with her bracelet that her mother had gifted her for today's wedding.

"I'm getting married," Elena said aloud to her empty house, which responded with silent judgement. "I'm getting married," Elena repeated, this time with a lot less conviction as she realised the magnitude of her statement. She breathed a little harder and felt panic grip her so much that she had to steady herself on the banister of her staircase. Elena suddenly reached for her phone, which was lying abandoned on the coffee table.

"Oh no," Elena said, noticing the several missed calls from Evan and frantically calling him back.

"Elena? Thank God, sorry for all the missed calls, you okay?"

"Yes I'm fine, what's wrong? Is it Alex?" she asked, half-hoping that he may have gotten cold feet.

"No, no, it's your wedding car. It broke down, but don't worry we've sorted it, John's on his way now to pick you up instead."

"John? Oh okay, great, how long do I have?"

"Ten minutes or so?"

"Okay, thanks Evan, I'll go and finish getting ready."

"No problem, see you at the church!" Evan clicked off and Elena was again left in silence, with fresh anxiety in her chest.

"John's coming here. Shit. Oh god," Elena again announced to the empty house. Elena still had her phone in her hand and opened up her search engine and began to type:

How do you know if you're marrying the right person?

She scanned the results and found several forum posts which had asked this very question. Some users had identified the feeling of trepidation before getting married, going through with it anyway and then being divorced less than six months later. Others had dismissed the feeling as nothing more than nerves on the big day. Others said that if you had to Google it, then he definitely wasn't the right person. Elena was caught somewhere in the middle. *Was* Alex the right guy for her? Was all this just satisfying some other need within her, simply that she wished to get married and have the perfect wedding? Probably. But it was too late now. She sighed, resigned to her fate and slipped into her sparkling silver shoes, completing her bridal attire for the day.

She hoped that he would like how she looked, unsure who the *he* was in this musing, and was again nervous, feeling the butterflies floating around her stomach. Just then, she heard the familiar rumble of John's car as it approached her house.

"Guess I'll find out," she said aloud, taking one last look at herself and opening her door.

John had barely pulled up outside Elena's house when he saw her exiting her front door. He stopped the car and sat there, with his mouth open in a comical way, such was his appreciation of how beautiful Elena looked.

"Fuck me," John whispered under his breath, taking in more of Elena as his eyes adjusted to the vision before him. He had never seen anything so mesmerising in his life. She looked amazing. If she was good looking before, John had no idea what to call her now. Stunning was what he settled on, and he got out of his car, ready to greet her as she delicately made her way towards him, her head bowed slightly out of shyness.

"Hi," John said, a little breathlessly. "You look...unbelievable."

"Thanks Buck," Elena said, smiling a little, but not fully relaxed. "What's so unbelievable about it though?" she asked, playfully, their old chemistry fizzing and sparking just as it always did.

"I suppose that you could scrub up so well," John answered, grinning broadly. He felt the pain of the last few months wash away in one smooth motion as she locked eyes with him for the first time and everything stopped for a lingering, wonderful moment. Elena felt it too, suddenly lighter and happier as though a cool breeze had whispered by on a humid day.

"Oh so you like what you see then?" she responded, her laughter permeating her words.

"You could say that, yeah!" John answered and he laughed, finally unable to resist any longer and pulling her in for a tight squeeze.

Elena felt weak in his embrace and she allowed her arms to gradually filter up John's broad back, joining again around the top of his neck. Her nose was buried into his collar and she inhaled his familiar yet addictive scent once again. It had been so long.

"I've missed you," John whispered.

"Me too," Elena answered, fighting back her tears. They remained like this for a while, yet simultaneously their embrace was over far too quickly as both of them began to realise the reality of the situation.

John pulled back from Elena, looked down at her face and said, with unmistakable sadness, "Right, let's get you married then!"

Elena almost choked on her words and could only muster one word, "Yep".

John quickly moved to the passenger door and opened it for Elena, allowing her to climb into his freshly washed and hoovered car, which he had fortunately cleaned the day before. He shut the door softly, made his way to the driver's side and clambered in with much less grace, but in a masculine way that immediately gave him authority over the vehicle.

"Off we go then," he said, not looking over at Elena, who was also staring straight ahead into the busy London roads and wishing that she could simply disappear into the crowds with John.

The drive to the church was only fifteen minutes and John wasted the first five by not saying a single word. Finally, as traffic halted once again to a standstill, John turned to face Elena.

"I'll only ask you this once," he began, choosing his words carefully. "Are you sure you're doing the right thing?" he finished, relieved to have eventually said what was on his mind.

"No," Elena said quietly.

"What do you mean no, don't you love him?"

"I do, I do, it's just…" she trailed off.

"If you're having doubts…" John began.

"Look, I can't, okay? I have to go through with this. I can't embarrass him."

"*Embarrass him?*" John repeated, incredulously. "I'm not being funny," he continued, "But fuck that. If this isn't right for you, you need to make it known. Doesn't matter if he'll have a moment of humiliation, this is for the rest of your life, you ca-"

"Yes I know, I know," Elena interrupted, her voice wasn't sharp, but it carried authority, as though she'd had this exact conversation in her own mind for months already. "I know, John. I know all this. But he's a good choice. He's steady, he's not unpredictable."

"Like me, you mean?" John asked flatly.

"No that's not what I mean," Elena began, her voice softer. Alex had kept her abreast of John's decision-making recently and she had observed, pained and from a distance, all the

195

trouble he was getting into with money (after having refused her offer of a loan).

"I just.." Elena started, struggling to find the words to justify her decision. "He's good for me, he's going to be a good husband and he's-"

"He's safe. I get it. He's the easy option and he's *there*," John finished for her, bitterness creeping into his voice with the last word.

Elena remained silent, she knew John was right. She knew her parents were right as well with their appraisal of Alex back in Seville. Everything was screaming at her to stop this wedding and to finally break free from her years of coasting with Alex. Yet she continued to stay quiet, as the church loomed in the distance ominously, the crowd of guests milling about outside all dressed for the occasion, all there for her and her big day. She couldn't back out now, she had no choice, her parents had spent so much money on today. *It will be fine*, she began to reason with herself again. *Everything will work out, Alex will be a good husband and will take care of me.*

She glanced at John, whose face was set with grim determination as he inched closer to their destination, his resolve finally broken as he accepted their joint fate of what was about to transpire. Elena again looked to the busy gathering of people as their faces began to focus into view and she recognised her family, who had flown over two days prior. Her spirits lifted at seeing them and she couldn't help but point this out to John, "Look! There's my Mama, my Papa, my sister! And my aunts and uncles!" she extended a perfectly manicured finger across John's vision to highlight who she was talking about and John followed her gaze, a broad smile breaking the stony expression he had worn moments ago.

"They look lovely, I can't wait to meet them," he said, rolling down his window and honking his horn, waving at the audience who had all turned to see the arrival of the bride.

As John did this, Elena forgot herself and suddenly felt like she and John were the married couple, waving to their adoring families and ready to celebrate their love.

Smiles broke out amongst those who spotted Elena and many waved back, particularly Elena's family, which John matched with equal enthusiasm. He laughed and put the window back up, turning down the road to where the church was located at the very end, acting as a termination of their journey in the most literal sense.

"This is it," he whispered, popping Elena's daydream bubble. "No turning back now." He switched off the engine and took one last look at Elena, who was silent and had her eyes fixed on the ancient structure that stood before them.

"No turning back now," she repeated, her voice barely audible.

CHAPTER TWENTY

The church was packed as the guests were finally settled. Alex shifted uncomfortably at the altar, nervously looking to his best man Tom for reassurance, who gave a thumbs up of support and a kind smile. Alex looked like he was about to be sick.

"Bloody hell, he looks ready to pass out," Henry whispered, which caused a ripple of sniggers to emerge in the sea of silence.

"Shh!" Leo hushed the others in the aisle, laughing himself as he did.

"Yeah, he don't look too clever does he?" Dom chimed in, leaning into John as he did, so that he could be heard by Henry, Leo and Evan.

"Definitely not. He's going to get so drunk later, you watch," Evan answered and the boys again muffled their laughter.

John had a look of stoic resignation on his face, and his silence was noticed by Dom.

"Everything alright, fella?"

"Huh? Oh, yeah. Fine," John lied. Outside when he had

arrived with Elena he was all smiles and acting his normal self, meeting and greeting as many people as possible before everybody was ushered inside. He didn't have a chance to say hello to Elena's family, save for a wave above the bobbing heads of the crowd, which was returned by someone he presumed was her father. Now, however, John had allowed the same impregnable stillness that had suppressed his emotions whilst driving Elena to the church, to once again return, as he processed the magnitude of the event.

"Can't believe he's getting married, ya know?" Dom said, echoing what John felt, though for a very different reason.

"Yeah, who would have thought?" John answered, staring straight ahead.

Dom was about to ask something else, when he was drowned out by the loud and sudden chords of the organ playing, which was to signify only one thing; Elena was here. Everybody in attendance rose to their feet and turned towards the entrance of the church with expectant faces. Elena glided into view, her head bowed and her veil covering her features. She walked silently next to her father, who was smiling politely at the congregation as he walked past. John was situated in the centre of the aisle and his heart was thumping in his chest as Elena drew closer. She didn't look towards him, but then she wasn't looking at anyone as she continued her slow march towards her fate. Her father made eye contact with John and for a second their gaze lingered, a sudden bond of knowing linking them in that moment as they both knew that this was all a big mistake. He eventually tore his gaze from John and he and Elena continued the last few paces towards Alex and the vicar, whose round face was welcoming them. Everyone was seated and the proceedings began, which John zoned out for. He had this constant voice in the back of his head urging him to say something, to do something, but all he could do was watch with sullen acceptance and simply sit there in silence.

～

Elena studied the ring on her finger which now bound her to Alex in holy matrimony. When those words "you may kiss the bride" were uttered by the vicar, she had almost recoiled, but had to steady herself and allow the deed to be done. She had forgotten what it was like to kiss Alex on the lips, for it had been so long and she felt awkward doing it.

"Right, we'll get you off to the location for the photos first, let the guests drink and mingle and then you'll join them, okay?" her photographer instructed Elena as her and Alex exited the church to loud clapping and cheering, confetti exploding into the air from the palms of the guests and raining down on the newlyweds. Words of congratulations fired upon them from all sides, Elena bowed her head and smiled, trying to flee the scene of the crime, but Alex was being his usual self and his pace was slow.

"Come on!" Elena said, with a forced grin fixed on her face as she almost dragged Alex along with her grip. They eventually made it to the now repaired wedding car that was to take them to Fordham Grange for the evening, where the guests would also be joining them.

"Hullo wife," Alex said with a grin which nearly made Elena vomit. She could smell alcohol on his breath.

"Have you been drinking?" she asked.

"Not really, had a few shots with the boys before the ceremony to steady my nerves, no big deal," he replied, trying to reassure her.

She shifted her weight and swivelled in her seat so that she was facing away from him and began staring out of the window at the disappearing huddle of guests as the car sped off towards its destination.

$$\sim$$

"Okay so Alex, I want you to hold her around the waist, that's it, good," the photographer directed as his camera flashed satisfyingly. Elena had never felt so rigid in her life. All her flair and panache had deserted her as she was simply going through the motions, doing as the man with wild curly hair and thick glasses asked.

"Elena, lean in and kiss his cheek, maybe kick your foot back a bit?"

Elena shuddered and did as she was told, her lips barely touching Alex's cheek. He stood there like a doorframe, emotionless and devoid of charisma.

"Beautiful!" the cameraman lied, watching all of this unfold. The first time he had met the couple, he was shocked at how far out of Alex's league Elena was. They seemed completely mismatched in every way and it was becoming more and more evident with every flash.

"This way, come on," he said, leading the couple into the ornate garden which was littered with spectacular plants and shrubbery, forming a dreamlike backdrop for a romantic picture.

"Here!" He halted Elena and Alex in front of a particularly dazzling array of flowers which popped with pinks and whites. Such was their beauty that even Elena found her spirits lifted.

"Elena, look away into the distance and Alex, I want your hands to wrap around her... yes that's it, that's it. Now look down towards her feet, nice and broody, perfect!" he clicked the shot and Elena could only imagine how utterly ridiculous they both looked as they stood there pretending to be models for a fleeting moment in time, when all she could do was think about how to get through this as quickly as possible.

"Okay now, same position, but Elena tilt your head back and let's have a nice big kiss guys!" said the photographer enthusiastically.

Elena's face lost a shade of colour and she couldn't help herself from holding her breath as she forced a kiss with her husband. She tried her hardest not to pull away due to the smell of alcohol now mixed with the stench of the cheese and onion crisps he consumed in the wedding car.

The final few shots were taken and at long last, Elena and Alex had finished their photoshoot, which had been an unmitigated disaster. However, now Elena knew the best part was coming where she could be free and dance and have fun with her family and friends, but it was cut short before it had even begun.

"Don't dance as we enter," Alex ordered.

"What?"

"Don't dance, you'll embarrass me. Just walk in and wave and smile, there's no need to try and show me up by dancing."

Elena was quiet and couldn't even think of a response before the thick oak doors were flung open. A cacophony of noise hit the couple as music blared from the speakers and the guests all cheered appreciatively. Elena smiled and Alex tightened his grip on her hand in warning as if to say, "Don't you dare." The couple walked around the huge open space which would later become the dance floor.

As the audience clapped in time with the beat, Elena finally broke free of Alex and danced with full enthusiasm and freedom and at this, everyone cheered louder and whistles of appreciation rained down on her, she smiled to herself, her head bowed and her mind escaping the reality of the moment as all she could see was her family also dancing and smiling.

Alex finally loosened up just as the song was finishing and did a few awkward leg movements that looked like a horse trying to kick a football. The beat subsided and the clapping continued, with the DJ announcing, "THE BRIDE AND GROOM!" to more applause. The couple took their seats at the top table and the food began to arrive.

With all of the speeches out of the way and the food digested, the evening had progressed to the part where everybody could fully relax, drink and dance and John was incredibly grateful.

"Johnny boy!" Carter slurred, his shirt already missing four buttons and a stain of beer somehow on his shoulder.

"'Ello mate," John greeted earnestly, pulling his inebriated friend in for a hug.

"Mate, loads of birds here tonight, you on the hunt?" Carter asked grinning, his eyes lighting up in anticipation.

"Nah, not tonight fella, gotta keep it classy," John answered, lying about the real reason for abstaining. His gaze looked past Carter as he watched Elena dancing with her sister enthusiastically, the former mesmerising John and enchanting him further. He noticed how little time Alex was spending with his new wife and thought to himself that had he been in his position, he would have been glued to her side.

"I'm gonna go and say hello to a few people, back in a bit," John said, patting Carter on the arm and moving towards the table where Elena's father sat. He was enjoying the festivities, clapping along in time with the music and watching his daughter proudly, a beaming smile on his face.

"Sir?" John said, introducing himself with a hand outstretched. "My name's John, I'm a friend of Alex and Elena's."

John took his hand firmly and Elena's dad squeezed back with the same pressure, both men smiling and instantly recognising the other as an equal.

"Hola, my name is Carlos. This is my wife, Maria and our other daughter Rosa."

"Buenas noches," John said, his attempt at speaking Spanish drew smiles of appreciation from the trio. "That's about as much as I can say, I'm afraid!" John added before taking a seat next to Carlos. "So, how are you all?" John asked, with genuine interest which was felt by all of them.

"Si, very good, we have our beers and our familia here, what else could we ask for?" Carlos responded.

"Some good weather?" John said laughing, the Viegas family also appreciating his humour.

"This is true, this is true. In Seville right now, wow," Carlos made a gesture with his hands to exaggerate the point before adding, "You will be sitting watching the football and sweating so much, my goodness."

"Ah, but won't that be from the nerves as you're worried about the other team scoring?"

"Hey, be careful!" Carlos said, jabbing a finger and raising an eyebrow.

"Come on, it's true, I'm an England supporter, I know how it feels!" John added.

"Well, yes, this is true!" Carlos said, laughing along and raising his glass to John's. "I like you, you're not afraid to joke around and say what needs to be said. How is your love life, John?"

John blew out a low whistle. "About as good as the English weather."

"Ah John, come on, it can't be that bad?"

"Trust me, it was!" John said.

"Well, what do you look for in a partner?" Carlos quizzed, Maria and Rosa exchanging glances of intrigue behind him.

"Family comes first," John began. "So, that means we both have to be spending time with our families and having big meals, lots of events, gatherings and so on. My mum and dad are so important to me, I still live at home actually."

"Well there's nothing the matter with that, it's good for a man your age to show so much care for family, it's not often you see that."

"I guess you don't, but it really is fundamental for me. Family has to be the most important thing. What else..." John pondered for a moment. "Well, she has to have a good sense of humour, you know? Able to make me laugh and keep me on my toes. Like Elena does." John went a deep shade of crimson at letting this nugget of information out. Carlos' eyebrows rose, Maria's head tilted backwards slightly and Rosa's eyes bulged. "You know what I mean, someone *like* Elena," John clarified with a smile, recovering the situation.

"I certainly do, John. You need a Mediterranean girl with the fire, passion, beauty and the brains."

"Yeah that does sound perfect, I'll agree to that!" and they clinked glasses again. "Well look, I'll let you guys continue your evening in peace and I'll be over later to discuss important subjects, like football." John winked as he left, shaking hands again with Carlos who overlapped with his free hand.

"It was good to meet you John, please do make sure you come back."

"The pleasure was all mine, don't worry, I will!" John left the table with a wave and as he turned his back, smiling with genuine pleasure at having met Elena's family.

As the evening wound to a close and guests started to leave, Elena began to feel a sadness creeping in as she saw John getting his jacket from the back of his chair in readiness to depart.

"I'm off," she heard him say to Alex. "Congrats, mate.

Really chuffed for you," he said, shaking hands with her new husband.

"Ah mate, cheers. Thanks so much for saving the day earlier! I wouldn't be married now if it weren't for you!"

John could barely muster a response to this. What he wanted to say was, "Yeah, if it had anything to do with me, YOU wouldn't be married to her." But instead, he said, "No worries. Have a nice night."

She saw him approaching her and she tried to steady her nerves. He looked so good in his suit.

"I'm going now," he said flatly.

"Oh. OK. Well thanks for coming," Elena replied, somewhat downtrodden. She reached forward and put her arms around his back, relishing the opportunity to be close to him, to breathe the same air, to be enveloped in his scent.

"Even after a long day like this, you still smell good." She couldn't believe she had said it aloud, but then she realised she hadn't and that John had. "Bye Elena," he said, pulling away.

"Bye John," she said, trying to force a smile.

Elena felt like she was suffocating by the time she got into her hotel room.

"Get this dress off me! I can't breathe!" she said to no one at all. Alex had gone to the bar downstairs with his dad and best man for a nightcap, so she had some time to process the events of the day. She was torn. She was both on cloud nine after such a wonderful party but felt as though a storm was imminent; a thought she pushed aside for a moment. She was thrilled with how the day had progressed and had thoroughly enjoyed seeing her family and dancing with them. The ceremony was beautiful, the evening had been full of laughter and she adored having all her family in one place, something which hadn't happened since a family reunion in Barcelona when she was eleven. Conspicuous in his absence throughout the day however was John. She hadn't spent any time with him at all, which was rare for the couple, especially at events where there was music playing. Normally she could count on him to be the first on the dancefloor with her, but today, he had really kept his distance. They had exchanged the odd smile and had danced together for the grand total of fifty seconds. It was weird, they had clearly actively avoided each other on today of all days. She felt that, had she spent any time with him, someone would have guessed her true feelings for him and called her out on the fact that she was in love with her husband's friend. *There,* she thought. She had said it, albeit internally. She was in love with him. And married. To someone else. *Brilliant.* She thought back to when they had said their goodbyes and felt with some level of certainty that she wouldn't be seeing John for a long time.

Elena shook her head, trying to shake thoughts of John both physically and emotionally and lowered herself into the bath in her hotel room, enjoying the sensation of the warm water enveloping her like a cocoon and easing various aches and pains that a day spent in a tight dress and high heels had caused her. Scrolling through the photos that she was beginning to be tagged in on Facebook, she smiled to herself as she saw various members of her family beaming into the camera. She lingered for a while on a photo of her with Alex cutting the wedding cake and shuddered at the memory. He was forced by the photographer to put his arm around her and kiss her as they simultaneously feigned lowering the knife into the sweet and elaborate creation. Body language analyst or not, it was clear to see that Elena was visibly pulling back from Alex as he did this. She swiftly dismissed the idea, choosing instead to send a message to John:

Thanks for driving me today. And for being there. It meant a lot. X

Within seconds, her phone vibrated in her hand with a new message:

I'll always be there. X

"Are you almost done? I think I'm gonna throw up!" shouted Alex through the door.

"Yes, I'll be out in a minute!" said Elena, a tear rolling down her cheek as she read John's message over and over.

CHAPTER TWENTY-ONE

"Alex! Alex, oh Alex, wake up!" Elena excitedly burst into their bedroom, shaking Alex from his sleep as he groggily poked his head out from underneath the covers, hair sticking straight up to attention and eyes no more than paper-thin slits.

"Wha..? What's going on?"

"Alex, *look!*" Elena exclaimed, producing a small instrument which showed a little 'plus' symbol. Alex's eyes widened in acknowledgement and he was suddenly awake.

"Oh my god, is that real?"

"Yes of course it's real!" Elena answered, beaming. "Alex, we're going to have a baby!" she squealed with excitement, jumping off the bed and throwing her arms into the air.

"I'm going to call my Mama right away, be right back!" Elena skipped down the stairs to the house phone which was docked neatly at its station in the kitchen. She quickly dialled the number for her parents' home and waited for the international dial tone to kick in.

"Si?" came her mother's voice.

"Mama! It's me, I have news!"

"What is it, chica, are you okay?" Maria could hear the frantic tone in Elena's voice and mistook it for something bad, so she was starting to panic somewhat.

"No, no, Mama it's good, it's good!" Elena reassured her mother. "Mama, I'm pregnant."

There was silence on the line for a few seconds as Maria processed the news.

"Pregnant? Oh mi amor, that's, that's great. With Alex, si?" she asked, hesitating.

"Yes Mama, of course!" Elena responded, laughing a little as she did. "Who else?"

"I don't know, but...anyway, doesn't matter, doesn't matter. My little girl is having a baby!"

"Si!..Okay Mama I have to go, I'll tell Papa later. Te quiero, speak soon!" and she hung up the phone before she had an answer. Elena docked the device and had tears in her eyes. Her mum sounded surprised and nowhere near as happy as she should be. *Why?* Elena shook these feelings from her head as she began to make her morning coffee.

～

"Carlos? Carlos? Where are you?" Maria called out into the garden, finally seeing Carlos emerge from behind the orange tree he was tending to.

"Here, mi amor, what is it?"

"Carlos, come inside, por favor."

"Oh, you sound serious, okay, one second," Carlos obeyed, putting down his shears and wiping sweat off his brow. He paced up the pathway to his house and came inside, taking a swig of water as he ventured further inside to his living room, where he found his wife sitting with a sombre disposition.

"Sit down, mi amor."

"Maria, what's happened?" Carlos asked, a worried expression forming on his weathered features.

"It's Elena," Maria began, which caused Carlos' eyebrows to almost disappear into his hairline as he raised them in surprise.

"What happened, is she okay?"

"Si, si, but.." Maria began.

"But what?"

"Carlos, she's pregnant," Maria finished, her voice trailing off as her head bowed.

Carlos let out a huge sigh of relief and for the first time in the conversation, a smile broke out.

"That's wonderful news, no? Why do you look so sad?"

"Because, it's Alex's child. Of course. But..."

Now Carlos understood. His expression quickly shifted from joy to concern as he gently put a loving hand on his wife's leg.

"You told her to be careful. To think before any big decisions, now look!" Maria said, throwing her hands to the sky as tears formed in her eyes.

"I know, I know," Carlos answered, patting her leg and doing his best to comfort her.

"Everybody knows he isn't right for her. Did you see how different she was when she was here? Her fire, her spark? Gone. He sucked it out of her, he's not right for her at all, I feel it in my soul," she said, inhaling sharply as she finally took a breath.

"Maria, we have to be happy for our daughter at this time," Carlos said, hugging his wife and staring into space as he processed the ramifications of this news. Maria pulled away from him and looked at her husband's eyes, her own now shining with fresh tears.

"We won't even see the baby, he's not going to want to come over here is he? Not for a long time."

The thought hadn't yet occurred to Carlos, but now he too was seeing the severity of the situation for what it was; they would likely miss out on so many magical moments with their grandchild.

"We need to just support our daughter, I'll talk to her," Carlos said, moving to the house phone in the corridor.

~

Elena had not long finished her breakfast, which consisted of porridge, banana and a touch of cinnamon.

"Finished, my love?" she said, smiling at Alex as she collected his bowl of mostly eaten sugary cereal.

"Yes thanks. I'm just going to call my mum and dad, tell them the good news."

"Okay, sure, say hi for me!" Just then, the house phone rang. "Who could this be...?" Elena wondered out loud as she moved to answer.

"Hello?"

"Hola, mi princesa."

"Papa! Oh have you heard!"

"Yes, yes, I have heard the news," Carlos answered, trying to sound cheerful as he looked at his weeping wife in the living room.

"I'm so happy, Papa!" Elena beamed.

"Good, good. Look, mi amor. You need to think about this, really think. This isn't just a small decision, it is life-changing and will set you on a new path forever," Carlos began to explain.

"Of course, I know that Papa," Elena responded, her smile fading. "Papa, you know how long I've wanted to have a baby..." Elena began, her voice trailing off.

"I know, I know. But this is not something you can just take lightly. A child not only is with you forever, but it also means you and your partner will be bound for the rest of time. He will always be part of your life. You need to consider that."

The appraisal hung in the air for a moment and lingered, the tension rising as the heavy silence oppressed both parties.

"Look, I know what you thi-"

"No, Elena, you don't understand," Carlos interjected, cutting her off. "This boy, this boy is not right for you. We all saw it, your mother and I have so many concerns about him and whether he will be fit to be at your side, let alone raise a child with you."

Elena allowed the words to permeate her mind as she absorbed the advice her father was giving her. What had begun as a morning of joy and celebration had quickly transformed into one of utter dismay. Her parents weren't happy for her. That was all she needed to hear.

"Okay Papa, bye." she hung the phone up like a zombie, her expression devoid of any emotion and her eyes staring blankly at the wall opposite, which had a crack at the top that Elena had never noticed before.

CHAPTER TWENTY-TWO

I'm so happy for you both! Congratulations!

John sent the text to Elena and sank into his sofa. He was completely conflicted; on the one hand he was genuinely thrilled that Elena was pregnant, she had always wanted a child and she would be a terrific mum. Yet, he was certain that the door was now firmly and completely closed to them ever coming together in a romantic way. He sighed heavily, just as his dad shouted in celebration as someone scored a goal in the game they were watching.

"Fuck me, what a hit! Ya see that boy, that's how it's done!" Bob looked over to John and saw that he wasn't even watching the screen. "John?" Bob asked, wondering why his son hadn't also leapt into the air in celebration.

"Yeah, wicked goal that," John responded, forcing a smile that was laced with sadness.

"What's going on, you alright?" Bob asked earnestly, turning the volume down on the television.

"It's nothing Dad, don't worry," John answered, his focus again on his phone.

"Son, I know something's wrong and you can always talk to me," his dad answered, his kind eyes studying his son with love and concern.

"It's..." John began, unsure of how to confess to his father, who patiently waited for him to continue. "Elena's pregnant," John finally said.

Bob took a second to process the information and seeing the look on John's face, knew that it didn't quite marry up to what should be good news. "It ain't yours is it?!" he suddenly exclaimed, adding two and two together and coming up with five.

John laughed quietly, "No and that's the problem," he finished, bowing his head.

Bob's eyes grew wide with realisation and he turned the television off completely, moving from his singular armchair to join his son on the sofa.

"Son, do you have feelings for her?" he asked the question delicately, knowing the answer already but wanting John to confront the truth.

"Yes," John replied, hastily adding, "but it's not like that. I don't want to break her and Alex up, far from it. I'm really happy for them, but she's just..."

"She's perfect for you, I know. That's how it feels," Bob gently finished.

"Yeah..."

"Look, son," Bob began, shuffling an inch closer to John and resting his arm on John's broad frame. "Life is funny like this. It's all about timing. You'll meet the right girl, but at the wrong time. You'll eventually discover that it's all about being in the right place at the right time."

"Yeah, like Alex was," John replied bitterly.

"Well, yeah. But you don't know where life is going to go, son," Bob said reassuringly.

"I think I've got a good idea now," John answered, a small laugh escaping.

"Well, all you can do is just be there for her. I know this isn't something you want to hear right now, but just have a little faith. You know how me and your mother got together don't you?"

"Sort of," John answered truthfully, not really knowing the full story.

"Well, we were both married before, right?" Bob began, allowing John to nod to show he knew this part of the story. "And we were friends whilst both being married to different people."

"Oh were you?"

"Yeah. So, one day, your mother and I were at a party, a boat party on the Thames," Bob recalled fondly before continuing. "I went up to her and said, well you know, that she looked good."

John smiled and allowed his father to carry on with the story.

"She says, well we're both married, so never mind!" John laughed as Bob chuckled to himself.

"Anyway, we stayed friends, then about four years later, I was helping your mother paint her house; this one. Again, still friends," Bob pressed the point once more. "After a while, it became pretty obvious we liked each other, but we were both still married, though she was separated with her husband and going through a divorce, I was still with that old bag," Bob said with clear distaste.

"So, what happened?" John asked.

"I packed my bags and moved in with your mother."

"Fuck off! Just like that?" his son exclaimed.

"Yep. I knew she was the one for me and she felt the same way, she was loyal to her husband though and waited for the divorce to be finalised. I told my wife it was over and fucked off out of it."

"Shit, I had no idea," John said, taken aback.

"Well there you are. My point is, you just never know. We were friends for years before everything worked out and now look, happily married again and we got you!" he said beaming at John.

"Yeah you're right," John said, pride swelling inside him at his father's admiration of him. "I just need to be there for her, no matter what."

"No matter what son," Bob agreed, pulling John in for a hug, cementing the point.

CHAPTER TWENTY-THREE

Alex finished his shift at the pub and threw his towel carelessly into the kitchen. He'd spent the last thirty minutes of his shift drying glasses and he had grown tired of it by the end.

"Right Mum, I'm off. We'll be round Sunday I think for dinner."

"Oh good, you can bring your glowing wife! Bet she looks radiant now! How far along is she?" his mum replied.

"Twelve weeks maybe? Yeah, she looks great," Alex responded rather disinterested, as he scrolled through his social media platforms on his phone.

"Well, take care, get home safe. Say hi to Mummy and baby!"

"Thanks, I'll see you tomorrow."

Alex headed for the door and walked the short distance up the road to the bus stop. He usually got the bus for thirty-five minutes when he would disembark to be picked up by Elena.

He fired off a text to let her know he was on the way and then pocketed his phone, unaware that she hadn't responded.

~

Elena was destroyed. Floods of tears poured from her as she processed the news she had received just a few short hours ago. What was meant to be a routine appointment to check on the baby's health had turned into a tragedy. The twelve-week scan was meant to be the first checkpoint of the long and beautiful journey, but instead it had been the worst day of her life. The doctors couldn't find the baby's heartbeat. Her worst fear had come true; she had lost the baby. Elena was booked in for a follow up appointment, known as a D&C, a term she didn't really understand. As the doctors were talking to her and trying to explain what had happened and why she needed the procedure, she felt completely numb. She felt as though she had floated out of her body and was watching the events happening from up above. All she took away from the appointment was that her baby was dead and that they had to get it out of her.

She didn't know how to process the information and was completely heartbroken. She was alone when she had received the news, as Alex had a big event at the pub which he had to set up for. On the way out of the hospital, she was trying to piece together what had transpired that day. She couldn't bring herself to call or tell anyone. She spent the journey home crying silently in the back of the cab, staring out the window as people continued with their normal lives. Why hadn't anyone stopped? Why wasn't everyone mourning the loss of her baby? How could they continue as though every- thing was normal?

"You alright luv?" came the gruff cockney voice from the front of the vehicle.

Elena couldn't muster the strength to speak, so she simply nodded at the driver as he watched her through the rear-view mirror. Her make-up was ruined, mascara beginning to run down her face as she stared out of the window in complete silence.

When she got home, she went upstairs, straight to the bathroom, and collapsed onto the floor. She continued sobbing, holding her knees tightly to her chest and occasionally whispering, "why me?" The front door suddenly burst open and Alex stormed in, a furious expression on his blotchy red skin, the result of over-exertion.

"Elena!" he yelled, his shoes being flicked off like a petulant child as he continued his loud entrance. "Elena!" he again screamed, this time his voice cracking almost comically as his rage was building.

Elena sat rooted to the spot, tears now silently cascading down her cheeks and her heart pounding in time with Alex's footsteps thudding up the staircase. He flung the bathroom door open and his wild eyes settled on Elena's crumpled and broken visage, yet there was no sympathy.

"Where the fuck were you! I was waiting ages for you to pick me up! I had to walk!" he yelled at her, still blissfully ignorant of the horrendous news he was about to receive.

Elena looked up at him, her emotions still failing to register and instead of answering she bowed her head back into the comfort of her knees.

"Answer me!" he again shouted, still somehow not processing how upset Elena was.

Finally, Elena regained her composure somewhat and again looked up at her husband and whispered in a small voice, "the baby's gone."

"What?" Alex spat, still angry, failing to comprehend the magnitude of Elena's words.

"I've lost the baby, Alex," Elena responded in monotone, now uncurling herself and beginning to rise to her feet.

Alex's eyes were still wide, but now with shock instead of anger, though his tone was still confrontational.

"Well, what happened? What did they say?"

"There's no heartbeat. I have an appointment in ten days where they're going to do something to me to get rid of the remains," Elena described with the coldness of an automated machine delivering an instruction. "Excuse me," she said, brushing past Alex.

"Where are you going?" Alex said lamely, attempting to hold her arm which Elena shrugged off with authority.

"Just leave me alone, like you always do. I needed you today. I had to listen to them tell me my baby was dead, on my own," Elena said, continuing her walk to the bedroom.

"But you know we had a big event on, that's not my fault!"

Elena turned and looked at him, tears pouring down her face as she looked upon her husband in disbelief.

Alex simply stood there, his anger bubbling again, but looking more ridiculous by the second as he failed to do his duty and comfort his wife.

Elena shut her bedroom door, reached for her phone and began to type a text to the one person she knew would make her feel better.

CHAPTER TWENTY-FOUR

John finished putting the dishes away for his mother when he felt his phone vibrate in his pocket. Normally, he would have left it, it was probably just the guys talking a load of rubbish as usual, but on this occasion, John decided to grab the phone right away and see who had messaged him. He pulled down the notification bar and saw it was from Elena. A text that simply said:

I need you.

John fumbled with his phone and almost dropped it straight into the soapy water left in the sink.

"Mum, dishes done!" John called out.

"Thanks love," came the reply from the adjacent room.

"'Ere boy, come on, game is about to start."

"Yeah I'll be right down Dad, two seconds," John answered as he ran up the stairs, taking them two at a time in a rush to get to his room and find some privacy where he could answer Elena in peace.

"Suit yourself," Bob said, relaxing further into his reclining chair.

John opened the message again and studied the words:

I need you.

Gritting his teeth, John began to type. It had been months since they had spoken, he hadn't even told her he was single. What could she possibly need him for? She was married to his friend and carrying his child. He shrugged those bitter thoughts to one side as he summoned up the courage to reply:

What's wrong?

Elena's reply came almost instantly:

I lost the baby.

John was caught off guard and his mind whirred, trying to process what he had just read:

What do you mean?

John was anxiously waiting for the response, his heart racing now:

I had my scan and they couldn't find a heartbeat.

"Fuck," John said to his empty room.

John: Oh shit. I'm really sorry to hear that. Are you okay?

Elena: *No. I don't know what to do.*

John: *Is Alex with you?*

Elena: *No.*

John paused upon reading this information, wanting to jump into his car immediately and drive to her aid. Instead, he sent another message:

Want to talk? I can call you?

Elena's reply came within seconds:

Yes. Please. X

Matching her speed, his fingers flew across the touchscreen of his phone:

Give me two minutes. X

Shit, despite these horrific circumstances, a kiss from her still got his heart racing, John thought. Right. Now was the time. He needed to be there for her as a friend and push his feelings aside.

"Hey Buck," she answered after just one ring.

"Hey Elena. How you holding up?"

"Buck, I can't...I don't..." she stuttered.

"Shhh. It'll be alright," John reassured her, his own heart breaking with every word she said through her sobs.

"I told Alex and he...Um. He just went to work."

"What the fuck? Is he a fucking idiot?" John reacted, all too quickly.

"He's not really upset. I don't know. I told him I have to go to um...I have to...They have to...um get the ba...I have a hospital appointment to..."

"When is it?" John asked, trying to avoid making her say the words she was struggling to say.

"The fifteenth. At ten," she responded, robotically.

"I'll come with you, yeh? Hold your hand? Take you for a milkshake when...?" John offered, unsure as to why or how he was having to deal with this but caring only about how Elena was feeling.

"Oh no, you don't have to. I know you're busy. I can go by myself. It's OK."

"You're not going on your own. Not to that. Look, I'll come pick you up at eight thirty, so we get where we need to be in plenty of time. And I'll come in with you. I mean if you want. If I'm allowed," John said, somewhat bashfully.

Silence met his response. He could hear her crying again.

"Are you sure?" Elena finally said, quietly.

"Of course, Elena. I'll be there."

"Thanks Buck," she sighed.

"Now, you need to take a deep breath and try to stop crying for a moment, so I can distract you. Ready?"

Elena sniffed and could be heard blowing her nose. "Ready," she said, clearing her throat.

"So, I'm going to tell you about the latest catastrophe that is my love life. I went on a date the other night, right. With this girl called Laura."

"John, I'm not sure this will cheer me up,"

"Just wait. It will! So I ordered a pizza, the usual pepperoni. Or so I thought. It turns up, absolutely covered in guess what? Peppers, not pepperoni. Of course, I can't send it back, this is a first date, how bad would that look? So, I start eating and at first it's fine, almost enjoyable. Then it hits me. The spices all of a sudden are causing chaos in my mouth, my eyes are watering and I'm turning pinker by the second and to top it all off, guess what? I fucking dribbled out of my mouth."

He heard Elena laughing and it made him smile.

"Told you it was funny!"

"Have you seen her since? Is she the one for you?"

"Nah, apparently she wasn't so keen on guys who dribble at the table," he said, adding, "So I'm still looking for the right one."

"Yeh, or someone who is willing to date you wearing a bib in public!"

They both laughed at this and the mood was lightened for a brief moment.

"Thanks for calling me, Buck," Elena said.

"It's OK. See you on the 15th."

CHAPTER TWENTY-FIVE

W hen the fateful day was upon them, they spent the
journey in silence, Elena twisting a tissue in her lap
the whole way to the hospital.

John parked and walked by her side to reception and spoke
for her as she couldn't. "Good morning. I'm here with Elena
Wickerman. She has an appointment at ten."

"Sorry, it's Elena Viegas," Elena said quietly to the receptionist.

John glanced at her sideways, wanting to ask why she
hadn't taken Alex's name yet, but deciding against it.

At that moment, Elena looked up at John, grateful to have
him with her to take the lead in a situation where she had no
strength at all.

"Down the corridor, first left, second right and through the
blue door," said the receptionist, a reassuring smile forming
across her lips as she understood the nature of their visit.

"Thank you," said John.

"I can't go in," said Elena, beginning to panic. "I can't. I
can't have them take my baby away from me. I can't breathe,
John I can't do it!"

"Hey, shhhh, it's alright. I'm here with you. I'll be with you the whole time," said John, pulling her in for a tight hug. She buried her face in his chest and he instinctively kissed her hair and they stood in the middle of the seemingly never-ending corridor for what seemed like hours while Elena sobbed. They finally pulled away from each other and John took Elena's arm, linking it with his as they began their slow walk towards the waiting room.

John held Elena's hand throughout the appointment until it was over and she had regained her senses after the sedation.

"We are so sorry for your loss. I've given you some leaflets about post-operative care and some information on counselling groups and one on trying to conceive again safely," the doctor said to both of them.

"Thank you doctor," said John, shaking his hand. "Right, let's go Elena. Let's get you home."

When they finally made it to the car, Elena managed to utter her first words since they arrived at the hospital that morning. "Throw that leaflet away."

"What? Elena there's some important stuff in here."

"Throw away the one on trying to have another baby. I can't go through this again. Not with him anyway."

"Are you sure? Maybe it's...."

"Throw it away. Please," she interrupted.

John did as he was told and opened the door for Elena as she climbed in. On the way home, as promised, John stopped off to buy them both a milkshake. Instead of drinking it in the restaurant, they walked to one of John's favourite spots in London; Primrose Hill, which overlooked the dramatic skyline of the city.

"Sit here for a minute, just look at the buildings and the sky and just be outside yourself for a bit," John said, lowering himself onto the grass, Elena following suit.

After about thirty minutes of silence, Elena finally spoke.

"It's nice here. Thanks for today and for bringing me here. It means so much to me."

"You're welcome," John said. "Can I have my hand back now? I need to go for a piss! You're welcome to come but…"

"Ew! I'm sure you can manage on your own!" Elena said, letting go of his hand which she had been holding the whole time.

CHAPTER TWENTY-SIX

"Put your back into it, Dom!"

"Oh fuck off, you try lifting this!" Dom exclaimed, struggling along with Alex to lift the heavy washing machine out of the house and onto the moving lorry.

"Yeah, easy for you to say Mr. Muscles!" Alex chimed, sweat forming on his brow as he struggled with the weight.

"Hey, you guys said you could handle it, I'm taking your wardrobe apart don't forget!" John called down the stairs from the landing, busy unscrewing the various bolts that held Alex's wardrobe together. The other two grunted and heaved the appliance out of the front door, careful not to scrape any walls or the doorframe. A moment later they returned, Alex puffing out a long breath and bending down over his knees.

"How much more is there?" Dom asked.

"Well, we've got the chest of drawers, plus about ten or so boxes filled with junk upstairs still."

"Great. Why couldn't you just pay a firm to do all this?" Dom questioned with an accusatory jab of his finger at Alex.

"We're not exactly rolling in cash, you know, we have to save where we can," he retorted.

John chuckled upstairs; Alex was famed for his penny-pinching and this was a prime example. He decided to rope in two of his friends to assist with moving house rather than pay professionals to do the job much more efficiently. John lost his smile at this thought, as he remembered the way in which Alex had left Elena to fend for herself not too long ago. She had to come to John for comfort, solace and support. Alex had done nothing to help her and had yet again let her down. Alex was coming up the stairs at that moment and John couldn't help himself.

"How's the relationship going then, happily married?"

"Yeah, I'd say so," Alex answered nonchalantly.

"How come you decided to move house?"

"Well, we both agreed it would be better for us, you know for the future."

You're lying, John thought. *You don't like it here. You've forced Elena to move closer to your own family and job, simply to make your life as easy as possible.*

"Yeah, makes sense," John answered, not looking at Alex. "Happy with where you'll be?"

"Oh very much so. Elena can be fussy, but we convinced her in the end that it was the right thing to do, better area to raise a family and so on."

Bullshit. You pressured her as always with your family backing you up, knowing she can hardly say no as she's here alone, what other choice does she have?

"Yeah, makes sense for sure," John instead answered.

"How's your love life?" Alex asked, eager to change the subject.

"Me? Oh great, great. Got a few dates this week, potentially one tomorrow night." This was an outright lie, but he didn't want to give Alex any indication towards his true feelings. It was becoming more and more obvious that at some point, he would have to tell Elena exactly how he felt and prepare for the consequences that would follow.

A week passed and it was Saturday night, the evening of Alex and Elena's housewarming party in their new home. John, Dom and Evan had met up at John's house for pizza before making their way to the party and were the last guests to arrive.

"Hi boys!" Elena beamed, answering the door and hugging each one in turn, lingering ever so slightly when she embraced John, her eyes locking onto his before she turned away, her brown hair flicking his face as she did.

"Oops, sorry, did I get you?" she asked, turning around with a twinkle in her eye.

"Don't worry, barely, try harder next time," he said with a half-smile.

"Ha, I just might! Can I get you guys drinks? Come! There's food over there, Alex's parents were really helpful in getting the spread sorted out."

"Beers fellas?" Dom asked.

"Not for me cheers," John replied.

"Oh yeah, you've knocked it on the head completely haven't you?"

"Yeah mate. Well, trying to anyway," John answered, smiling sheepishly as he caught Elena's look of wonder.

"So, two beers and a coke?" she asked.

"Perfect," John answered, watching her walk away with a longing in his eyes. She had on a pink dress which complimented her figure perfectly and as usual, highlighted her tanned skin, which he noticed had flakes of glitter on, just as it had years ago at his birthday party.

"Few birds in here tonight," Evan pointed out for the benefit of Dom and John.

"Yeah, can't wait to strike out with all of them," Dom answered, making his friends burst out laughing.

"Oh come on, you'll be fine mate," John offered.

"Easy for you to say, you don't even seem to be trying anymore! What's up with that?"

"Other priorities mate," John said, watching Elena as she came back with the drinks.

"Here you all are, two beers and a coke."

"Thanks sweetheart," John answered, forgetting himself for a moment and feeling the colour in his cheeks change, which apparently went unnoticed.

"So, any of your friends single?" Evan asked.

"Why, want me to put in a good word for you?"

"No of course not, for these two," he said, pointing with his thumbs at Dom and John who were either side of him.

John noticed Elena's smile falter just for a fraction of a second before she answered.

"Yeah, there are some. I can introduce you if you'd like?" she turned and faced John, her eyes meeting his.

Holy shit, she is pretty, John thought, forgetting himself for a moment. He shifted awkwardly on his feet, increasingly anxious for the conversation about finding him a match to be stopped before he would be forced to answer a difficult question, which of course, followed immediately.

"What do you say John, up for it?" Dom asked gleefully.

"Nah, not feeling it tonight, you can though by all means," John stole another glance at Elena who was suppressing a smile.

"Right, in that case, you two, come with me," she linked arms with Evan and Dom to whisk them away, turning back to speak to John, "Back in a minute."

"I'll be here!" John exclaimed, giving a thumbs up to the

three of them. He scanned the room properly now, able to digest who was actually there. He spotted Carter engaged in an animated discussion with Leo and Tom, likely putting the world to rights with his own unique spin on how everything should run. Not too far away from them was Alex, two bottles of beer in his hand and laughing loudly with Freddie. His parents were also in the same circle of conversation and appeared very much at ease. Scattered throughout the large living room were other faces John did not recognise; he assumed they were colleagues of Elena's. He remembered back to meeting her family at the wedding and wished they were here now, he wanted to talk to her father, let him in on the secret that had been growing inside him like a flower in bloom. "Carlos, I love your daughter," would be his opening gambit, one that he was sure would be met with approval.

"Alright mate!" Henry suddenly shouted, as he spotted John.

"Henry! How's it going fella!" John replied, embracing Henry and in truth, glad of the momentary distraction from his internal monologue.

"Good, mate, wish our team was doing a bit better," he mused.

"Tell me about it. How's things been tonight so far?"

"Yeah, good, Alex is getting mortal though, never seen him drink so much!" Henry proudly announced.

"Oh dear, well I suppose if he voms at least he's in his own house!"

They both laughed at this assessment.

"So, how's the love life?"

John sighed with exaggeration. "You must be the thousandth person to ask me that. Well you know I broke things off with Chelsea ages ago, right? Fucking nightmare that was. Anyway, since then, really just been focusing on myself, ya know?"

"Right, hitting the gym definitely, you've bulked up again!" Henry commented, noticing the extra girth in John's chest and shoulders.

"Ha, thanks mate. Yeah, it's been the one thing I can pour my energy into, that and clawing myself out of debt!"

"Yeah, the boys said that you'd been taken to the cleaners by her. Sorry to hear mate, can't have been easy for you."

"Toughest period of my life actually. But thankfully, things are looking up. I'm not getting texts off my bank every evening and can finally look at my account without shitting myself," John answered, smiling as he did, realising for the first time that things were actually much better financially and he had turned the situation around in a relatively short amount of time.

"Good to hear mate, good to hear. What you drinking?"

John brandished his coke with a smile.

"Woah, straight edge! How come?"

"Just had enough mate, don't feel the need to drink at the moment, turns out I can have a perfectly good time at events sober!"

"Good on you, pleased to see things are working out for you again mate," Henry clinked his bottle of Budweiser against John's coke before taking his leave to talk to Carter. John sipped his drink with a smile, unaware that things were about to explode in a catastrophic way.

"Oi oi! You.. you lot!" Alex slurred as he stumbled over to John, Dom and Evan.

"Hello mate! Fuck me steady on!" Evan replied as he caught Alex just as he was about to fall forward.

The very much inebriated host waved a hand dismissively announcing that he was "fine."

"We were just saying how nice it is here mate, congratulations," Dom offered, to which Alex simply smiled in agreement, his left eye hovering between just barely open and being completely shut.

"We also discussed how Dom here is never going to get laid again," Evan chimed in, resulting in raucous laughter from John and Alex and a disgruntled Dom punching Evan's arm.

"Leave it out, it didn't go that badly."

"Yeah, in the same way getting punched in the face isn't that bad. She couldn't wait to escape!" Evan mocked, again drawing further laughs.

"Look, I'm sure she was genuinely taking a phone call, even though her screen definitely wasn't on a call and just on Google and she faked the whole thing," John said, putting an arm around Dom in comfort.

"Alright, alright, it wasn't my best effort, but fuck it, plenty more fish in the sea, right fellas?"

"True that," Evan said, raising a glass, Alex drinking deeply from his bottle and spilling some beer down his top.

"So, boys..." Alex began as he moved to lean against the mantlepiece, missing completely and pushing an ornate vase completely off its perch causing it to smash loudly, pausing every conversation in the room. All eyes turned to the three of them, Alex was seemingly oblivious to the sudden attention everyone was paying him and carried on talking as if nothing had happened.

Elena was walking towards them, containing her anger for a moment, but then she noticed how drunk Alex was and she felt a fresh wave of frustration take over.

"Alex, what happened?"

"What?" he said, with a disgusted look on his face.

"You broke my grandmother's vase!" Elena suddenly exclaimed, noticing the shattered ornament on the floor.

"Oh, shush, it will probably be alright," he answered.

"Alex...it's completely broken," Elena said quietly, tears filling her eyes as her family vase lay in pieces at her feet.

"Oh yeah! You know what else is broken?" Alex suddenly spat, his eyes wide in a sudden, maddening rage.

John's eyes flicked from Alex to Elena, he felt like he knew what was coming, but like witnessing someone falling from a great height, there was nothing he could do to stop it.

"Alex...please," Elena whispered, her eyes looking imploringly at her husband.

"YOU!" he screamed. "Fucking you! You can't even keep a baby alive in your body, *that's* how broken *you* are! Probably because you were touched up by your mate's dad, if that's all that happened!" he finally unleashed, his fury amplified with every word, his features contorting into a grotesque fashion, like a gargoyle from the depths of hell.

A stunned silence fell at the climax of his rant. Several women put their hands to their mouths in shock, Alex's parents came over and grabbed him by his arms and dragged him away, his mother could only muster a "sorry" as she rushed out of the room. Alex's head lolled from side to side and just as he was about to leave the living room, he emptied the entirety of his stomach onto the floor in a final flurry of disgrace.

John took his eyes away from that disaster and found Elena.

He rushed to hug her, but she turned away, running through the bi-fold doors into the empty garden, onlookers offering glances of pity.

John followed her, "Elena!" he shouted.

She carried on running to the far end of the garden and to the swinging chair and collapsed onto it, in floods of tears.

"Elena! I'm sorry, I'm so sorry!"

"H-ho..how, how could he!" she managed through sharp intakes of breath and sobs, large tears spilling onto her dress.

"It's okay, it's okay," John put his arms around her again, comforting her.

"I can't. I can't do this Buck, I can't! What am I meant to do? We're married! We have a house! I can't!" she repeated over and over.

"Sshhh, it's okay, it's okay," John answered, his arms squeezing tighter and tighter as Elena finally allowed her own limbs to wrap around him, mimicking his pressure.

They stayed there for minutes and the embrace was the most comforting thing Elena could have ever asked for. John's smell filled her nostrils, her tears subsided and she released her grip while he did the same.

"Elena," John began, finally deciding the time was now, it was the moment. "I have something to tell you."

"What is it?" she asked, her big brown eyes looking up into his, shining with tears and reflecting the many stars that dotted the night sky.

"Just...forget about what he said. He isn't important. I'm here for you, Elena," John announced, feeling a rush of disappointment as he realised he couldn't tell her what he so desperately wanted to.

Elena's mouth was working into a reply just as Dom announced his arrival.

"John mate, we have to get Alex out of here, he can crash round mine or something."

John knew Dom was right, but he couldn't leave Elena.

"John, come on, his parents have him outside. Look, they're ringing me." Dom implored John to leave and John knew it was the right thing to do. He had driven Dom up and taking Alex away with them was the best decision right now, but he couldn't leave Elena.

"Here," he said, tossing his car keys to a startled Dom. "I can't leave her. Take him away." He looked at Elena, her silence giving him no indication of how she felt, but the look in her eyes was new, something was different.

"Mate, come on, he's so wasted, I need your help," he said as he scooped up the dropped keys.

John was torn; he desperately wanted to stay with Elena, to make sure she was okay, but at the same time wanted to ensure Alex was out of the house and out of the picture.

With that, John rose from his seat and said, "Text me if you need me, alright?"

"Wait," Elena said, standing up with a rush of confidence. She took a deep breath and began marching towards her husband.

"Woah, what are you-" Dom started, but backed down when he saw the look in her eyes.

Elena kept walking and felt the entire room watching her as she came face to face with Alex. His eyes struggled to focus in on her and his mouth twisted into a half smile. Just as it looked like he was about to say something, Elena got in first.

"I want you to leave now! Go! You broke my trust and I don't want you here!"

Alex stood there, a bemused look on his face as he tried to process what his wife had just said to him. Before he had a chance, Dom and John swept in and turned him away, walking the drunkard out of his own house. John glanced over his shoulder at Elena standing there all alone and wanted nothing more than to run to her and tell her everything would be okay.

CHAPTER TWENTY-SEVEN

Elena slumped down into a free chair, silent tears still falling down her face as she watched John depart with Dom. A sudden quiet enclosed her new house, the buzz of gathered friends in a happy atmosphere expelled by Alex's hateful outburst. She wept again at this thought, holding her head in her hands, despair all but consuming her when she abruptly stopped, adjusted her posture and stared wide-eyed at her house, remembering one key message delivered to her that night.

She got up, picking her phone up from the kitchen bench where it was charging. She rapidly dialled her mother's number and awaited her answer.

"Hello? Elena? Are you okay?"

"Hola Mama. Si, well no, actually. I need to talk to you. Is Papa there? Can you put me on speaker?"

"It's very late, si, of course, what's wrong, what's happened?"

"So much Mama, you wouldn't believe. Tonight was the housewarming party, everyone was here," she started, her voice catching as she spoke. "We were all having a nice time, I was talking to my friends and Alex's friends, but Alex, he was drinking and... Mama he told everyone," she said.

Silence met this announcement, finally broken by the words of her father.

"What do you mean he told everyone? What did he...?"

"About Teresa's dad and me losing the baby and he said I was broken and that it was because I was abu..." she started sobbing down the phone to her parents.

"Ay *pobrecita*," her mother said, trying to console her daughter and wishing she was with her to hold her.

"Never mind *pobrecita*, Maria! This idiot, this boy, Alex! How dare he say this to my girl, in front of everyone! *Estas bien*? Are you alone? Is someone with you?" Carlos asked, concern clearly evident in his voice.

"No, I'm on my own. But it's fine," she paused, trying to suppress her tears. "Papa, I don't know what to do."

"You don't need to do anything right now, chica, go to sleep, rest and speak to Alex tomorrow when he is calm," her mother answered on her father's behalf.

"What Alex? No Alex! She should leave him and that's that! Maria, por favor, this is crazy, she cannot stay with him! He was never right for her in the first place!" retorted Carlos.

"Papa, don't say that, please. That's unkind. I'm married to him, I can't just leave him! We have a house! We were trying to start a family! I can't just abandon him, he's a nice person, he just had a... a moment, that's all. We all make mistakes," she attempted to pacify her father, not believing the words she was saying.

"Ay, Carlos, you have such a temper," said Maria, "Don't listen to your father, Elena. You're right. You are married. You cannot just give up at the first *problema*, you know? Sleep on it, speak to him tomorrow, I'm sure he will say sorry. Alcohol is an ugly beast sometimes," Maria said.

"Si Mama, OK, I will try to rest. Buenas noches."

"Buenas noches, Elena. Speak to you tomorrow."

As Elena hung up, she tried to put things into perspective. On the one hand, her father had a point. Was he even right for her? However, she couldn't leave Alex because of one stupid outburst. She was sure he would apologise. She looked up at the sky and recalled her vows, sighing a breath to try and still her nerves.

"For better or for worse," she said aloud to her empty kitchen, and set about tidying up after her housewarming party.

∿

Meanwhile, as he was driving, John glanced in his rear-view mirror at a dishevelled Alex, who was rambling something to Dom. John didn't care to listen as he knew it would just frustrate him even further.

Fuck. That got ugly very quickly. Surely she won't take him back after that outburst. What a prick. Molested? When? Why didn't she tell me? When was this?

Stopped at a red light, he checked his phone. Nothing from Elena. He decided to fire off a quick message:

`Hey, sorry I had to leave. Are you OK? X`

As the lights changed, his stream of burning questions and thoughts kept spinning around in his mind. *I wanted to tell her I loved her. Shit timing, John. What the hell made you think that TONIGHT, after she was clearly distraught, was the right moment for that? Maybe I should call her when I get in, just to check on her. As a mate.*

CHAPTER TWENTY-EIGHT

Elena left work the next day and immediately began to feel an overwhelming sense of dread. Alex was due back later that evening and she felt like she was walking headfirst into doomsday. She squeezed into the packed train with her fellow commuters, all eager to return to their homes and put the day behind them and found herself a seat. Elena recalled the conversation she had at lunch with her colleague, Rachel, who had offered sound advice. "Just tell him flat out that what he did last night was unacceptable and that you think you need to see a counsellor together."

"But I don't think he can handle it, Rach," Elena had replied.

"He's going to have to. Trust me, it's better this way. You need to tell him you want to see a marriage counsellor as you feel you have issues that need addressing. The fact that he blames you or what happened to you when you were younger for your miscarriage...it's just *beyond* ridiculous!"

"He's going to go crazy," Elena warned.

"Let him, it only strengthens your position. Just keep your

calm, hold your nerve and be strong. Your decision has already been made, hasn't it?"

"Yes, I discussed it with my family this morning. I feel that we need to see a professional or it won't end well. Or I'll blame myself for not trying, or have regrets or whatever my Mama said," Elena answered quietly.

"Well then, there you go! There's no point dragging this out any longer than you have to."

"Yeah, you're right. Thanks Rach," Elena had hugged her colleague and thus concluded the pep-talk. She was feeling more nervous as each station passed her by, the thundering sound of the train on the rails matched her racing mind as she went over the countless possibilities. *What if he starts crying? What if he hits me? What if he refuses to listen? How can I get him out of the house if things get ugly?*

She inhaled deeply and turned the volume up on her music to drown out the constant flurry of questions, but yet they remained all the same, prodding at her from a distance.

Hey, I'm almost home. Hope you're OK? x

Elena sent the text off to John and dearly wished he would reply quickly; she wanted to know he was on hand should things start to get messy.

Okay, I've just finished work, so let me know if u need me. x

For the first time in hours, Elena relaxed into a smile. John was ready for her, she knew he would be.

Elena: Thanks, feeling scared x

John: *I know sweetheart. U got this. Just be honest with him x*

Elena: *Okay, thanks Buck xx*

John: *I'm here for you, always x*

Elena allowed another smile to surface as she absorbed John's comforting words, bracing herself for the impact she was about to face. Her key turned in the lock and she wished with all of her might that Alex wasn't there yet.

"Hullo?"

Her heart sank the minute she heard his voice, he sounded very stiff and formal. "Hi," Elena replied gingerly, her heart beginning to race as her adrenaline spiked in preparation for what was about to occur.

"What's for dinner?" he called out, almost making Elena laugh with how trivial the question was compared to the discussion they were about to have. She kicked her shoes off, hung her coat on the rack and walked softly into the living room where, as predicted, Alex was sitting on the sofa watching television. He turned to look at her, his expression blank and she couldn't read him.

"Alex, we need to talk," she began, taking a seat on the armchair, some distance away from him.

"Okay," he replied flatly, with the television still on in the background.

"Can you turn that off, please?" Elena asked.

Alex sighed like a petulant child and clicked the power button.

"Thank you," Elena began. "Alex, there's no easy way to say this but-"

"Hold on, hold on," he interrupted. "First things first. You kicked me out, why haven't you apologised?"

"Excuse me?" Elena asked, utterly bewildered by this statement and throwing her off the objective entirely. "Me apologise to you?"

"Yes, you embarrassed me by doing that, what must everyone have thought? That we have problems?"

"Alex, we do have problems!"

"What do you mean?" his voice rising an octave, along with his anger.

"Alex, this isn't right."

"I know, so what are you going to do about it?"

"Alex-"

"Tell me what your plan is, are you going to tell my parents how sorry you are for making a scene? What about my friends?"

"Alex-"

"You can't kick me out of my house, I put money in here as well you know!" he was verging on shouting at this point and Elena was trembling, partly in fear, mostly in her own anger at how oblivious he was to the damage he had caused.

"Alex-" she tried again, only to be interrupted.

"No, you listen here. I-"

"ALEX! I want us to see a marriage counsellor!" she said as loudly as she could, finally unable to contain herself any longer or be stepped on by this person who refused to treat her as a woman, who never let her be who she actually was and who didn't embrace her quirks, qualities and unique attributes.

Alex was stunned for a moment, his mouth working into a response but unable to formulate the words, so Elena seized her moment and pressed on.

"Alex, I think we should see a professional," she reiterated, softer this time. "I'm not happy, I haven't been for a long time and after what you did, you proved your true colours to me and I'm not going to live like this. We need to get help before...well, to fix us," Elena concluded, waiting now for the response.

Alex's eyes were wide in shock, his face was flushed and he too was beginning to shake, though this was most certainly through anger. Instead, he laughed, almost a psychotic cackle that caught her totally off guard.

"A therapist? Don't be so stupid, we've only just got married! We don't have problems!" he continued, mocking Elena for even suggesting the notion.

"Alex, I'm serious," Elena replied, desperate to make him see how very real this situation was.

"No, you're not thinking. You need to calm down," he said patronisingly.

"I'm actually using my head for the first time in a while, Alex. You and I have had issues for some time. I thought we could work past them, but I can't do this anymore. You're not who I thought you were."

"Oh isn't that convenient!" he roared from nowhere, making Elena jump back in fright. "You get me to buy this new house with you, and now you think we have problems?" he jabbed a finger in her direction and she could almost feel the force coming off of it. "It's bullshit, you've got to think with your head. Get the dinner on and stop this shit."

"Excuse me?"

"You heard!" With that he threw a coaster at Elena, it narrowly missing her face and clattering with a thud against the wall behind her. She was paralyzed, unable to move and now he was advancing towards her and she could do nothing about it. He grabbed her arms, pinning them to her side and brought his face uncomfortably close to hers, talking in a low voice, "We are *not* seeing a counsellor. People don't do that after six months. Don't be stupid."

"Alex, please just listen. We don't have sex. When we do, I have to get myself in such a headspace to be able to...and most of the time it doesn't work. And we were meant to be trying for a baby! I had to beg you to let us start trying but you kept saying no, and eventually you obliged for no other reason than to shut me up. Then when we got pregnant, it was as though you didn't care, you weren't happy, you didn't come to the scan, you weren't there when they told me the baby..." Elena took a deep breath and tried to regain her composure. "I had to go to my hospital appointment with Buck as I was too distraught to go alone."

"Elena, I told you I had to work, it's not my fault," Alex suddenly interjected.

"Alex, I had to deal with my baby being taken out of me, with one of your friends by my side instead of you. I would have thought that it was a bit more important than a shift at your parents' pub. Last night, well. It was the final straw. Things haven't been right for a while now and we need to see someone. You clearly have an issue with me and blame me for everything and anything that goes wrong in this relationship. Please, let's just go to a therapist and if it doesn't work, then fine, at least we tried."

"Your reasons are stupid. We don't need a therapist. I'm sorry if you feel this way, but really, you're being a bit dramatic." Alex turned back towards the television and turned it back on.

At this, Elena shut down. It was as though someone had extinguished a burning candle in one breath, as though Alex had poured scorn on the very fibre of her being. He had no idea of how she had been feeling. If she was completely honest with herself, she didn't realise just how miserable she had been and how well she had been disguising it until this very moment. He just couldn't get his head around what she was trying to say. He wouldn't accept any blame. Of course, she was emotionally damaged and that definitely had a part to play in the slow but inevitable demise of their relationship, but there was nothing she could do to convince him.

"I'll go and make dinner then," she said, resigning herself once again to the monotony of their coexistence.

CHAPTER TWENTY-NINE

Elena walked into her office the next day and sat behind her desk, exhaling deeply and reclining as she did. She unpacked her bag and switched on her computer, bracing for impact against the tide of "urgent" emails that would be sitting in her inbox ready for action. It was just after 9:30AM and Rachel, her assistant, walked in with the usual cup of coffee.

"Thanks Rach," Elena said, collecting her cup from the tray Rachel was holding. "Say, Rach. Do you have a minute?"

"Erm, yes, sure, let me put this down," she replied, heading for the door.

"No, no it's okay, just have your coffee here. I want to ask you something on a personal level, following our talk yesterday."

"Oh...okay, of course."

"I need you to be honest with me and tell me the reality, okay?" Elena began.

"Sure," Rachel answered, looking noticeably nervous.

"You were divorced at a young age, weren't you?"

"Yes..."

"And now you're happily married again, with two children?"

"I am. Elena, what's this all about? Did you tell him you wanted to see a counsellor?" she quizzed.

"Yes," Elena began, the words catching in her throat. "Rach, I think I've made a big mistake and I need to fix it. But I want to know what I'm getting into."

"What happened?" Rachel asked, flicking her greying hair away from her glasses.

"I made a mistake," Elena repeated, bowing her head a little.

"Did you cheat on him?" Rachel inquired timidly.

"No, no. Okay," Elena said, exhaling and rolling her eyes to the ceiling. "I made a mistake marrying him in the first place. He was the safe option, no trouble, easy life. Except it's not, at all. I did what you said, I told him I wanted to see a counsellor and I listed my reasons, but he laughed. Like he literally laughed."

Silence descended in the room as Rachel absorbed the information.

Elena felt a sense of relief at having admitted to someone other than John what her situation was. It felt liberating to have taken another step forward down this path of no return.

"He laughed?" Rachel asked.

"Yes, told me outright that my reasons were stupid," Elena said forlornly.

"You're joking! What a twat! Sorry. I mean..."

"No, it's fine."

"What are you going to do?"

"I have no idea. I can't just walk out. He doesn't want to try at all though Rach, he just wants to continue as though everything were normal. Meanwhile I feel like I'm suffocating," Elena said flatly.

"In that case, be prepared. It might get ugly. I left my ex-husband for similar reasons actually. He was *fine*, but he didn't excite me or really look after me. I felt alone and trapped, just like you. Seven years I tried to stick it out, but I was getting more and more miserable. I buried myself in my work to avoid going home, that's how bad it got. Just a completely sterile environment, no passion, no desire. Just existing, day after day. So, if that's how you feel, then I fully support you. But be aware, this will blindside him, even though you've told him you want to get help, he'll become petulant, he'll make things difficult as he can't understand your reasons why. Mine told me I had mental health issues!" Rachel finished with a laugh.

"Oh gosh," Elena replied, "Well that sounds awful! But thank you for being so honest."

The ladies were interrupted by Elena's phone ringing, which Rachel took as a sign to vacate the room.

"Elena Viegas speaking, how can I help?" Elena answered with a smile and mouthed a silent "thank you" to Rachel as she left. It occurred to her in that moment that she still hadn't adopted his name since their wedding. Elena Wickerman just didn't sound right.

"Hey. My parents want to come over for dinner tonight, hope that's OK?"

Elena squirmed upon hearing her husband's voice. "Alex, could we not wait until we've sorted us out first? I feel like we need to talk some stuff through still?" she asked hopefully.

"No it's fine, we said it all yesterday anyway. Besides, they won't stay long, just a quick dinner. Is that alright?"

Elena paused for a while and realised that she couldn't think of anything that she would rather do less than have an evening at home playing happy families.

"Oh no, sorry Alex, I forgot I actually have a work meeting tonight, invite them over though, you can eat without me!"

"Have you got anything left over from what you cooked

yesterday? Don't fancy a takeaway!" Alex made a futile attempt to lighten the mood.

"Yes, think there's some lasagne in the fridge but it's not nice to give your parents leftovers from our meal last night," Elena said, a little embarrassed at the thought.

"Nah, it's fine, unless you fancy coming home to whip something up before your meeting?"

"I do hope you're joking," said Elena, dismayed.

"Obviously. Ha. Well, have a good day. Love you!"

"You too," Elena gave a non-committal response and placed the receiver back down.

Picking up her mobile, she made an impulsive decision to message John:

Hey Buck, fancy meeting for a coffee after work tonight? Just as mates obvs haha! X

Too emotionally fraught, she packed her phone away and resolved not to look at it until after her conference call this afternoon. Besides, if he said no, she could always make an appointment at the beautician and get her nails done. Alex wouldn't notice the change in nail polish, that much was for sure.

"What the fuck man, think this bloke must have hit a deer with this thing or something! Look at it! It's fucked!" Dom said to John as they both inspected a people carrier suspended above them.

"Yeah. Fucked," John said, all of a sudden clearly distracted.

"Who's that then? That bird off Tinder? The one from

Wales?" Dom said, peering over John's shoulder as he looked at his phone.

"Nah mate, it's Elena. She's asking to meet up for a coffee tonight," he blurted out.

"Holy shit...It's happening!" Dom shook John by the shoulders. "This is it, this is your chance. One on one with the Spanish beauty! God, what I'd give to..."

"Hey, it ain't like that. She wants to meet as mates. What do I do?"

"Ah mate, that's shit. Friend-zoned already."

"She's married in case you've forgotten!"

"Yeah but surely, *surely* after the other night they're gonna be on the rocks, it's your time to swoop in, be her knight in shining armour," Dom said sincerely.

"Argh, I don't think it'll be that easy. She seems to keep going back to him. I know a lot of stuff he's done to her and said to her and take it from me, he ain't no saint. Fuck it, I'll go. What's the worst that could happen?"

"Yes mate! That's the spirit. Tell me all the deets tomorrow, positions, everything!"

"Shut up, it's not like that with her," John hit Dom on the arm as he began typing back to Elena.

Hey you, sure, I'll see you at 6.30. Let me know where.

He contemplated putting a 'x' at the end of the message but decided against it at the last minute, realising the magnitude of her words *'Just as mates, obvs'*. Leaving his phone on the bench, he got back to work, putting the radio on loud to drown out both his own thoughts and Dom's chides.

∼

John disembarked from the crowded train and emerged into the centre of town with his heart racing. It was 5:25PM, meaning he had precious little time to compose himself and prepare for his date (*Was it a date?* he asked himself) with Elena. John had never been nervous before seeing her, but this time it was different. Since the party, there had been a shift, certainly from where he was standing, yet he was anxious that Elena didn't reciprocate the feeling. *"Just as mates, obvs"*, the text Elena had sent reverberated around John's mind, did she really mean that? Was she shutting herself off from him? These questions only served to make John more apprehensive. His feet carried him automatically towards *Costa Coffee* and he found himself flinging the door open with slightly too much force. John winced as it bounced carelessly off the poorly placed bench to the left, a few eyes turned to the momentary distraction before the onlookers resumed their coffees and conversations. John felt colour rise in his cheeks, which made him even more self-conscious and did nothing to settle his rapidly out of control nerves.

"Smooth entrance, Buck."

John looked down to his left where he saw Elena, hidden somewhat by the supporting pillar that held the roof in place.

"Jesus, sorry, didn't see you there," John replied, his heart racing even faster now.

"I picked a good spot then," Elena said with a smile as her eyes averted his gaze.

Was that nerves or did she not want to look at me? John thought.

"Very well hidden. Do you want a drink?"

"Sure, flat white please, here."

"Oh, behave," John said, dismissing her attempt to hand over some money.

"Are you sure?"

"Yes! See you in a sec," John left his coat hanging on the

back of the chair and proceeded up to the counter where he would order their drinks. *Well that went well*, he thought. He couldn't shake the feeling he had, that this was more than a meeting of two friends. So, would tonight be the night? Admit how he feels and see what happens? What if-

"Hello?" a curt voice cut into his thoughts as the barista demanded John place his order.

"Oh, sorry, erm yeah two flat whites please."

"Anything else?" she didn't even look at John when asking.

"No that's it thanks. Oh actually, I'll take one of those marshmallow biscuit things."

"Sure. Eight fifty."

John paid the amount and dared to glance back at where Elena was sitting. She was looking out of the window, people watching and apparently deep in thought. The way the late-afternoon sun glinted off her hair seemed to bathe her in a golden light, she looked beautifully calm and tranquil, John thought. He collected the cups and the brown bag containing the biscuit, took a deep breath and made his way back to the table.

～

"Hey, thanks Buck," Elena said as John sat down and took a sip of his drink.

"No problem. Oh here, I got you something else. Coz I know you like marshmallows!" he said with a wink.

Handing over the paper bag, Elena looked inside to see a biscuit in the shape of a heart, covered in mini pink marshmallows and drizzled with chocolate.

"Oh, this is cute! Shall we split it?"

"Sure! So, how are you?"

Elena blew delicately into her drink before daring to raise it to her lips. She looked at John over the brim of her cup and their eyes locked and for a split second, a fire burned as hot as the scalding coffee as their souls met, both equal in their desire for another.

"Honestly Buck, a bit rubbish," she answered.

"'Cos of the other night?"

She smiled sadly, "How did you know? Yeah. It's made me realise a few things."

"Oh really, like what?" John pressed, intrigued and excited at the same time, a fluttering feeling rising from his stomach.

"Okay so this is all between us, right?" Elena began, not even sure herself what she would divulge.

"Of course," John reassured.

Elena paused, now wrestling with her own moral dilemma. Despite everything, she didn't want to disrespect Alex too much, after all, he was still her husband. Yet this was Buck. She loved him, but couldn't tell him, not yet. So what could she say?

"I've asked Alex to come to marriage counselling with me," Elena finally spoke, omitting the fact that Alex had been less than willing to oblige.

"I think that's a good move," John said without too much emotion.

Elena couldn't read his reaction, so continued to speak. "I'm feeling like I live with a housemate, or like in a shared accommodation with a friend from university, you know what I mean?"

"Not really, I didn't go to uni," John replied with a half-smile.

"Oh Buck," she responded, lightly slapping his arm. "You know what I'm saying here." Her tone becoming more serious.

"I do, I do. Is it really that bad?"

"There's nothing there Buck. No spark, no passion. I feel so alone all the time. We just meander through the days, both with our routine and then off to bed, separately may I add."

"Seriously?" John was legitimately surprised to hear this. He imagined their life to be a lot more exciting and to be brutally honest, involving a lot more sex. I mean, it was Elena we were talking about here, how could anyone *not* want her?

"Yes Buck. Seriously. It feels like I'm living with a friend." Elena finally admitted what she had known and been feeling for years. Alex was a good friend, but nothing more. Even that was now a stretch, considering the despicable way he had treated her.

"I had no idea. So, you hope the therapist will get you back on track?"

"I'm not sure there is a track to get back on, if you get my meaning," Elena said quietly, taking another sip.

"So why bother?"

"Because he's my husband."

"So, you're doing it out of duty?"

Elena again paused. She supposed she was. Her duty to him as a wife but also to herself. If she followed this line of thinking to its inevitable conclusion, a divorce would be a big deal to her family and she would surely have to provide some evidence of having at least *tried* to salvage the relationship. Plus, there was the house which they'd only just purchased, joint savings accrued. It would be a long and drawn out process.

"I have to," she answered flatly, plucking a marshmallow from her half of the biscuit and placing it gracefully into her mouth.

"What do you hope to get from it?" John asked, his own thoughts now swirling. There definitely seemed to be more to this than the other night, Elena had clearly not been happy for a while.

"I really don't know," Elena replied with honesty. "I want him to understand how I'm feeling. I want him to know that what happened the other night was disgusting and I've not felt so low in a long time. I need him to take responsibility." She stopped short of continuing, realising that she was getting emotional, not at the thought of her marriage breaking down, but rather at the time wasted with the completely wrong person for her, when she knew her match was sitting directly opposite her this very moment.

"It's okay," John said softly, reaching out and squeezing her hand. "You're doing the right thing."

"Am I?" She asked, eyes shining as she looked up at John. "What if this breaks him? What if he gets angry with me? What if, on the other hand, he gets so distraught that he does something unthinkable? Oh Buck it's such a mess, such a mess."

A silence followed this, John wrestled with what to say next, wary of putting Elena under more pressure by admitting his own feelings for her.

"The truth is, he wasn't exactly open to the idea."

"Of what? Therapy?" John probed.

"Yeah, he kind of, well. He made me feel stupid for feeling the way I was feeling, he like, laughed at me and got so angry," she finally admitted.

It took all of John's strength to stop himself from calling Alex every name under the sun. Instead, he took a sip of his coffee, which burnt his tongue slightly. "What about you, though? What do *you* want in order to be happy?" John framed the question deliberately.

Elena wasn't blind to his tactic and allowed herself to smile for only the second time during their meeting. "I think you know what."

"Do I?" John's heart began to race, could he dare allow himself to believe that she wanted the same thing he did?

Their moment was interrupted by the shrill ring of Elena's mobile. She frantically hunted for it in her bag and brought it out, sighing as she saw the caller ID.

"Sorry, hold on, don't say anything," she said to John. "Hi Alex," she said into the phone. A pause. "I don't know, maybe in about half an hour or so? I am finishing up this document with Rach and then I'll be leaving." Another pause. "Don't worry, tell them I'll see them another time." They said their goodbyes and Elena stowed her phone away again.

"Why didn't you tell him?"

"What? That I'm out with you? That would look really odd!" she said, laughing nervously.

"Why? It's not like I'm at your house and we're watching a movie!"

"Oh god, that would end well!" Elena said blushing.

"Depends on your definition of well," said John, looking Elena in the eyes until she felt herself getting flustered and she had to look away.

"I should probably go soon," she said, looking sad.

"You don't have to, we could grab something to eat?" John offered, aware of the shift in Elena's mood.

"I don't know. I shouldn't. But at the same time, I really don't want to be at home alone with him right now. When he said I was ridiculous for wanting to see a marriage counsellor, I don't know, something shifted in me. I wanted to try to salvage something and that's why I suggested it and then at least I would know that I had done all I could before making any decisions."

"Look, we don't have to stay ages, we could grab a quick burger or something and then you can head off."

"Maybe next time, Buck. I'm not great company at the moment."

"I disagree, but alright. I'll hold you to that," he said, as they prepared to leave.

CHAPTER THIRTY

"Hi Alex, I'm back!" Elena shouted into the air. She looked into the kitchen and saw a mountain of washing up to greet her.

Her husband came thudding down the stairs in his dressing gown, "Oh hi, how was it?"

"Good, fine. Got stuff done," she lied.

He walked towards her wanting a hug and she moved away.

"Don't, I feel like I need a bath. The tube was rammed and there were loads of sweaty people near me," she said, not wishing to divulge the truth that she had briefly embraced John and could smell the faint lingering scent of his aftershave on her skin.

"Ah, rank. OK, no prob. I'll whack the kettle on and we can have tea when you come down yeah? It's been a mad few days."

"Yes, OK. What did you guys eat?"

"Chinese. Was great actually. From that new place down the road. There wasn't any left, sorry!" he said, not realising how famished Elena was.

"That's OK, I'll whip something up after my bath. Be right back."

As she turned on the taps and started undressing, she looked at herself in the mirror. She wasn't sure what she was feeling when her reflection stared back at her. A sense of impending doom was on the horizon and she didn't know who she could turn to. She had felt good confiding in Buck, but she felt that she needed to hold back with him as he was hot-headed and was worried that if she told him everything he would have come home with her, made her pack her bags and leave with him. She couldn't tell her parents and sister everything as she didn't want to make them worry, and she didn't have many friends in England, so trying to explain to anyone from home what was going on didn't seem worth the hassle. Closing the lid of the laundry basket after she had placed her underwear and clothes inside, so too did she place a lid on her emotions, bottling up the multitude of thoughts swirling around in her mind.

Lowering herself into the warm water, she picked up her phone and saw that she had one message from John:

Hey, thanks for confiding in me. I'm here for you. Please let me know when you get home safe. X

She replied immediately:

Sorry, phone was on silent in my bag. I'm home and in the bath. Thanks for tonight. Was so nice to see you. X

Her phone buzzed again within moments, and she felt her heart skip a beat upon seeing his name.

John: *Is it weird talking to me while you're naked? I kinda feel like a creep.*

Elena: *That's because you are one! I do this all the time, I just never actually disclose that I'm in the bath during messaging sessions! X*

John: *ALL the time? Jeez, you must stink needing to wash that frequently!*
Elena: *You know what I mean!!! Anyway, you're the one that hugged me earlier, tell me, do I stink?*

John: *Yeah of fuckin, roses and flowers and shit.*

Elena: *Oh, sorry, didn't realise you didn't like my perfume. :(*

John: *Never said I didn't like it. X*

Elena: *Oh. X*

John: *Anyway, you always bang on about how my aftershave 'wreaks' (your words if I recall correctly) and that when you leave me you always stink of me! Guess that's why you're in the bath, huh? X*

Elena paused before replying. Should she tell the truth? Should she tell him that smelling John on her skin is her favourite thing? *No. Not appropriate, Elena. Stop this, you're on a slippery slope.* So she held back and replied:

*Something like that. Right, got to go and
make myself something to eat. Speak soon
stinky x*

Elena walked to her bedroom in her towel and a shudder went up her spine as she felt Alex touch her shoulder from behind her.

"Hey," he said, in a low tone. "Why don't you take your towel off and lie down?"

"Alex, don't," Elena said, feeling physically sick at his touch.

"What do you mean don't? You said we don't have sex enough? Well, come on then? Lie down," he said trying to take the towel from her.

Elena pulled away, gripping the towel tightly around her. "Alex, I can't. I'm not happy, I told you as much. I can't just have sex with you just like that. Not when you won't work with me to resolve anything." She felt bad for rejecting him, he was her husband after all, but she couldn't bear the thought of allowing him to touch her. For the first time, she felt disgusted by him. That was when she knew that something in her had truly and irreparably shifted.

"I'm hungry. I'm going to get dressed and go and make something to eat. I'll see you downstairs," she said, getting her clothes out of the wardrobe.

"Come on, it may help with how wound up you're feeling," he proffered as a solution to their issue.

"I can't just force myself to have sex with you Alex. It doesn't work that way. I'm not in the right headspace. Sorry." With that, she walked back towards the bathroom to get dressed, not wanting to do so in front of Alex. She was about to send a message to her sister to see how her parents were coping with the potential demise of her relationship, but she was distracted by a question which popped up on her phone:

*I know you see all my pics. How fucking good
do I look? Like honestly it's pretty fucking
dope.*

Elena actually laughed aloud, knowing exactly what John
was talking about. In the past year or so, John had really
honed his physique into a work of art. She had never been
'into' muscly guys and never realised she liked that particular
look, but on John, it made her stomach flip. She quickly went
onto John's Instagram profile and scrolled through the countless pictures of him topless, showing his carved chest, his six-
pack, his bulging shoulders and strong arms. She sighed and
went to her favourite picture of him. It was a black and white
photo of John sitting at a dinner table, looking into the
distance, wearing a dark shirt which fit him perfectly. It was
slightly unbuttoned at the top and he had rolled his sleeves up,
revealing his toned forearms. Elena pushed aside the thought
that the photo had probably been taken by his ex, Chelsea, and
instead started formulating a response to his message:

*Very. I'm saying it. You're very sexy. I
can't 'like' any of your posts, it's really
frustrating. This? This photo is just. UGH.
SO hot.*

Attaching one of her favourite photos of him, she pressed
send, panicking slightly as she did.

What am I doing? This is bad, she thought.

*John: Seriously? I'm screenshotting that
message LOL. For the record, that photo you
posted the other day of your new haircut?
You looked so damn good.*

Oh. My. God. He said I looked good? Not just good - SO DAMN GOOD?

Elena: HA. This is awkward. Let's change the subject. Um, OK, do you think Pizza Hut should start serving breakfasts?

John: I can't imagine many people want a whole pizza for breakfast. By the way, just wanted to say, at Tom's wedding, you were the most stunning woman there. Just looking at a photo of you from that night. You look incredible, holy shit.

Elena: What photo?

John: I took one when you were sitting at the table waiting for dessert. I thought you looked so pretty sitting there so I took it. Hope you don't mind. (Too late if you do LOL). It's part of my private collection.

Elena: Excuse me? Your private collection? What kind of photo is this? A close up of my cleavage LOL?

John: Haha I wish.

Elena: !!!!!!!

John: Nah, it's just you sitting there in that bloody gold dress. God, when you got out the car and I saw you - honestly I was speechless. You're a Goddess.

Elena: *Sorry, while we're on this topic. You at Tom's wedding. God. It's inappropriate but you looked SO good in your suit. I was so excited for you to see me. I only cared about whether you thought I looked pretty or not.*

John: *There's a photo from YOUR wedding, of us two walking towards the church, and I like to imagine that it was our wedding. ANYWAY, yeh, pepperoni pizza for breakfast sounds good tbh.*

Elena: *I wanted to dance with you but I was trying to keep away from you.*

John: *Like proper dance or goofy dance?*

Elena: *Proper dance.*

John: *Huh. How about that. Me too. X*

Elena: *Oh dear. X*

John: *Indeed. X*

Elena: *How do I know that Alex hasn't put you up to this and this is all just a cruel trick to catch me out?*

John: *How do I know that you're not actually Alex and I'm about to be murdered for talking to you like this? I need proof.*

Elena: *How can I prove it to you?*

John: *Selfie.*

Elena: *No! I'm in my towel.*

John: *That would be what Alex would say.*

Elena: *John...*

John: *Alright, was just trying my luck.*

Elena: *I look like a slob.*

John: *Oh believe me, I'd very much love to come home to that slob.*

Elena: *Stop! Would you actually eat a pizza for breakfast?*

John: *Probably. On that note, you owe me a dinner. When can I take you out?*

Elena: *Tomorrow? Haha*

John: *What time?*

Elena: *Any time. Alex is away on a stag do for the weekend.*

John: *I'll pick you up from yours at 7?*

Elena: *This isn't a date.*

John: *Of course it isn't. We both find one another hideous.*

Elena: *Good. Night Buck. x*

John: *Night sweetheart. See you tomorrow. x*

Elena put her phone down and felt like she was floating. It had all happened so fast, but so naturally. Now she was going to see John and she felt excited and happy for the first time in a very long time. The euphoria was punctured as she heard the television blare out from downstairs and Alex laughing at something on the screen. He was apparently unfazed by the rejected proposal moments ago and Elena sighed, realising the butterflies, rainbows and sunshine with John would be on hold for the moment. She finally got dressed, loose baggy jogging bottoms and a t-shirt and trudged downstairs to the kitchen, where she would still need to do all of the washing up and fix herself some dinner. Elena rummaged in the cupboard for something substantial as the noise from the living room drowned out her clanging, with yet more laughter from Alex adding to the symphony of misery in the grand, lonely house.

CHAPTER THIRTY-ONE

Elena couldn't bear the suspense and had spent the entire day with her stomach in knots, unable to concentrate on anything. Alex had been preparing to leave for the stag do in the morning and she of course had to iron his shirts and pack his bag as she always did, with him watching over her. She had felt relieved once he had left for the airport but at the same time, she was completely terrified of what would happen that evening with John. At numerous points during the day, she had drafted and deleted many a message giving her excuses and telling John that she couldn't see him, but something within her had held her back every time.

As she looked in the mirror at home, she felt a wave of anxiety and finally sent him a message, telling him how nervous she felt about it all, to which he responded:

Hey, it's only me, don't worry, I'm not gonna do anything! It's just us, going out as mates for a meal alright? I'm not gonna jump you! ;)

She felt a little calmer reading his words and once again glanced at her reflection. Elena hadn't planned this outfit like she had others when she had known that she would be seeing John. This time, she merely chose her favourite items of clothing. A pair of light blue jeans, a strappy grey crop top which revealed her tanned and toned stomach, over which she wore a white lace strappy top her sister had made her several years ago. On her feet, she wore gold sparkly sandals she had bought one year whilst on holiday in Greece. Her hair was loosely curled and draped over one shoulder and she had a variety of dainty diamond hoops and studs in each of her ear piercings. Applying another coat of lipstick, she blotted it onto a tissue to soften the colour a little like she had always watched her mother do as a child. Picking up her handbag, she went downstairs and waited in the silent living room, feeling more nervous as each minute passed. She jumped at the sound of John's car outside, stole one last glance at herself in the hallway mirror and walked out.

At first, she couldn't bear to look directly at John. Lowering herself into his car, she'd briefly smiled and said hello but had retreated into herself as reality struck her; she was going on a date with someone who wasn't her husband. What was she thinking? What if someone saw them?

"I know what you're thinking and you need to breathe," John's voice broke the silence between them. "Just try and calm down. We're only going for a meal, it's no big deal, I'm not asking you to come home with me," he finished, smiling that crooked half-smile of his that made her weak.

"Sorry, Buck. I just...I don't normally do this. Much less with Alex's friend. It all feels a bit weird to be honest," Elena admitted, shifting uncomfortably in the passenger seat.

"Hey, I know, but it'll be alright. It's no different to our coffee yesterday, OK?" he said, squeezing her hand which was fiddling with the strap of her bag in her lap, his touch soothing her slightly.

"OK," she sighed, looking out of the window again as they pulled up in a parking space.

"Here we are, I hope you like it, I've been before and the food was great," said John, gesturing to a cosy looking restaurant tucked discreetly amongst some trees.

"Oh, it looks lovely," Elena replied in earnest. She took a moment to look at the establishment, admiring the fairy lights surrounding it, the soft glow of the tealights in the windows and the little lights dotted in the trees. "I love it! It's basically sparkling!" she laughed, relaxing a little for the first time that evening.

"Ha. Suppose it is. Matches your sandals then!" he said, surprising her with his attention to detail.

"Yes, well, no outfit would ever be complete for me without some glitter somewhere!" she said, walking through the door he held open for her.

Taking their seats at the reserved table, Elena fiddled with the table sign which read his name.

"You look so good by the way. I was gonna say earlier but I couldn't really respond in an appropriate way when I first saw you to be honest. Pretty much story of my life with you!" said John, looking at Elena as she was illuminated by the light of the candles.

"It's because it's dark in here!" she retorted. "But you look good too," she finally admitted.

Their meal went as they both had assumed it would, full of laughs and jokes and banter. It was just like always; they felt completely comfortable, as though they were two halves of the same whole.

"So, I'm gonna say it, just get it out there, what was last night about?" John blurted out into the silence, asking the question that had hung over them throughout the meal.

"I don't know what came over me, I'm sorry I said anything," said Elena, beginning to blush.

"Oh, so you didn't mean it then?" asked John teasingly.

"Oh no, I didn't say that, I just, shouldn't have said it. I'm married to your friend for God's sake!" Elena answered with wide eyes.

"Yes. I'm aware," John responded, the playfulness having left his voice all of a sudden.

Elena sensed this change in tone and decided to take charge of the situation.

"I meant every word last night, but it's just not right. I need to work through my nightmare of a marriage, work out what I'm doing and then..."

"I get that. But I feel like we're ignoring the elephant in the room here," John interrupted.

"What elephant?"

"That I'm in love with you. And I think you have feelings for me too," John calmly announced.

A rush of emotions hit Elena and she didn't know what to say. Instead, she gulped and took a sip of her water to bide herself some time.

"You don't mean that, you can't be in love with me. I'm a mess," she said finally, hoping he would counter that.

"Well, it's true and has been for a long time now. I've tried to ignore it, I've tried to move on with other people but the fact is, no one compares to you, they never have and they never will," John admitted, exactly as Elena had dared to hope.

She felt warm inside, finally hearing those words from

John made everything around her seem more colourful. The lights twinkled like stars and her mood was entirely changed.

"You're not just saying this to try and make me feel better?" she asked with trepidation, a nagging doubt still lingering in the back of her mind.

John laughed, "Definitely not. Do you remember back at Tom's wedding?" Elena felt a flash of anger rise at the thought of him kissing Josie Black and then running off to his girlfriend's house. "That night, I thought you looked like the most beautiful girl in the world."

"Yeah, me and Josie," she said forlornly, sinking back to her previous sullen mood.

"Listen, that skank kissed me, not the other way round. I didn't even know who she was. I pushed her off straight away, but I guess you didn't see that part," John explained.

"Sounds like an excuse to me. Not that it matters. You can kiss who you want to, you're single! You're allowed," Elena answered, a hint of petulance in her voice that was more playful than angry.

"Well, it's not. But my point is, that night, I wanted to tell you everything, I wanted to tell you how I felt, how good you looked and how I much needed you. But in the end, we both managed to make some bad choices but that never changed how I felt about you. I'm sorry it's taken me this long to say it but ever since I first saw you, at that stupid, shitty pub, I've been crazy about you and I can't stop thinking about you. And I want you to be mine," he finally finished.

Elena was stunned into silence. She wanted to tell him how she felt but was worried that it would sound insincere or that he wouldn't believe her.

"You don't know how long I've waited to hear you say those things," she whispered.

John started to say something and she put her hand up to stop him, ready now to fully commit to her feelings.

With a deep breath, Elena began. "The first time I met you, I knew you were the one for me. I kept thinking, this guy, he's so handsome and funny and intelligent, and you made me laugh so much. Your charisma and confidence blew me away and when we left that first night I just wanted to be near you and message you and I just...It was weird but from that moment it was as though you showed me that you were the man for me, and everyone else paled in comparison to you, including and especially Alex. At your birthday, I wanted to be around you all the time, and the group was just, I don't know, boring without you. It was as though I had something missing in me when you weren't there. Then at Tom's wedding, when you arranged that heater to keep me warm, I just felt so...it just felt right. I felt like I was your girl and it's all I wanted and all I want. Seeing you in your suit looking so good, and when you hugged me...God...I remember every time I moved I could smell you on my skin and I loved it. Your opinion of how I looked was all I cared about. I wanted to look good for you. I made an effort for you. You're my superhero, Buck. You save me from everything and everyone. You're the only one I can be myself around. I even told my sister about how I was in love with you. But I didn't think you felt anything for me so I went ahead with the wedding. I didn't think you wanted me at all or liked me in that way." Elena finally finished. The air settled and she looked at John expectantly.

John shook his head, smiling and began to laugh.

Elena asked, "What's so funny?"

"Isn't it just all ridiculous how we've been feeling this way for each other for so long, for all these years? And it took this major, complete disaster on Alex's part for us to finally be honest with each other!"

"I suppose that is a little bit funny," Elena admitted, "in a tragic and depressing way."

"Why tragic?"

"Because I'm married, Buck. There's nothing we can do. It's too late," Elena again felt the weight of her situation press down upon her.

"Leave him. What's the point in staying after all that's going on at home? He's shown you his true colours. Do you really want to be spending the rest of your life waiting for the next outburst? Is he right for you?" John asked.

Elena sighed, "I can't leave him. I'm married to him. It's not the same as a relationship where you just break up and it's done. We have a house together. It's not straight-forward."

"You don't have any kids, so you won't have any ties to him. You just need to get divorced and sell the house and you'll be free of him," John countered.

Elena shook her head, repeating again, "It's not that simple, John."

He grabbed her hand and comforted her. "I know it's going to be difficult and it will be a long road ahead, but you're not going to be alone. You've got me now," he said with a calming authority that instantly made her feel better.

They had spent the rest of the evening telling each other about their true emotions; how they had both felt about one another at various events over the past. Deepest desires and secrets that had been bottled up for years were finally being revealed in a dreamlike haze of wonder. An overwhelming sentiment of disbelief, awe and love washed over them both in the car journey back to Elena's house. As they pulled up, Elena gathered her belongings together and prepared to exit her bubble of happiness which would pop the moment she left John.

"Thank you for a lovely evening," she said, turning to look at John.

"It was my pleasure. I had an amazing time with you. God, finally! I can say it!" John said.

"Me too. Gosh, this all feels so surreal. Yet sad, as nothing can ever happen between us."

"Never say never," John said, and while he tried to sound confident, his voice was tinged with sadness.

Elena reached over to hug him goodbye. As she did so, she could smell his intoxicating scent. Her arms were wrapped around his broad shoulders and they stayed like this, John's arms around Elena's waist, for what seemed like hours. Elena began to pull away and move to open the car door, when John grabbed her wrist.

"Wait." With that one word, he completely controlled her. She turned and saw the look in his eyes.

"John, I…" she said, leaning towards him.

"Shut up," he said, pulling her closer.

She gulped, inches from his face.

"I can't resist anymore," she said, her lips moving against his mouth as she spoke. She allowed him to cup her face with his hand. For a moment, they remained like this. Lips ever so slightly touching and both trying to avoid the inevitable. His mouth finally sought hers and kissing her softly but authoritatively, she became his.

The kiss only lasted a moment, but when it was over, Elena began to laugh and shake her head in dismay.

"Oh no," she said. "No, no, no! What are we doing? What am I doing?"

"Sorry, I couldn't help it," John admitted.

"No, it's not your fault. That was…Yeah, that was just…The best ever and now we're in a right pickle."

"Is that what you call this? A pickle?"

"Yes. If you wouldn't mind telling me what I'm meant to do, Mr Buckston, that would be greatly appreciated."

"Well Little Miss Pretty, I suggest you get your fine ass into that house before I try and follow you in and have my way with you." She blushed at this. "And try not to overthink things. Just go and have a bath and text me all night."

"But we…!"

"Yes. And it was fucking phenomenal. So let's just accept it and there's no pressure here. You know where I stand, what I feel for you, and I'm not going anywhere. So get out of your head and text me. OK?"

"OK," she said, opening the car door. "Buck?"

"Yeah?"

"You're just. Everything I've ever wanted. I'll text you when I'm naked," she said, sticking her tongue out.

"As always. Can't wait. Night beautiful."

Walking up the steps to her house, she allowed her fingertips to cross her lips and closing her eyes, she re-lived the events of the evening and the kiss of her life.

"Just gonna stand there and think about me all night?" John shouted from the car.

"Yeah, actually, I was."

"Ditto. Now get inside. You're too pretty to be standing there like that."

"Night Buck," Elena said, turning her key in the lock and disappearing with a final wave.

CHAPTER THIRTY-TWO

I t had taken Elena a further three weeks to finally convince Alex to go to see a marriage counsellor with her. She had tried as much as she could to distance herself from John and the events of that night in order to have a clear head as to whether or not she would be abandoning her marriage. Elena kept reminding herself that she didn't want to allow her ever-growing feelings for John to cloud her judgement in terms of what would happen with Alex. To assist with this, John and Elena hadn't seen each other since their meal, but, despite their best efforts to stop communicating, they had been texting and calling each other daily. Meanwhile, Elena had withdrawn further from Alex and had even moved into one of the spare rooms. Try as he might, his advances towards Elena remained futile, the space between them growing more and more each day, until at last he had called time on it all, accepting her proposal of therapy. She glanced at her phone before stepping inside the marriage counsellor's office and saw a text from Rosa:

If you don't love him anymore, if he's hurt

you too much then you need to be honest and
tell him - do it quick and rip it off like a
plaster. Either way, I love you so much and
will support anything you do. Xx

She closed the message without replying and inhaled deeply. Alex had already entered ahead of her and was sitting down, refusing to acknowledge her. She took up the singular armchair away from him and sat down, nervous about the whole ordeal.

"So, what brings you here today? Mrs Wickerman? I understand that you were the one who organised this meeting?" said Dr Seth.

"Yes, um, for a while I have been feeling distant from my husband. There have been many things I feel aren't right with us and I want to see if we can work through them," Elena admitted.

"I see. And Mr Wickerman, how do you feel about being here today?"

"I think it's a load of crap to be honest, think Elena needs to see a therapist, I mean, she's used to that but, you know, I don't think WE have issues," Alex said sharply, crossing his arms in front of him.

The doctor nodded patiently. "In many cases, partners feel as though they don't have issues until they are in this space and it is then when they realise that they need to be honest with each other and indeed themselves, to address any present issues."

"Hmm," muttered Alex, unconvinced.

"Well, Mrs Wickerman, why don't you start then?" Dr Seth adjusted the glasses on his nose and opened his laptop to type the notes from the session.

Elena sighed, stretching her hands down her legs, holding her knees. "A lot of things really. I don't know where to begin."

"Perhaps just tell me how you are feeling about your relationship with your husband," Dr Seth offered, before continuing, "Mr Wickerman, it is important that you remain open and receptive to the things Mrs Wickerman says, so that this becomes a forum and a safe space for you both to discuss how you feel."

"Well, I feel that we are like friends. There's no spark or passion and I don't actually feel like his wife. I never really have," Elena began, not looking at Alex.

"Yeah, there's no passion coz she refuses to have sex with me!" Alex interjected, his voice shrill and opening his arms wide in protest. "Every time I go near her, she pulls away or makes an excuse. It's been like that for weeks and weeks now."

"And Mr Wickerman, has it always been the case that your wife rejects your advances?" probed the therapist.

"Sure as hell feels like it."

"Alex, that's not true," Elena answered, glancing at him before turning her attention back to Dr Seth. "Doctor, we had been trying for a baby for a while and so of course we had been having sex, but then we got pregnant and..." Elena stopped, holding back tears. "Well, we lost our baby and ever since things have gone from bad to worse. I can't be physical with him at all."

"And why do you feel like you can't be intimate?"

"I had to go to the appointment alone, he wouldn't come with me. When they were removing...um..." Elena said, looking down at her hands in her lap.

Alex opened his mouth to defend himself, "I had an important work thing, Doc, I was there when she got home."

Elena felt a surge of sadness rising up within her as she remembered clearly how Alex abandoned her when she needed him the most. "It's not just that though, even when we were trying for a baby, he wouldn't go to the hospital with me for fertility tests and check-ups. Not even when they thought that I might have been infertile. I felt really alone and it was something we should have been going through together."

"Oh big deal, what's the point in me being there while they do tests on you? What use am I?" Alex said, without a hint of compassion and looking more and more like a sulking teenager who was in the headmaster's office for misbehaving at school.

Despite the interruption, Elena pressed on. "Then things went from bad to worse. We had a party at home, and Alex got drunk and told everyone that it was my fault that I had miscarried and that it was because I had been sexually abused when I was a teenager. In front of all our friends and family. I can't forgive him for that." She finished her sentence with emphasis, her courage in finding the right words giving her renewed strength as the session progressed.

"I've said I was sorry for that. I can barely remember it anyway, I was pissed," Alex protested in a whiny voice.

"Mr Wickerman, how do you feel about what your wife is saying to you?" the doctor asked without looking up from his note taking.

"That she's being a bit of a drama queen. I mean, sure, I'm not perfect, no one is, but that doesn't mean we need to be in separate rooms or that we even need to be here talking to you really. She's a bit like this; loud, overdramatic. Her whole family are. I'm here to get her to stop moaning about it so we can get on with our lives," said Alex, his arms still folded and his tone defensive.

The doctor looked over the rim of his glasses with mild surprise on his features, it was difficult to remain impartial when he was witnessing such a complete dismissal of his client's concerns. Before he could ask Elena for a response, she spoke up and finally looked at her husband fully.

"I don't think that's fair, Alex. I'm just trying to tell you how I feel so we can maybe work through this." She shifted her body to face Dr Seth. "Doctor, I don't know if there is anything to salvage for me. I feel very distant from Alex and what he did at the party, not to mention during the pregnancy, have left me feeling broken and alone. Even before all that, we were living together like we were friends, not lovers, not husband and wife or anything - it was almost as though he was like my little brother who needed looking after; like me doing everything for him. That's why I wanted to come here, to see if you could help us, so he could see what is really going on and come to terms with it." Elena said, her confidence growing with each word and her posture straightening from the slumped and broken woman she was upon entry to the office.

"Mrs Wickerman, it is not something that can be resolved in one session, we have to have frequent visits, I would say at least ten, to establish a long-standing open conversation between the two of you. A lot of the work needs to be done outside of this room in terms of communication as a couple," Dr Seth answered, maintaining eye contact with Elena and silently communicating that he did understand her plight.

"Well I for one am not planning on making this a regular thing. Sorry, Doc, but I don't see what spending lots of hours and even more money on this is going to do for us. Elena just needs to get over this so we can both move forward," Alex said, cutting across the room with his voice.

Elena bit her lip and recalled her sister's words earlier this morning, *"If you don't love him anymore, if he's hurt you too much then you need to be honest and tell him - do it quick and rip it off like a plaster."*

"Alex, I think we should separate for a while. I'm not sure I can work past this. Not the way I'm feeling. And I think a bit of space will do us both good."

The announcement caught Alex off guard and he took a moment to process what she said, looking at her in dismay.

"Excuse me? Separate? This isn't one of your stupid Spanish soaps, this is my life here! No, we are not separating. What a load of nonsense. Come on Doc, surely you're on my side here, she's being a bit ridiculous," he spat, his hand pointing from Elena to the doctor imploringly.

Dr Seth adjusted his glasses and addressed Elena, "Mrs Wickerman, please think seriously before making any rash decisions. I think you need more sessions before…"

"I told you, Doc, we won't be having more sessions," Alex interrupted.

"See what I mean?" Elena remarked, remaining calm and allowing Alex to dig his own grave, before turning to him to continue the conversation, "Alex I don't understand you! One minute you want to save us, the next minute, you're not willing to work on us. This is why we need space. I will go and stay with my parents in Seville, I will see if I can work remotely for a few weeks. We can then see how we feel about reuniting."

"There's nothing *I* need to do, Elena. You're the damaged one. You're the psycho here. You're making up all these issues that are frankly a load of shit." His eyes bulged with anger as his voice rose an octave, "I'm not leaving *my* house, so yeah, whatever, you need to go to Seville or somewhere else if you're that hell-bent on space, coz I ain't budging. I paid half for that house, fair and square, I'll be staying there." He glared at Elena before shifting his focus back to the doctor. "Doc, it was nice to meet you but no offence, it's been a bit of a waste of time. Maybe you should see Elena on her own and see if you can make her see sense, coz I sure as hell can't seem to. Elena, I'll see you at home. I'm going to do my shift."

Elena was dumbfounded as she watched Alex rise from his seat and move towards the door.

"Oh, and another thing, if you think *any* of this is my fault, then you're delirious. You need to sort your head out. See ya Doc."

Slamming the door behind him, Elena looked at Dr Seth and shrugged. "Maybe I am damaged. Sorry to have wasted your time, Doctor. It was nice to meet you." She didn't wait around to hear any final pieces of advice the therapist might have given her, it was futile. The entire visit had been a waste of time. Or had it? Had it served a purpose in that it had reaffirmed her realisation that her marriage was indeed over?

Three days later, Elena had packed her suitcases and finalised the arrangements for her one-way trip back home. Her parents had been shocked to hear the news but supportive of their daughter and were looking forward to having her back home so that they could look after their little girl. She heard a car-horn outside signalling that her lift had arrived, so she checked her hand-luggage for her passport, phone and ticket and wheeled her cases out of the front door. Stopping to turn around and take one last look around the house she had been ready to call a home, she felt a cold emptiness creep into her heart, signalling the beginning of a long and hard emotional journey towards the end of her marriage.

"Hey you, let me get those," John said, lifting both suitcases with ease, one in each hand.

"You really didn't need to take me to the airport you know," said Elena, a hint of sadness to her voice.

"Yes I did, it's the last time I'll see you for a while, I couldn't miss this opportunity. Are you sure you won't stay in London?

You could stay with me you know?" he offered sincerely, knowing his parents would welcome her with open arms.

"What and be the talk of the town, the married woman shacking up with her husband's friend? No, thank you. I would have loved to, but I feel I need a break from it all here for a while. It will be good for me to be with my family and clear my head." Elena smiled in earnest for the first time in what felt like years. John always made her smile.

"Yeah, you're right. Listen, we'll talk every day and it'll be like you're still here. Who knows, I may even grace you with the odd FaceTime call so you can see my ugly mug, what about that?" John offered, knowing that it might ease his own pain of missing her as much as it would for Elena.

"That sounds perfect. I'm going to miss you so much, Buck." Reaching her arms around his shoulders, she hugged him tighter than she ever had before.

"Me too. Me too," said John, breathing in the scent of her hair, his arms around her slender waist, stroking the small of her back. "Come on. Let's get you to the aeropuerto!"

"You practicing for when you come over?" she laughed at his terrible accent.

"Si, mi amor, ready for when I see Big C!"

"Big C?" she said, clearly missing the joke.

"Big Carlos! Your dad!"

"Oh! Ha! I think already likes you, I don't think you need to learn Spanish to impress him!"

"Nah, it'd be nice. I can speak to your whole family then and you can all laugh at my shit Spanish!"

She laughed as she always did when she was with John, and they pulled away, leaving the big house and some of her worries behind them.

CHAPTER THIRTY-THREE

Elena woke from a deep sleep, the best night's rest she had managed in a long time. A cool breeze floated delicately into her room from the open window, the curtains blowing wide to invite the morning sun in. She was used to this kind of awakening by now, just over two months had passed since she had left her home in London to be with her family and more importantly, to be away from him. Contact with Alex had been limited, but necessary. After the initial two-week period had elapsed, Elena had phoned Alex to let him know she would be staying in Seville a little longer.

"But why?" she recalled him asking on the phone.

"Alex, there's no point in me coming back home," she had said in an almost defeated tone. "Do you really feel like you want me back?"

"Not if you're still being a lunatic. When are you going to snap out of this shit and be normal?"

"Bye Alex," Elena had clicked the phone off and left Alex to stew in his own failure and anger. The marriage was finished, Elena knew it. Whether Alex would accept it or not was another matter. Elena naturally confided in her family about everything. Their initial reaction was a little surprising, her mother was deflated that her daughter's marriage was for all intents and purposes over, however she soon recovered upon hearing of how bad it had truly been for all this time. Carlos was secretly thrilled this was all coming to a conclusion and when Elena finally let slip that she had feelings for John, he was over the moon.

"Johnny boy, ha! I knew it! He's a good man. The right man for you. But daughter, you have to be careful. Make sure you are separated officially before starting anything with him, you don't need the overlap of a broken marriage to start your beautiful new journey with John."

Elena heard these words and only a few days after speaking to Alex, called him again.

"You what?!" Alex's tone was incredulous, his anger already spilling over and they were only thirty seconds into the phone conversation.

"A divorce Alex. We're done. This needs to end for both of our sakes, we can move on, we're still young and let's just use this all as an experience to learn and grow from."

"Oh cut the fucking shit. You're so full of it. Fucking bitch. So sick of you and your psycho tendencies."

"Alex-"

"No, I'll save you the trouble. I'm filing for it. My lawyer will be in touch." The line went dead and Elena cried, not from the sadness of her marriage ending, but from the hostility, the abuse, everything. The conversation had been a lot shorter than she had anticipated, but the end goal had been reached. Less than forty-eight hours later, the official paperwork was sitting in Elena's inbox. He had filed for divorce. She was stunned at how quickly this had moved; Alex was never one to make something happen with any great haste, so it spoke volumes as to how he must have been feeling about the whole shambles of a marriage. She told her parents and Rosa, who comforted her with her favourite meal.

"Why don't you invite John out here?" Carlos asked.

"Papa! You can't be serious. I've been separated for five minutes!" Elena replied, scooping another portion onto her plate.

"I know, I know, but why not?"

"What do you mean why not, isn't it too soon?"

"No sis, it's not soon enough if you ask me," chimed Rosa with a smile and a wink.

"There you go, your mother agrees as well, don't you?" Carlos said, prompting Maria for input to the conversation.

"My sweet girl. You must do what makes you happy. You're going to be here with us for a while, so why not invite him out?"

"Okay, I'll see how he feels about coming, maybe let's give it some weeks and let the dust settle?"

"Well done my daughter," Carlos said, kissing Elena on the head. "Let's finish this feast!"

Elena exchanged texts with John that same night, confessing how she was missing him and also updating him on the situation; that she was separated and that the divorce was now in the process of going through, albeit in its early stages. In truth, she wanted to invite him over that same night, but didn't think it was appropriate, nor that John could likely just drop everything for her. Elena's fingers danced around her keys, deleting words, yearning to ask him to fly out but she kept restraining herself. However, as the conversation progressed and John said again how he missed her, she decided to take the leap of faith:

Do you want to come out here for a visit?
Maybe at the end of the month? x

John's reply was instant:

I'd get on a plane tonight if I could. I
miss you so much. Let me get the time booked
off from work and I'll let you know
tomorrow xx

For the first time that day, Elena had smiled and those butterflies returned in her stomach, making her feel excited; something that only happened when John was talking to her, either in the flesh or through other means. It didn't matter, his effect on her transcended all planes of existence. She was utterly enraptured by him and couldn't wait to see him.

Elena had to wait a little longer however, as John couldn't get time off for another four weeks. Work was busy and others had annual leave already booked in. So, they kept their distance, texting every day, calling whenever they could and sharing a conversation via video chat. This continued up until today, when Elena was waking up to the fragrant smell of the orange trees outside her window.

"Good morning mi amor," Elena's mother's voice floated into her room as she made her way up the wooden staircase, a freshly made coffee in hand for her daughter.

"Mmm, hola Mama," Elena said, stirring from her bed and stretching out.

"Oh, come now, you need to get ready, he'll be here soon!"

"Mama, he's not arriving until four!"

"Si, I know, but it's ten now. By the time you have breakfast, have a wash, go to the shops, time will be gone before you know it!"

Elena laughed before responding, "Okay, okay, I'm up. What do you need from the market?"

Maria paused, thinking about the food required for tonight's welcoming feast. "We need *chorizo*, *jamon* and maybe some more steaks. Does John like his meat?"

"Oh just wait, Mama. He loves all food!" Elena felt a sense of pride speaking about John like this, as if he was *hers*, which she supposed he now was.

"Good! Now get up, your breakfast is downstairs!" Maria lightly slapped Elena's bum as she walked past her.

Elena paused at the top of the staircase and turned to her mother. "Thank you, Mama. For everything."

"De nada my angel."

Her left foot crossed over her right as she waited with some degree of impatience in the arrivals foyer of San Pablo airport, just twenty-five minutes from her family home. John's flight had landed about ten minutes ago, according to the electronic display hanging high above her. She craned her neck again to check it, for no real reason other than a fleeting hope that John might burst through the doors as she did. "Come on Buck," she whispered, feeling tense. She was so anxious to see him. It had been almost four months since she had left London and she was longing to feel his strong arms, smell his signature scent and taste his lips again. Lost in thought for a moment, she jumped when she saw him emerge from the open door and immediately beamed a huge smile.

"John! Buck! John!" Elena shouted and waved to get his attention.

John looked around for a moment, trying to identify the

source of the noise before his gaze settled on Elena. As soon as he saw her, his face lit up with genuine happiness.

"Elena!" he shouted back, not caring about whether there were onlookers giving him a glare as he rushed past people. "Elena!" he shouted again, drawing closer until finally they met, John's bag dropped carelessly to the side as he picked Elena up with ease, spinning her around and kissing her deeply on the lips.

"Wow, hey mister," Elena said, wobbling a little when she felt her feet touch the ground.

"Hey yourself. God, I missed you," John replied, that huge smile still plastered on his face.

"Did you? You don't act like it," Elena teased.

"Ha shut up, come here," John pulled her in for another kiss.

"You're quite nice actually, aren't you?" Elena said, smiling dreamily as she savoured the lingering sensation on her lips.

"Not as nice as you. Shall we get out of here?"

"Yes, let's not keep everyone waiting," Elena said, glancing sideways at John and wondering if he would pick up on the deliberate choice of words.

"Yeah, can't wait to see everyone. Hope Big C has stocked up on the meat for me," John responded without breaking stride.

Elena smiled, knowing already this was far more like how things always should have been.

They were greeted by a wall of noise as soon as they entered the house. Elena's mother, sister and father were at the front of the crowd, smiling and shouting their welcome as Elena and John walked through the door.

"Ohhh!" John exclaimed, dropping his bag by the foot of the stairs and embracing Maria in a hug, kissing both cheeks as he did. "Maria, como estás? You look wonderful!"

"Ey Johnny boy be careful that's my wife!" Carlos said jokingly as he approached John, shaking his hand firmly before pulling him in for a hug.

"Like I'm going to mess with you!" John replied squeezing Carlos' arms in admiration. "I tell you, if I can be in this shape when I'm your age I'll be happy. To be honest, I'd be happy with it now!" John said earnestly, generating more laughter. "Hi Rosa, how are you?"

"Bien, gracias. Nice to see you John. Welcome to our home," she replied.

"Come, John. Let me get you a beer," Carlos said.

"With respect, if I could just have a coke? Or something like that? I'm not drinking tonight."

"Of course! Maria, can you get John a nice cold bottle?" Maria dutifully obliged, handing John a drink from the fridge.

Elena was quietly stunned, she hadn't expected John to turn down alcohol, in fact she assumed it was a given that he would be drinking, he usually had one or two drinks whenever they were out with the group.

"Thanks so much, now, where is everyone I need to say hi!" John said enthusiastically.

"This way, come!" Carlos led John into the dining area where extended members of the family were already seated.

"Everyone this is John!" A large chorus greeted him and John threw up his arms in faux bewilderment.

"Oh! Hola everyone! How are we all tonight?" John asked the crowd. A cacophony of noise answered, he could make out a few "bien gracias and you?" here and there, but it was mostly just a jumble of phrases. He smiled kindly, making eye contact with everyone at the table from his position in the doorway.

303

"Thanks so much for having me here and inviting me into your family home, I can't wait for this feast!"

A wave of approval met these words as Carlos pulled out a seat for John next to him, opposite Elena. "Here Johnny, next to me, I can keep my eye on you," he joked.

"Hey, I'll be keeping an eye on you I think! You better not steal my food!" He clapped Carlos on the shoulder and everyone laughed, just as Maria burst into the room with the first platter of Mediterranean food.

"This smells lovely Maria!" John said enthusiastically as he assisted with clearing a space for it to go.

"Gracias, John," Maria said, blushing a little. Elena followed soon after her mother, carrying yet more food for the table.

"Johnny, here try this first," Carlos said, heaping a great spoonful of paella onto John's plate.

"Yeah then add some of this!" Rosa said, ushering John's plate towards some chicken in a pot surrounded by almonds and cherry tomatoes.

"Try this!" Another voice, this one belonging to Elena's uncle steered John towards some more meat to try.

Elena watched all of this unfold, conscious of how uncomfortable Alex had been in this environment a few years ago, yet John was thriving. He was smiling broadly, engaging with everyone and making sure to sample everything on the table. Finally, Maria sat down and then John stood up.

"Por favor," he said confidently, drawing cheers of appreciation, which he accepted jovially. "I just want to say thank you so much for inviting me here to your home, letting me share in this wonderful meal and being so kind. Gracias." He raised his glass to the air, signalling he was finished and everyone copied his gesture, drinking as they did. He sat down and Carlos patted him on the back, all the while Elena couldn't take her eyes off John, who noticed and gave her a wink and a smile.

～

"Wow, that was amazing," John said appreciatively at the conclusion of the banquet. His plate was spotless save for some chicken bones, mirroring Carlos' plate, which didn't go unnoticed by Elena's father.

"You like the food we have here?" he asked John.

"Oh my, if you eat like this every day you won't ever see me leave!"

"Ha! Well not quite like this, but the food here is so good, you're going to love spending a week here."

"Oh I don't doubt it, I already love the place!"

"Ha! Good man," Carlos said, his hand on John's broad shoulder. "Come, we'll go next door. I think there's a game on."

"Champions League tonight isn't it?" John asked, knowing the answer already.

"Si, big match. We have Milan away."

"Tough one. They're not what they used to be though, so I think you have a good chance," John said knowledgeably. The men walked into the room and Carlos and John sat down next to each other.

"John I just want to say thank you," Carlos said just as the match started.

"Oh, for what?"

"For supporting my daughter, helping her through such...difficult times."

"It's my pleasure. Besides, she's been there for me for years, always supporting me no matter what stupid decision I made!"

"Ah you two. She looks happy John, even with everything going on. As soon as you got here, she looked *alive*, truly herself again."

"I'm glad, because I feel the same way with her. With all of you actually, you've made me feel like I've been here my whole life, like I've known you all for years and years. It was the same when I met Elena for the first time. We just clicked."

"You're a good man John, thank you again for showing my daughter what it is to be happy." They clinked glasses and settled into the match in a comfortable silence.

~

Members of the family began to drift off to their respective homes, eventually leaving Maria, Carlos, Rosa, Elena and John.

"We're going for a midnight stroll, you two can stay here, catch up," Carlos suggested to his daughter and their guest.

"Gracias, Papa," Elena said, a surge of anticipation rising inside her at the thought of being alone with John.

"We'll see you soon," Maria said, waving to the pair as they walked out. Rosa gave Elena a studied look accompanied with a wry smile, which puzzled Elena but again got her heart racing. The family left and it was now just John and Elena, alone at last.

"What a day," John said grinning. "Come here." He pulled Elena in for a hug and squeezed her close, embracing her tightly. They pulled apart slowly, their faces still close together. With a burst of passion, John planted a deep, firm kiss on Elena's lips, which she gladly accepted. Her arms wrapped around his neck and their tongues intertwined, John's hands now moving down Elena's figure. They pulled away from each other, panting.

"John, we shouldn't...."

"I love you." With those words spoken by John, Elena paused for a moment and then moved closer to him and they resumed kissing, until she was on his lap, her legs wrapped around him. John ran his hands through Elena's hair and kept pulling her closer to him as he kissed her, holding her head. John then proceeded to pick Elena up, his hands lifting her with ease and their lips locked, as he carried her up the stairs, increasing the urgency of their connection with every step. John reached Elena's room and let her go. She gasped, landing on her back on the bed and looked both surprised and at the same time, full of desire.

"What are you doing?" she asked, breathless, wriggling a little. The anticipation was escalating to new heights and she could barely contain her excitement.

"Nothing," John said in a low voice, taking his top off and leaning back down to Elena.

"Oh god," she moaned, her hands dancing along his broad back as she felt his lips on her neck, his hands exploring her body. He returned to kissing her lips and as he did, Elena dug her nails into John's back, a pain which he relished and only served to heighten his own enthusiasm.

"I can't take anymore. I need you," she said, as John lifted her dress above her head, revealing her lace lingerie.

"You're so fucking sexy," he said as he looked at her. His eyes were filled with passion and desire, he took off the rest of his clothes and Elena could see how much he wanted her. John carefully removed Elena's underwear exposing the rest of her body and this desperation grew to an unbearable point. John kissed each of her nipples as he pinned her legs on his shoulders, finally easing himself into her, making her moan with pleasure. The love making was intense, frantic and passionate. They watched each other throughout and between their moans they could be heard repeating the same phrase to each other.

"Look at you...you're so beautiful."

Years of wanting one another finally unleashed in an

explosion of ecstasy as they both reached climax together. When they managed to pull their bodies apart, John lay down next to Elena and kissed her softly on the mouth.

"I love you," he said with earnest.

"I love you too," she replied. After such a long time, it was everything they could have imagined and so much more. John and Elena were finally one.

At the conclusion of John's visit, Elena shed tears, not wanting to be away from her love, but new job commitments had forced her hand and she had to remain in Spain for a while longer. John parted with the family having forged deeper bonds of trust and respect with everyone and was sad to say goodbye.

"We'll be on video every day," he had said at the airport, kissing and hugging Elena.

"Yeah," she nodded, tears falling down her face as she squeezed him tighter. "Have a safe flight."

"I'll see you soon. I love you."

"Love you!" Elena had exclaimed, waving and blowing a kiss, which John mimicked catching and putting in his pocket.

"Saving it for later," he said with a wink and he was gone, leaving Elena missing a crucial piece of her. With John's departure, her thoughts realigned to matters involving her soon to be ex-husband. She wondered what was happening with the house, which was now on the market after a heated debate. Alex wanted to keep it, Elena wanted it sold. Alex's parents had stepped in to try and buy Elena out of the property so Alex could remain there, but their offer had been way under value. It caused yet more friction between the couple and only served to solidify Elena's decision even more. She couldn't wait to be away from him, his foul language and lack of respect for her came through with every phone call, particularly where money was involved. She took comfort in the fact that the divorce was moving ahead and that eventually she would never have to speak to him again.

CHAPTER THIRTY-FOUR

A few weeks had gone by since John's visit and Rosa, having returned from a fortnight's stay in Sicily, finally managed to catch up with her sister about it in their favourite cafe, *La Fontana*.

"So," started Rosa, stirring her coffee. "Did you?"

"Did I what?" replied Elena, feigning ignorance.

"Did you two, you know...have sex?"

"Yes," said Elena, blushing slightly and taking a bite of her toast.

"And?? How was it? Tell me all the details!"

Elena and Rosa had a very close sisterly relationship, so much so that they had always shared the details of their respective amorous liaisons. As Elena began to recount the events of the first passionate night she had shared with John, along with the following six nights of his stay, Rosa's jaw dropped.

"Ay Dios! I'm so jealous! You two sound like you were at it like rabbits!"

"Well, only when Mama and Papa were out, I mean, I'm sure they knew, but they didn't say anything."

"They definitely knew. Mama called me and told me that you two had been walking around like two lovestruck teenagers all week the day after I left for my holiday. So... what happens now?" asked Rosa.

"I don't know. I mean I love him so much, I can't even tell you *Rosita*, I've never felt this way about anyone before. It's like we've been together for always. He's perfect," Elena said with a wistful smile, which swiftly turned into a look of worry.

"Qué? What is it?"

"Nada. It's nothing," said Elena unconvincingly.

"Come on, I can see it in your face. You miss him, right?"

"Of course. But that's not it. I'm late."

"But I thought you didn't work on weekends?" her sister asked, totally missing Elena's point.

"No, I'm late. My period, it hasn't come and I'm normally like clockwork."

"Oh shit!!! Sis!!!! Have you taken a test?"

"No, not yet. I'm too scared."

"But you have to! You have to find out!"

"What if I am, Rosa? I'm still married! And John and I have only been dating for a little while - it's a lot for him to deal with."

"Look, your divorce is weeks away from being granted, right?"

Elena nodded in response, sipping her chocolate milk.

"And you both love each other, si?"

Elena replied, "Of course we do! I love him so much!"

"Right, so let's do a test and we'll deal with the rest after!"

The walk home felt long and cumbersome to the two sisters. Pregnancy test stowed in her bag, Elena ran through various scenarios in her mind. What if she was pregnant? How would it work? She couldn't leave Seville due to her work and anyway, what if John didn't want her to keep the baby? How would she even tell him she was pregnant in the first place? Over FaceTime?

"Stop, you're thinking and getting ahead of yourself. Just wait and see OK?" Rosa said, reading Elena's thoughts.

Locking herself in the bathroom, Elena took a deep breath and tried to steady her nerves.

"It's just peeing on a stick," she said to her reflection in the mirror. "No big deal."

"Have you done it yet?" her sister's voice called through the door.

"No! Give me a minute!" she called back, taking a seat on the toilet. "Here goes," she whispered, holding the pregnancy test in her hand.

"OK. Set the timer," she said to her sister, unlocking the door.

"OK done. Three minutes and counting." They both stared at the phone until it beeped to signal the time was up. "Go on," Rosa said. "Take a look."

"I can't. You do it," replied Elena.

Rosa moved towards the test and Elena sat down on her bed, watching her through the open door to the ensuite.

"I think you'd better call John," said Rosa.

John was under a Nissan Juke when Dom shouted over to him, barely audible over the sound of the radio playing in the garage.

"Hey, mate, your phone's ringing. It's Elena."

"Ah fuck, pass it here mate, put it on speaker, I'm covered in oil!" Dom obliged and John called out from underneath the vehicle, the phone beside his head, "Hey sweetheart, you OK?"

"Hi mi amor. Are you busy?" he heard Elena's voice, crackling slightly with distortion.

"Not too busy for you bub, what's up?" John said, biting his tongue in concentration as he twisted a bolt tightly.

"Am I on speaker? I just need to tell you something."

John sensed a tension in Elena's voice, so he wiped his hands on a nearby rag and picked the phone up, taking it off speaker.

"Not any more. Is everything OK? Are you alright? Your family?"

"Si. Well no, well yes. So, I kind of have massive news to tell you, are you ready? Are you somewhere private?"

John moved towards the office, which was in essence a cupboard with a computer in it, closing the door behind him. "Yes sweetheart, go for it."

There was a pause and Elena gulped, biting her lip in anticipation. She cupped the phone close to her mouth and slowly announced, "I'm pregnant."

John let the sentence sink in. His heart was racing, and an enormous grin erupted on his face. His heart thumped in his chest and he finally spoke, "Holy shit, really?"

"Really," Elena answered, smiling as she heard the excitement in John's voice.

John's enthusiasm was contagious, "Fuck! No way! Holy shit! We're gonna have a baby! Elena!" he said loudly.

She began to laugh at the sound of his joy, feeling nothing but happiness at his reaction. "Yes, mi amor, we are. Are you sure it's not too soon? We've only recently started going out," she cautioned, wary that this might be all too much too quickly.

"Well, as far as I'm concerned, I've loved you since the day I met you, so no, it's not too soon. It's long overdue as it happens," he laughed, still bearing a huge smile on his face.

"You mean it John?" Elena asked hesitantly.

"Of course I do. I mean, how do you feel about it?" John

replied, suddenly aware that she might be frightened due to her past.

As if reading his mind, Elena answered, "I'm scared. Of...you know. What happened last time. I mean of course I want a baby with you! It's like a dream come true! But what if..." her voice trailed off and John interjected.

"Shhh," he reassured her as best he could through the phone. "Look, let's take each day at a time. God, this is the happiest day of my life! When's the scan? I'll fly over."

"Papa has booked you a ticket already, it's on the twentieth. I said to Papa to wait and see if you wanted to come first, but he said that he knows you better than I do, so he booked it right away."

John laughed at this. "Quality. What did your parents say when you told them?"

"I didn't actually tell them, Rosa was so excited, she ran and told them before I could stop her. I wanted to tell you first. They're really happy. I think Papa's words were, 'I told you, Maria, I said it would happen before my 60th birthday!'" Elena beamed, remembering the precious moment she'd had with her family before calling John.

John laughed heartily, "That's hilarious. Oh sweetheart, this is the best news. Wait 'til I tell my mum and dad, they'll be over the moon!"

"I love you John, so much. We're having a baby! We're actually going to have a baby! You and me!" Elena said, almost in disbelief.

Laughing again, John replied, "Yes my sweetheart, we are. Right, as much as it pains me, I better get back to this shit-show of a Nissan Juke. Honestly, it looks like the owner drove directly into a pile of trollies at a supermarket or something. Fucking nightmare. I love you. I'll call you when I finish, OK?"

"OK mi amor. I love you."

"Bye sweetheart."

Hanging up the phone, both John and Elena had a spring in their step as they went about the rest of their days, messaging each other whenever they could. That evening, John and his parents called Elena and her parents on FaceTime and they all rejoiced at the happy news.

As expected, John and Alex hadn't exchanged a single word to each other after the divorce was finalised two weeks later. Their relationship had been deteriorating for a while anyway, so it didn't arouse suspicion that they no longer spoke. John really wanted to send Alex a spiteful text confirming that he and Elena were together, but she had coaxed him out of it. He wasn't aware of the new relationship and neither were any of his friends, apart from Dom of course.

"He deserves it though!" John protested with a smile.

"Just don't! We love you so much, be safe okay?"

"I will, say hi to everyone for me," John said waving and blowing a kiss to Elena as they ended their video call.

"You done with all that soppy crap?" Dom said from behind him.

"Ah shut up man, you ready?"

"Yeah, cab's here and all, look," Dom answered and the pair left Dom's house ready for a night out with their friends.

They climbed into the back of the taxi, *The Bucket and Spade* please mate," Dom said to the driver. The cab pulled away and began the short fifteen-minute trip to the pub. John fiddled with his jacket.

"You okay mate?" Dom asked, noticing the movement.

"Yeah, yeah. Just wondering how the lads will react, you know?"

"If they're your true friends they'll back you."

"Thanks mate, you really are a good man, you know that?"

"Course I do," Dom said.

The cab arrived at the busy pub and John and Dom quickly found their friends who had arrived just a few minutes earlier.

"Fellas!" John said as Evan, Freddie and Henry rose to their feet to greet him.

"Been a while mate!" Freddie said.

"Yeah, blimey where ya been?" Henry chimed.

John slid into the booth with Dom and made himself comfortable. "Well, I got some news," he started.

"Well wait five minutes, Alex will be here, and we can all hear it at the same time!" Evan said.

John's stomach dropped. He shot Dom a sideways glance, his wide eyes confirming that this was a surprise to him as well.

"Oh, speak of the devil!" Freddie said, waving over to the entrance.

John looked up and felt his chest tighten as his adrenaline spiked. There he was, the man who had caused Elena so much pain, reduced her to tears time after time, making the divorce as difficult as possible. Alex waved back and started to walk over.

John got out of his seat and made himself visible to Alex, who was smiling. Their eyes locked and Alex froze. His face contorted and he snarled, *"You!"*

John didn't back down. He stood his ground and let Alex come closer. Confused looks were exchanged between Evan, Henry and Freddie. Alex got nearer to John's face and prodded his chest. "This is all your fault! You ruined my life."

"Alex, don't be a prat. Not the time or place," John said, keeping is words steady and his breathing controlled.

"Do you know what he did!" Alex said loudly to the table. "He had an affair with my wife, *that's* why we're divorced!"

John looked back at his friends, who all had shocked looks

on their faces, except for Dom. "That's not true," he said to them.

"Liar!" Alex said, pushing John with all his strength, catching him off guard. John stumbled into the table, the corner of it jutting into his leg painfully. He grimaced and looked at Henry, Freddie and Evan in turn and realised with sorrow that they believed Alex. They looked at John as though he were dirty and suddenly, he felt completely unwanted.

"He kept it a secret from all of you," Alex continued, "thinking I would never find out. Oh, but I did. I did, Johnny boy!"

John rounded on Alex, his temper barely in control, he brought his face close to Alex almost nose-to nose. He whispered, so only Alex could hear, "You don't know a thing. Just accept that you're a failure as a man and a husband."

John withdrew and saw the blood filling Alex's cheeks, as his eyes flared with hatred and then he swung a closed fist at John, catching him awkwardly in the temple. John was rocked, more from the shock than the impact. He looked at Dom briefly as a second attack from Alex landed on his nose. John got his hands up and swiftly guarded against another hit and in an instant, countered with one forceful blow which immediately knocked Alex backwards.

John stood over Alex, contemplating his next move.

Dom grabbed John from behind. "Mate it's not worth it, let's just go."

John's fury dissipated as he immediately thought of Elena and their unborn child. He left Alex writhing in pain on the floor and turned back to the three still seated at the table. They looked at John with a mixture of disgust and fear, John becoming overwhelmed with the feeling that he had lost them forever.

"Come on, we'll get a cab and watch the footie back at mine," Dom said, pulling John away from the group.

"Yeah, fine. You can't tell Elena about this, she'll go nuts," John replied.

"Don't worry mate, I doubt she'll want to hear about you hurting yourself on a table!"

John smiled and realised with sadness that Dom was the only friend he had left.

CHAPTER THIRTY-FIVE

"Are you sure I look good in this?" Elena moaned, studying her figure in the hallway mirror.

"How many times do I have to say it? Yes! You look amazing as always," John answered her with a reassuring kiss to her forehead as he glided past her to his bedroom.

Elena ran her hand over the bump that was now a part of her body. She was seven months pregnant with John's child and as much as she was thrilled by the whole experience, days like today weren't quite as glamorous as they had been pre-pregnancy.

John's mother climbed the stairs, beaming at Elena as she did.

"Tina, am I fat?"

"Oh, behave yourself! I'm fat, you're pregnant! Big difference sweetie," Tina reassured, lightly touching Elena's exposed arm from her purple dress.

"You're not fat!" Elena exclaimed, just as John walked back into the hallway having secured his tie.

"Nobody's fat, you're both nuts though," he said bravely with a grin.

"Oi!"

"Cheeky!" the duo answered in unison.

"You'd best get a move on," Bob helpfully called up from his position in the living room.

"Cheers TomTom, how long is it gonna take ya reckon?" John called back.

"How long's a bit of string?"

"Fuck me. Alright Dad, Mum, we're off," John said, kissing his mother on the cheek as he scooted past her.

"Bye loves, don't forget to take lots of pictures together!"

"Bye Tina, we will don't worry!" Elena answered, hugging and kissing her as she did. Bob met the pair at the foot of the stairs, arms wide to embrace them as they left. "Be careful out there, look after my grandchild!"

"Always, Dad, see you both later on," John answered with a hug.

"Bye love, good to see you as always."

"You too Bob," Elena answered, and with that, they were out of the door and heading to John's car, walking hand in hand.

"What's the matter?" John asked kindly, seeing Elena's glum expression.

"I just want to always look pretty for you, but now I'm big an-" John cut her off before she could continue.

"You're the most beautiful girl in the world, now you're carrying our little baby. That's the best thing to ever happen to me. So yes, you do look pretty, more than that. You're enchanting." Elena smiled at these words, finally accepting John's sincerity.

"I love you, John."

"I love you too."

~

The pair arrived at Broadwick House where the "evening" portion of the wedding would take place. John and Elena had invitations for this part of the day as they didn't know the couple very well at all; John knew the groom, Peter purely from playing football and there were no connections to any of his other friends. He didn't actually know what Peter's wife was called, so that was something to look forward to when introductions were made.

"Wow, big crowd," Elena observed as they entered the grand hall, which must have housed two hundred people at that moment.

"Yeah, oh there's Pete!" John waved at the groom who was busy getting drinks at the bar some distance away and received back the same gesture.

"Come on, let's say hello," John said to Elena, holding her hand and beginning to move off, but he felt resistance.

"Babe?" John asked, turning around to see her rooted to the spot, staring into the crowd of people. "Elena?" John followed her gaze and instantly realised why she was paralysed with silence. "Well, fuck me!" John exclaimed. Across the room, sitting alone with a drink in hand was Alex Wickerman. John's eyes bulged in amazement, *how the fuck is he here?* He wondered. John walked in front of Elena and held her waist. "Babe, if you want to go, we can go. It's fine."

She didn't answer.

"Babe?" he repeated.

"No, it's fine," she said with a faraway voice, continuing to stare at her ex-husband.

"Hey, come on sweetheart, we can go if you want."

"No, no, it's really fine," she said, snapping out of her trance and facing John, putting on a smile that was a little strained.

"Nothing's gonna happen okay. We'll keep our distance, if he sees us, then he sees us. Oh shit, he's seen us," John suddenly said as he made eye contact with Alex. Even from that distance, John could see the colour drain from his face. He stared at John, then at Elena and then finally her stomach and if it was possible, became even paler.

"Do you want to go over to him?" John asked, to himself as much as Elena.

"I don't know," she answered flatly. It had been almost a year since she had last seen him and was quite content in the thought that she would never see him again, yet here he was, at some random wedding of someone she didn't even know.

"He's still sitting there staring," John whispered to Elena, conscious that he too had not taken his eyes off of Alex.

"Let's go over there," Elena suddenly said with authority, her head held high and her confidence soaring. "Come on," she said, linking her arm with John's and beginning the march over to where Alex was seated.

"Here goes nothing," John muttered, striding with purpose as he kept his gaze fixed upon Alex. Before they realised, the pair were mere feet from Alex and could make out every feature upon his weathered face. He still wore the same expression of shock, his mouth began to work towards a sentence as John and Elena came to a halt at the other end of the table, conscious to keep some distance between them still.

"Hi Alex," John said coolly, his tone even.

"Hi," Alex responded curtly, averting his eyes and taking a gulp of his beer. His eyes flicked towards Elena and the corner of his lips twitched into a snarl for a split second, which John of course noted.

"Surprised?" John asked, deliberate with the ambiguity of the question. He knew Alex would be stunned to see Elena pregnant.

"Yeah. Didn't expect to see you here," he answered coldly, finally looking at John with a stern face. John's eyes glinted, inviting the challenge, but it was Elena who alleviated the tension.

"How are you?" she asked earnestly, still holding John's arm.

Alex studied her and was about to answer when a voice suddenly cut into the conversation.

"Excuse me, sorry, do you mind if I squeeze past?" The owner of the voice brushed past John and sat beside Alex, her eyes yet to turn their attention to John and Elena.

"Holy shit," John said as he recognised the woman. She glanced up at him and her mouth opened in shock.

"John?!"

"Hi Kate," he said stiffly, his turn now to be utterly taken aback. Elena started laughing, soft at first but then a full-blown chuckle.

"What a small world!" she exclaimed, upon seeing the girl that had confessed to stringing John along all those years ago. John looked at her with surprise but seeing her laugh, his smile appeared and before he knew it, he too was joining in, appreciating the ridiculousness of the situation. Kate smiled politely but was clearly uncomfortable. Alex remained silent and motionless.

"So, you two huh! How about that! Good for you!" John said good-naturedly, still suppressing a laugh. "And how the hell do you know Peter?"

"I know Sarah," Kate answered automatically without emotion.

"Oh Sarah! That's her name, John!" Elena replied, seemingly a lot more relaxed now she knew Alex had a new partner. Her statement was met with another awkward silence, which John broke.

"So how long have you two…?"

"Six months," Kate said, answering John's question before it was asked.

"Oh cool! Well, it's been great guys. Enjoy the rest of your night." He turned, and Elena did as well.

"Wait!" Alex called out. The couple froze and turned back to him. "Congratulations. On...you know," he gestured to Elena's stomach with his eyes. "I hope it goes OK."

John was stunned by this unexpected warmth from Alex and nodded appreciatively.

"Thanks Alex. You take care, okay?" Elena replied for them both. With that they turned and made their way back into the crowd, content that finally the past was behind them, with only their future to look forward to.

EPILOGUE

"**M**ia, come for your hot chocolate!"

"Not yet Mama! I'm skating!" Elena's daughter replied. Tossing her brown curls around as she glided around the ice rink.

"Well Mia, how are you going to do that if Daddy catches you! "John shouted, surprising his daughter from behind and swiftly picking her up.

Mia squealed with delight and thrashed her legs in protest. "No Daddy! Put me down!"

"Not until you've had your drink!" John insisted, pulling her in for a cuddle as he moved to the exit. Defeated, Mia accepted and buried her head into John's neck, nuzzling into his warmth as he carried her over to the table Elena had secured.

"Thanks for picking something close," John said grinning.

"Yeah you need it, with your dodgy knees!" Elena said teasingly.

"Yeah, yeah, very funny," John answered, wincing as Elena slapped John's right shoulder with a laugh.

"Mama said that you're silly Daddy," Mia chimed, now sitting at the table and clumsily reaching for her drink.

"Thanks Mia," John said with a broad grin. He sighed thoughtfully, the cold night air whipping around them.

"Whatcha thinking about Daddy?" Mia asked.

John looked over to his daughter, her big brown eyes the same as Elena's looked back at him expectantly, awaiting some valuable insight.

"I'm thinking..." John began slowly. "That we should get Mummy a chocolate brownie!"

"Yay! And me!"

"Okay, finish your drink and then we'll go," John instructed as Elena looked on fondly.

Mia didn't need any further motivation, she quickly finished the remnants of her hot chocolate and proudly proclaimed she was done, tugging at John's arm to leave.

"Come back soon I miss you already!" Elena said, waving as they left.

≈

John walked the short distance to the stall selling all kinds of desserts and treats with his daughter, who was merrily skipping along. John breathed out a deep sigh and turned to his little one. "Okay, Mia. Before we get the brownies, Daddy has something important to tell you."

Mia looked up at John, eyes now filled with wonder.

"What is it Dadda?"

"Well..."

≈

Mia skipped ahead of John, holding two chocolate brownies in her hands. They were identical in size and luckily she had managed not to drop them yet whilst skipping, as she'd done once with ice creams on holiday in Miami which had led to no shortage of tears. At the time Elena had placated her daughter with a new ice cream, which had delighted her five-year-old.

Elena waved as Mia drew closer, John behind her when it happened. Mia dropped her brownie, mere feet away from her mother. "Mama!" she wailed, without tears for the moment.

"Alright bubba, it's okay, it's okay," Elena said, coming over to comfort her.

Mia crouched down and began to finger the dropped treat.

"There's something there Mama!" she exclaimed with excitement.

"Oh really? Be careful, let Mummy see," Elena bent down to assist her daughter, but Mia had already found what it was. Elena gasped and only now did she notice John was on bended knee, smiling up at her.

"Elena, my love," John began.

"Oh god, John!" Elena said, immediately whimpering and putting her hands to her mouth.

"Will you do me the honour of becoming my wife?"

"Say yes!" Mia shouted, making her parents laugh.

"Yes! Of course, yes!" Mia gave her mother the ring and clapped with glee, jumping as she did. John rose and embraced his fiancée, kissing her deeply on the lips as Mia joined them in a loving embrace.

"You've just made me the happiest man in the world," John said, beaming.

"John Buckston, you've been the man of my dreams since the day I met you. I love you so much."

"Chase me, chase me!" Mia exclaimed, tugging John's arm.

"Alright, but you better be fast!" John said, allowing Mia to get a short distance ahead. He faced his future wife and winked, before chasing his daughter around Winter Wonderland.

ACKNOWLEDGEMENTS

I wish to start by thanking my amazing partner, without whom this book wouldn't even be possible. She has worked tirelessly to edit this novel and ensure it can be the best possible story. I literally couldn't have done this without her.

Secondly, my good friend and fellow author, Richard, who provided me with some fantastic and helpful feedback against an early draft of this story. His input helped transform sections of this book for the better and he has been a constant supportive influence throughout this process. I cannot stress how privileged and fortunate I am to have you there and willing to chat about any ideas and issues I had with this book.

My advance readers, who were handed early copies of this novel to read and critique. I am so thankful for the valuable time you took to not only read the book, but let me know what things worked and what needed tweaking. You know who you are and I am so appreciative that you were there for me.

Last but not least, to my truly wonderful friends and family, who always support me no matter what I do, despite how ludicrous my ideas may be. I'd be absolutely nothing without you all, so thank you from the bottom of my heart.

ABOUT THE AUTHOR

Chris Kenny is an emerging author in multiple genres, with this debut The Love Story his first fiction work. Chris balances working a full time job with creating new stories and keeping fit. More importantly than that, Chris ensures his two year old cat is well looked after and loved, often taking naps together on lazy Sundays.

If you want to know about his next release , please visit his website at https://chriskennyauthor.com, where you can sign up to a monthly newsletter containing updates on new releases and free content.

facebook.com/chriskennyauthor
instagram.com/ckennyauthor